LANDINGS

JG WALLACE

JG Wallace
Justin, TX
jgwallace249@gmail.com
JG@HardTurnSeries.com

Hardcover ISBN: 979-8-9885846-4-3
Paperback ISBN: 979-8-9885846-5-0
Ebook ISBN: 979-8-9885846-6-7

Cover design by Lance Buckley
Book design by Brian Phillips Design
Edited by Carlo DeCarlo

First Edition

Printed in the United States

Landings is here.

Departures wouldn't have even been reality without
the love of my life, Beverly.

Now I am publishing *Landings*, Book Two of the
Hard Turn series, with more books to come.

Thank you, mahal ko, you have encouraged and enabled me.
You are the light in my life and the power that keeps me going.

I love you!

PROLOGUE

Major Dan Hatfield had been summoned by the aide to the base commander, General Stacy McHugh. The aide was not forthcoming with a reason for the meeting, but he did note the others attending could safely be described as "command-level officers." The lowest rank in the room was an air force full-colonel; everyone else was wearing stars.

Major Hatfield walked into the room and immediately came to attention facing General McHugh. He saluted the general as crisply as he could manage. When the general returned the salute, he was given the "at ease, major" command. Major Hatfield looked around the room, taking in a very deep and very involuntary breath as he did so. He'd never been in a room with so much brass before. He knew something was up.

General McHugh spoke. "Major Hatfield, I know you've told the story now probably a dozen times, but we need to hear it again, in detail, right now. As you can see from the camera, it is being recorded this time, for several reasons we can go into after your narrative."

Not knowing exactly what was going on, Hatfield carefully recounted the story of the night of his rescue. He began with the pre-mission briefing, how his fighter jet sustained missile damage, the need to eject behind enemy lines, and ultimately how he took out the Iraqi soldiers manning the SAM missile site. As he wound carefully through the tale, everyone in the room sat and listened intently, silently. He felt a pang of shame when he related losing his communication radio in the dark. That shame spiked tenfold when he watched several people in the room close their eyes and wince when he said it. But he continued on, giving his detailed account all the way to his post-rescue medical examination. The debriefing lasted about fifteen minutes, but it seemed to Hatfield like an hour. The time had given him the chance to look around the room more carefully. There were officers from every branch of the service there, and Hatfield couldn't imagine what had possibly brought a navy admiral to this meeting.

"... as the doctors found no serious injuries, the minor injuries sustained, superficial in nature, were attended to, and I was dismissed to my quarters for bed rest. The first full debriefing was scheduled for the following morning." Major Hatfield finished his debriefing.

A silence lasting an eternal ten seconds hung in the room as the officers looked at each other wide-eyed. Several were shaking their heads. The room felt to Hatfield as if they were unsure who should speak next. General McHugh had called the meeting, so a few were looking to him to take the reins. Hatfield drew in a breath, as if to break the silence, but the army general on General McHugh's left held up a finger.

The army general spoke. "Before anyone says anything, I want to put out there that my colleague across the table from me in the marine corps, and myself, personally oversaw the forensic examination of the mobile SAM site. I can tell you with complete confidence that absolutely every detail you gentlemen just heard from Major Hatfield is backed with solid, factual evidence recovered from the site. If anything, Major Hatfield is downplaying his actions of that night. Damnedest story I've ever heard, and I've been dying to hear it since my first visit to the site."

"Gave me a hard-on!" Everyone laughed hard at the marine corps general's remark. It was as hilarious as it was typical of the hard-charging marine. As the laughter died down, Hatfield could see that everyone was nodding in agreement. It was probably the most heroic, first-hand account any of them had heard and the room was swelling with pride. As the noise level in the room subsided, Major Hatfield was still standing in the position of "at ease."

What in the hell is going on? Where is this going? Dan thought.

1

Nick Tuber was the Central America Region Supervisor for the CIA, and his meetings usually were attended by several people. It wasn't lost on Mexico Field Supervisor Mario Eliazar that it was unusual for Nick to meet with only one person, and Mario wanted to be anywhere but in that room. Tuber was angry.

"It's been *six fucking months!* You need to get me something, and it needs to be soon, or you go up for internal review. I'm sure you understand that is code for 'make progress on this or you are gone.' What you need to understand is that internal review isn't just about your job. The incompetence, disregard for procedures and protocols, the loss of assets, and three agents disappearing, that rises to the level of possible prosecution. Now, I want to go over this entire shit show from the beginning again."

Eliazar started to tell a story he'd told countless times. "Six months ago, Field Agent John Bayan checked in with me on the phone, gave me a status update, and finished the call by telling me he was going to check something out. He gave me no details. Three days go by before I reach out to him again. That amount of time with no contact was not unusual. I thought maybe he was in Mexico. I tried calling him; it went straight to voice mail. So, I called his partner: same thing. I then called the cell phone number of the IT engineer who was operating in the El Paso house: same. Now I'm concerned, so I drive from my house in Del Rio to El Paso. When I get to the El Paso house, it's stripped. Safe is empty, no computers, no servers, all files and records are gone. House has been stripped, ransacked, and trashed by kids. Nothing of value, nothing to suggest exactly what happened."

Tuber stared at Eliazar as if he was waiting for more. When the silence became uncomfortable, Tuber shifted in his seat, never breaking eye contact with Eliazar. Thirty seconds after that, Tuber broke the silence. "Not much of a fucking story, Mario. Seems to be missing an ending. And what about Villareal? A whole fucking drug cartel evaporates overnight? Do you even have any theories?"

"Sir, we developed the connection with the Villareal cartel over the last seven years. The connections were solid, the cartel was stable. What happened exactly, we are still piecing together. What we know is that the leader of Villareal disappeared. The same day, his number-two man, his enforcer, was killed in Mexico. Word got out quickly that Villareal was in the crosshairs of someone powerful, that it had been decapitated, and was now leaderless. And that all Villareal assets were up for grabs, so the other cartels moved in quickly. I've been thinking about that, sir, and I think that may present us with an opportunity."

"Oh? How do you figure that?" The skepticism in Tuber's voice was obvious.

Eliazar explained, apprehension in his voice. "When the Villareal assets were snapped up by the other cartels, they took the personnel with them. That means we now have low-level contacts in some, maybe most, of the other cartels. We are trying to redevelop the contacts now, with some success."

Tuber laughed. "Agent Eliazar, does 'with some success' sound like enough to save you here? Do you think 'trying' is a characteristic I value here? I feel like I need to remind you that we are the fucking CIA! Do you think we have gotten it done or that we do get it done by 'trying'?"

Eliazar let out a sigh. "No, sir, I don't. But I think you would agree, this whole mess has some events that are without precedent. Those men were agents of the CIA, but they were also friends of mine. We were building something huge, and now it's all gone. I want to get to the bottom of this. I want to find who is responsible. Damn it, I want heads on spears on this one, sir. I will pursue this wherever it takes me, and I will burn to the ground whoever is behind this."

It wasn't something Eliazar did consciously, but as he spoke, he leaned further over the table toward Tuber's face until he was only a few feet away. He recognized that Tuber was sizing him up, probably making a mental assessment of him. *If the tables were turned here, I'd be trying to decide if I was the right guy for the job. I need to sell this.* What Eliazar said next made up Tuber's mind.

"I will lay my career on the line on this, boss. I come through for the Agency, or I step down and apply to the Border Patrol. This was a direct assault on the CIA, with casualties, and it cannot be allowed to stand. Sir, whoever is responsible needs to be publicly and dramatically made an example of. I, we, need to make this story a cautionary tale that they tell for two hundred years about what happens when you fuck with the CIA. Those men need to be avenged. I will do that. I will dedicate my life to that, but ..."

It was Eliazar's turn to be dramatic. He let his words hang in the air until Tuber bit on them. "But what, Eliazar?"

"Sir, I'm going to need access to Special Assets."

"Special Assets. Eliazar, what are you talking about?"

"Sir, with all due respect, you of all people know exactly what I'm talking about."

Eliazar had Tuber cornered. He couldn't admit to knowing what Eliazar was requesting, as access to the Special Assets section, maintained by the CIA, was highly classified. And yet, Tuber also knew that Eliazar was correct. If Eliazar was to pursue their new enemy wherever they lived, he was going to need special help. The next words from Tuber were carefully measured code that Eliazar understood as he heard them.

"Agent Eliazar, this attack on the CIA is without precedent and requires a far-reaching, overwhelming response resulting in the elimination of all aspects and assets of the organization in question. I am authorizing the use of all means necessary and available to achieve the goal of threat elimination, and I will make sure that you have all means necessary and available at your disposal."

When Region Supervisor Nick Tuber finished speaking, an understated smile spread across Eliazar's face. A smile of satisfaction at having been given a task he desired, and a smile of resolve that he was going to be given the tools to complete the task. The two men nodded to each other. Eliazar collected all of his materials and walked out of the conference room without another word.

The two men set in motion something that no one could predict how or where it would end. The only thing both men understood completely was that people were going to die before this matter came to a close.

2

Even as Dan climbed the stairs to the second floor of his home, he heard the sounds emanating from "the" bedroom upstairs. Sindee was in the middle of a "show" on her website. This particular show was one that involved a coworker from the club, and Dan marked his time in the office, waiting to go upstairs and check on Sindee. The sounds of two women obviously enjoying themselves filled Dan's ears as he reached the top of the stairs. The air was also filled with the sound of website visitors depositing money as they enjoyed the show.

He turned the corner and stood in the doorway of the bedroom. Dan was greeted by the sight of his beautiful Sindee on top of a brunette in a position that made it impossible for Dan to see the other woman's face. Sindee tracked the movement in the doorway and quickly flashed Dan a huge smile. She tilted her head to the side and mouthed the words "come here." Dan's open mouth converted quickly into his own huge smile as he simply shook his head no. The pout Sindee made almost changed Dan's mind.

Almost.

Sindee turned to the camera and announced, "In ten minutes, this show will come to a climax," — she smiled devilishly — "so plan accordingly!" She took her eyes off the camera to flash Dan one last, smoldering look, then buried her face between her friend's thighs. Dan watched the next ten minutes from the doorway and wished it would be over quickly.

The sight of two beautiful women in lingerie pleasuring each other vigorously made his breath quicken.

After saying some goodbyes, Sindee reached for a small remote, blew a kiss, then turned off the camera. As the two women untangled their bodies from each other, Dan finally recognized Mali, a sublime Asian dancer from the club. She was five-foot-two with a meticulous and ambitious brain, which sat one foot above engineered thirty-four double-D breasts. Dan had recently hired Mali to take care of the financials for his life, which had become quite complicated. Between Sindee's two increasingly lucrative businesses, Dan's side work with Angelo, and Dan's day job as a pilot, it had become too much for Dan to handle alone. And he also loved the way Mali looked when she worked naked in an office chair in his office, at the new desk Dan installed just for her.

"Time to take my nose out of your woman and put it to the grindstone," Mali announced to Dan as she glided past him and headed for the stairs.

It was Sindee's turn at Dan. "Hey, flyboy. Is it time our show?" She strutted up to Dan and grabbed his crotch. She didn't let go; she used her skilled grip to guide him to the stairs.

Dan said, "Careful on the stairs in those heels, lover."

"There's little I can't do in four-inch heels, but then you know that already." She squeezed him a little tighter in just the right place. He groaned with delight.

At the bottom of the stairs, Dan caught the breathtaking sight of Mali in her chair, one leg over an armrest, one hand on the keyboard, and the other hand busily doing something else.

Dan whispered, "Jesus, Sindee, she really *is* like you. She never gets enough. That is some impressive multi-tasking."

Sindee purred back. "Well, baby, right now, she's missing what I believe I'm about to get a whole lot of."

When they cleared the bedroom doorway, Dan turned around to close the door. He heard the sound of Sindee jumping onto the bed; when he turned back, Sindee was already posing for him.

"Good lord, woman, I swear you could stop midday traffic!"

"You'll be lucky if I don't stop your heart in the next hour, but that's about all the time we have. Remember, lunch at Vincent's with Angelo."

Dan held up a finger as a thought came to mind. "I know, baby, and that reminds me. We need to ask Mali to print some reports for the meeting. I'll be right back."

Sindee stopped Dan from moving with the gentlest of hands on his shoulders. "Oh no. I'll go. You might not come back." She laughed as she glided past him toward the door.

. . .

Nico was concerned about certain decisions Angelo had made regarding the computer equipment that had landed in their laps. It's not that he didn't trust Angelo's judgment, but information was only as valuable as it was fresh. "It's been six months, boss, when are we going to start making some moves with the intel? You're kinda keeping me in the dark on this one."

Right at home behind the enormous desk in his office, Angelo sighed heavily. "Fuck, I don't know when we are going to be able, but I can tell you, it ain't gonna be for at least another month. I'm not keeping you in the dark; it's that I don't have a lot to tell you. We sat on everything for a month just to make sure we got away clean. Then, IT guy and Manny started working on all the documents and paperwork. I talked to IT guy yesterday. He says the shit still has his head spinning. Those two have been trying to organize everything to create a picture of what was going on in that house. At first, none of it made sense. He said he couldn't figure out the links to the drug cartel. It's obvious now that it was a CIA intelligence operation, but he's developed a theory that these agents had some double-dipping going on. Whatever the fuck it is, I think we need to go slow. He hasn't started on the computers yet. What he's going to need to crack those computers might be in the paperwork, so until they are done sifting through that, they are holding off on the computers. Even when they get to them, he said they need to be extremely careful about each step. He sounded like they were talking about disarming a bomb."

"Boss, I'd follow you into a burning building. I've never met a man with better instincts. You plan like Frank Sinatra sings. If you think we need to go slow, we go slow."

Angelo couldn't hide the small grin that materialized on his face. He valued Nico and his contributions to his outfit greatly, and the compliment was well-appreciated. "Patience, Nico, patience. We are predators in this food chain, but we aren't the only predators. One of our survival tools must be to always keep a low profile. When we make a move, we move slow when we can, fast when we need to, always careful to watch where we put our feet. If IT guy is right, there's a bear trap out there we don't want to step in."

Looking at his watch, Angelo noted that he had to leave for Vincent's in about ten minutes. Almost simultaneously, he heard his email notifier. Glancing at his monitor, he saw that it was from Mali.

"Excuse me, Nico, I have something I need to look over before I leave, and I've only got a few minutes before I go."

"Sure thing, boss. I'll go get a coffee."

3

"Miss Simpson, Captain Hatfield, what a delight to see you again." Vincent greeted the pair warmly, as he always did.

All heads turned as Sindee entered the front door of Vincent's Italian Restaurant, on the arm of Dan. Vincent Ricci, the owner, took the time to greet every patron, most of them by name. While he tried to make every patron feel special, Sindee and Dan actually *were* special. Vincent's demeanor, his voice, and his gestures conveyed his feelings for them genuinely, but no one in the restaurant or the bar was looking at him. All eyes were on the stunningly beautiful blonde in the tight red dress, which was nearly too short. Nearly.

Sindee closed the distance between herself and Vincent and placed a light kiss on his cheek. Dan reached out a hand, which was firmly shaken. "It's nice to be here again, my friend. I've been missing your pasta. It seems like months since our last visit."

Vincent nodded with appreciation. "The meeting room is ready; your friend is already here."

"Early as always," Dan said.

Vincent opened the heavy doors; Dan and Sindee strolled through as the doors closed behind them. Angelo smiled from behind the table, glass of red wine in hand. "Aah, the lovely couple. Sindee, you look like a million bucks. Sit, my friends. We have so much to talk about."

The pair sat across from Angelo. Dan placed a folder in front of him on the table. Angelo glanced at it, then back to Dan, who saw the anticipation on his face. It wasn't lost on Dan that a good businessperson loves to talk business when the business was good. And for Dan and Sindee, and Angelo as well, business had been thriving. Dan assumed that the reports in front of him were neat, thorough, and informative — *thank you, Mali* — because Dan hadn't even peeked in the folder. Sindee took every minute of their hour in bed, and then did her best to distract Dan as he drove to Vincent's, though not for any reason than her own pure enjoyment.

Dan opened the folder in front of him, and said, "Angelo, I'm not sure where you want to start, but it is all good."

As with everything, Angelo knew exactly the order of business he wanted to conduct. Without hesitation, he opened the meeting. "I'd like to dive into Sindee's business venture first. But before that, let's give the waiter something to work on. I could eat a horse, ya know?"

Dan and Sindee both nodded in approval as Angelo signaled the waiter. The familiar hidden door opened, and a waiter Dan recognized entered the room. Out of respect, the waiter turned his attention to Angelo first, but Angelo made the slightest nod toward Sindee. The waiter picked up the cue to take her order first. True to routine, the waiter memorized the specific meal requests of the three guests seated at the table, hands behind his back as he listened. Then with a nod to his guests, he disappeared into the kitchen.

Angelo went right back to business. He smiled at Sindee. "So, tell me, *bel fiore*, how would you report the maid and the online businesses are doing?"

"Well, big guy, they are doing so well that Dan and I are trying to decide how to proceed from here. That's one of the reasons we were glad you called this meeting. I'm online doing shows a few times a day, subscribership has exploded, and the money is flooding in. The club supplies a good talent pool that provides a good variety to the shows so that we're able to satisfy all our viewers' many tastes. But Sugar, what's most surprising is I now have some subscribers requesting to be in a show with me. That can be one possible and very profitable area of expansion. We'll just need to figure out the logistics of that. And the best news is that all of what goes on with the web is completely legit, the books are above board, taxes paid, and everything."

Dan noticed the look of satisfaction on Angelo's face. "That sounds great. And the Maid business, how is that going?"

Sindee continued, but the look on her face became more serious. "Also booming. And that's what brings us to this meeting. I'm getting too busy to handle it all, Angelo, and we want to be smart about our next moves. Not all of the Maid biz is legit. I got basically four types of clients: ones who want a clean house, ones who want a hot maid to look at while they get a clean house, some who only want sex, and some who want a combination of both. So, it's all about organization and detail. I have some girls that only clean. I have babes from the club who are open for anything, and some who are only willing to put on a show. The way I have been running it, no matter the client, the only fee I see is either a full-day cleaning, or a half-day cleaning. Once the girls are there, they negotiate their own fees for the services they provide. Strict confidentiality is required of the girls, and fortunately that has not been a problem."

Dan added, "Don't forget about the—"

"I got it covered, Sweetie." Sindee put her hand on Dan's leg. "Expanding Maid for You is going to happen, and it's exciting, but we need to be careful. Obviously, we need to keep a low profile, but I feel like we are just one accidentally fucked husband away from a knock on the door from a cop. On its face, it's running right now as a legitimate business, but if we are going to continue to expand from our present level of about forty clients, maintaining that legitimacy is going to be increasingly difficult. I'd like to bring on someone to help keep everything, all of the business details, organized. I love Mali. She's killing it handling the financials, but she's only available part-time."

Angelo nodded as she spoke. By now, Dan recognized when Angelo's gears were turning, doing something he excelled at: problem-solving and scheming. He was filling in Dan and Sindee's unfinished puzzle with the pieces in his head. Sindee let her last thought hang in the air and waited for Angelo's head to stop nodding, which meant that he'd arrived at a solution. Finally...

"I don't like to walk away from money," Angelo said. "Whenever possible, that is."

Dan and Sindee exchanged a concerned look. *Did Angelo want out?*

"I believe we can move forward here with the right person to assist, and I have a few that I'm thinking of," Angelo said to the couple's relief. "Give me a few days to narrow the list, make a few calls. What I'm thinking is you need a business manager. We put him, her, whatever, in charge of the daily operation and scheduling. They can be the face of the business, in charge of the calendar, talking to clients on the phone, interviewing workers, meeting clients. The manager handles all Maid for You business, and if the manager gets overwhelmed as the biz grows, we will get them help. Your role, Sindee, is behind-the-scenes leadership — a sort of big-picture CEO position — with your main concentration on the website biz. Dan continues to share the decision-making in any major rulings. Mali can become a full-time and well-paid bookkeeper for all of it. But darling, please, keep her in your shows. That show today, oh my God, was as hot as anything I've ever seen."

The look on Angelo's face, the way he went smoothly from business to his review of her show, was a deep compliment to Sindee. Dan knew that Sindee would take the compliment for what it was. Angelo was a busy man, one who had seen and experienced a lot in his lifetime. Dan also knew that the compliment from such a man would turn her on. Dan noticed her lean forward, slowly slide her right hand off the table, and settle between her legs.

Angelo smiled at Sindee's subtle reaction. "Anyway, I'll let you know what I come up with in the next few days. I believe lunch is ready."

The hidden door opened, and the waiter appeared with a large tray on his shoulder.

Dan chuckled at the timing. "Angelo, how do you do that?"

Angelo smirked. "I can't give away all my secrets."

With precision and obvious experience, the waiter laid out an amazing lunch in front of the three. The only words spoken were a "thank-you" from each. It wasn't until he was back in the kitchen that the conversation continued. Angelo set the tone for the next few minutes. "Let's enjoy this lunch and stop talking business for a while." As he twirled his fettuccini around his fork, Angelo paused. "One last thing before my pasta, though. I want to make sure we are clear. Maid for You, the web biz; they are yours, and yours one hundred percent. Clearly, we can help each other here too, but also there is the potential to affect each other. We have overlapping interests. If Maid for You blows up in your faces, it could affect the club as well. I consider you two good friends of mine, not partners in business. *Capiche*?"

Dan spoke. "We appreciate that very much, we appreciate you, and we consider you a good friend as well. But we couldn't do this without you, so Angelo, there will be tribute."

Impressed, Angelo just nodded as he gave the couple a warm smile, then turned his attention to his fettuccini.

4

It was close to one P.M., and Angelo was enjoying the first food he'd been able to get in front of since dinner the night before. He enjoyed giving Dan and Sindee detailed descriptions of the three entrees on the table, their preparation, history, and what wines went best with them. It was light conversation. That was something Angelo did purposefully, as he knew the next conversation with Dan was going to be much more serious.

Sindee barely touched her food. She sampled everything and ate very slowly, actions not lost on Angelo. *She's gotta keep that smoking body somehow*, he thought. Angelo heard a chair slide across the floor and looked up to see that Sindee had backed her chair from the table. *She's done with lunch?* He glanced at Dan, who clearly didn't know what was about to happen next either. They both leaned back as Sindee stepped onto the chair and then the table.

"I'm done with my lunch, and I didn't want to just sit there. I thought maybe my two favorite men in the world would like a show with their lunch. How about it?" Sindee's smile was as wide as it was seductive. Looks of pleasant surprise washed over Dan's and Angelo's faces. Neither man said a word as her body began to sway to dance music softly emanating from her phone she'd placed on the table. Slow-moving hands reached up to the zipper on the back of her dress. She turned seductively and gracefully so that both men could see her deliberately peel the zipper down her back. As she guided it lower and lower, Sindee slowly bent at the waist so that by the time the dress parted and fell to the table, she was bent at a right angle. The only thing she had on were her stockings and her heels. Both men leaned back in their chairs, sitting with only wine glasses in hand.

The look Angelo gave Dan said, *I guess we're all done with our lunch, too*. Dan raised his eyebrows in affirmative response. Sindee turned and sank to the table while bringing her body upright. The pose finished with her on her wide-spread knees and her hands on her breasts.

"The waiter is going to be coming in to clear the table soon," Angelo warned.

Clearly the idea turned her on, as Sindee put on a huge smile at the notion. That and the fact that she began touching herself was a dead giveaway.

"Let him," she purred. "I hope the sight of this makes him want to come work for you. He'll be the hardest working guy on your payroll."

Angelo laughed. "Hardest working. I see what you did there. But seriously, he is actually on my short list for a possible manager for you." That comment got Sindee and Dan's complete attention. "I've known him since he worked here while in high school. He just graduated with a business degree, is very intelligent, has a great memory, and can clearly keep his mouth shut. Plus, he's gay, so I know he will be able to concentrate, even with you in the room."

"Gay? Really? We'll see about that. Call him in." Sindee then slowly leaned back into a reclining pose, turning her attention to her body more vigorously. Just as the first sigh escaped her lips, the door opened, and the waiter emerged with a large, empty tray. Sindee kept him in sight in the corner of her vision. Her actions continued as the waiter cleared the table, and she reached climax as he lifted the tray to his shoulder.

The waiter looked around the table. "Is there anything else I can get you?" Both seated patrons shook their heads. The waiter turned toward the hidden door with tray lifted high and took a step; Angelo stopped him.

"Actually, Carleton, if you could put the tray down, I would like to introduce you to my friends. This is Dan Hatfield and Sindee Simpson, two of my closest friends. As a matter of fact, they could be your future employers."

As Angelo spoke, Carleton placed the tray back on the table and reached across to shake Dan's hand. He proceeded to reach for Sindee's hand, then paused.

She chuckled lightly, then held out her left hand.

Carleton winked at her, then took Sindee's left hand into his and kissed it respectfully. "I already knew that Mr. Genofi and Mr. Ricci held you both in very high regard, so it's my pleasure to formally meet you both." Carleton then turned back to Angelo with a querulous look.

Angelo answered it. "Dan and Sindee need a business manager. I believe you would be a perfect candidate for the job, the position will pay considerably better than you're making now, and I know you already make good money here. It would also be a better use of that business degree you just earned. If you take them up on the offer I will be making for them, I will smooth things over with Vincent. I'm sure he knew he was going to lose you soon, and I hope it'll be a small consolation that he lost you to me. Sindee and Dan and I have discussed the scope of their needs in a business manager. Our businesses are interrelated; I'm using my organizational skills to make sure all of the businesses work together like a Swiss timepiece. If it's okay with everybody, I would like to talk to Carleton when Dan and Sindee go?" Dan and Sindee nodded approval.

"Of course, Mr. Genofi. Again, it was delightful to meet you both. I hope we can come to an employment agreement. I'm confident that if Mr. Genofi is involved, it will be sensational." Carleton then picked up the tray and disappeared through the kitchen door.

Sindee slid off the table after the introduction, so by the time Carleton last answered Angelo, she was fully dressed. She held up her hand, mouth open as if to say something, but looked like she didn't know what to say.

Angelo turned to her and said, "Told you he was gay. I saw you keeping your eyes on him; I don't think he looked at you once."

Dan said, "I think we've found Sindee's kryptonite. He completely robbed you of your superpowers, baby."

Sindee gave Dan a playful slap across the shoulder as they all enjoyed a laugh. Angelo's face took on a slightly pleading look. "Darling, could you please do me the favor of heading to the bar and driving all the men out there crazy while I discuss something with Dan?"

"Certainly, big guy. I'm going to go out there and do exactly that, but not just because you asked. I'm going to drive them all crazy because I enjoy it."

Angelo smiled as he tried not to think too much about Sindee's lunch matinee. "I know you truly do, baby. One of the things I love about you most."

5

Mario Eliazar stepped off the regional aircraft, which took him to the Del Rio airport, and onto the jet bridge. *So much better than the days of turboprops and walking across the tarmac in one hundred-plus–degree heat.* He walked into the terminal and headed toward the parking lot where he left his car. In his mind, he was already pulling into his driveway in Del Rio. *I have to go straight to the office when I get home. I've got so much to do, so much to get ahead of.*

. . .

Both men watched Sindee leave the room. Neither took their eyes off the doors until they were shut behind her. They then both pulled their chairs closer to the table and took business-ready postures.

Angelo began, "I've got something huge that I've been working on for a long time now, and it is almost ready to launch. There's a large casino outside Houston, the Silver Star casino. Right now, I'll just give you the basics of the job, but you'll get a full workup when we get closer. It seems the casino president and the head of security have cooked up a little plan to rob their own casino. I know this because I managed to get a friend into the vice-president position at the casino. My friend, Andy Powers, is a guy I've known a long time and can be trusted. He knows all about it, but they don't know he knows anything."

"Convenient for us."

Angelo taps his nose and points to Dan. "Exactly. Part of their plan is to frame him as being a participant in the robbery, and they think he has no idea. That part of Texas is my territory, and they haven't brought me into it. In fact, they've been stiffing me on my tribute. The last emissary I sent to talk about it to them ended up needing an IV and a bunch of stitches. They actually think I'm leaving them alone now." Angelo let loose a guffaw.

"Clearly, they don't know you," Dan said.

"Clearly not. What they did do is serve up to me what is going to be an amazing score: an armored car deal. Those two idiots plan on making off with millions in casino loot, pinning it on my guy, and, since the money in the armored car is insured, they figure there's no real victim. They can just disappear."

Dan sat back in his chair. "Millions?"

Angelo smiled, "Yep. Many. Course we won't know exactly until we count it. This is where you come in. Right now, the plan has too many moving parts. The head of security has to go first before they initiate their plan. The president will still go with their plan, as it's all set, *plus* he won't have to split the money. With their entire plan in place, they're just waiting for that one specific day when the haul will be enormous. So... that's a long way of saying, can you do your magic and get a Houston overnight sometime in the next few weeks? Maybe get a few in case we need to postpone. This is big."

"Will do, boss. We overnight a few crews every night in Houston. I can get a couple no problem."

Angelo opened a laptop he retrieved from the end of the table and set it in front of himself. He turned it around and pushed it across the table to Dan. "See if you can find a couple of them now. I don't like to leave loose ends. And while you're hard at work, I'll retrieve your better half from the bar, before she sends half the place into cardiac arrest."

Dan laughed as Angelo headed for the bar. Angelo was not at all disappointed when Sindee came into view. Seated at the bar with her beautiful legs crossed, heels dangling on one end of each leg, and just a bit of her perfect ass peeking out of the dress on the other. Three men surrounded her, all trying to talk her up even though she was clearly out of their league. As Angelo approached, all three men backed away from Sindee. They may have known who he was, or had no idea at all, but his confident stride and her smile at him told those men all they needed to know. They were striking out.

"Hey, big guy, did you miss me?"

"Always, baby. Ready to join us?" Angelo held out his arm as Sindee slid off the barstool. Taking her drink in one hand and Angelo's arm in the other, they strode through the restaurant and back through the heavy doors of the private room. Dan was leaning back in his chair, in a posture that said he was successful on the computer.

Dan smiled when he saw them walk through the doors. "I booked one next week and one a few weeks from now."

Angelo nodded. "I'll let you know." Sindee sat down next to Dan, sliding her chair up close to him. The sight of Sindee cuddling up to Dan gave Angelo a warm feeling inside. He asked the both of them, "So, how are you two? There've been a lot of changes, most of them seem to be for the better. You two solid?"

* * *

Sindee always wondered what these two were up to when they had their private talks, but she knew better than to dig. Angelo usually didn't dig into their business either. So, it was a surprise to her when Angelo asked about their relationship.

Dan said, "We are great, Angelo." Dan looked to Sindee as if for confirmation. She nodded with feigned enthusiasm. "Yup, happier than I've ever been. Sindee is awesome. We are building a future together."

Angelo's question brought something to the surface in Sindee that had been bothering her, though she couldn't put her finger on it. Dan's words, however, brought emotion out of her that she rarely felt, and even more rarely displayed, and thought she hid well. So, she was surprised when both men looked at her, clearly expecting her to echo Dan's words, but she couldn't speak. She was equally surprised to discover tears running down her cheeks. Dan's face dropped, and Angelo quickly stood. As he leaned across the table, Dan put his hands on her shoulders to comfort her. She could see he was torn up, believing that he'd hurt her or their relationship made her unhappy.

"What's wrong, sweetheart? What did I do?" Dan implored.

Sindee desperately wanted to put her emotions into words, but it wasn't something she was comfortable with. She struggled to express herself. "I... I... for the first time in my life, I have a man, a real man in my life who makes me happy. A man who I want to make happy. Someone I want to travel with, be with for the rest of my life."

Both men had puzzled faces. Sindee clearly saw that they were waiting for the reason for her tears. "It's just, I'm afraid it could all be gone tomorrow. Dan hasn't said a word about what the two of you do, other than that I have nothing to worry about. But that's just it. Whatever you two are doing, you feel like it is best that I don't know what it is, so it could be dangerous. The not knowing, it may be what you think is best, but it is also what makes me the most afraid. It makes me think about all kinds of things I don't want to think about. Like where I would be if Dan didn't come home. If he was in jail or worse, what would happen to me?"

There was a long silence. She looked at Dan, but she could see it wasn't his place to reveal anything.

Finally, Angelo spoke. "Sindee, I'm going to ask for your patience for just a little while. Dan can attest that I plan carefully what things I choose to endeavor in. Your man climbs into a metal tube, flies thousands of miles through the air, miles above the earth, hundreds of miles an hour, through every kind of weather. And yet, his flying is safer than the drive to the airport. Planning. Caution. Experience. That is what makes flying safer than driving a car. I feel the same way about all my business, and not just when Dan and I cross paths. Trust me that I will figure out a way we can make your worries go away, and in the meantime, know that Dan is not in any more danger than when he is in a hotel van. As for you, darling. You know how I feel about you both."

"And baby," Dan added, "I will make sure that no matter what, you are taken care of for the rest of your life. I'll take steps tomorrow with regard to your future."

Angelo smiled as he said, "I just need your patience and your trust for a little longer."

Sindee's mind was racing. She was still worried about the unknown, but she felt the sincerity in Angelo's words and the expression on Dan's face. *What choice do I have but to trust them anyway?*

"Angelo, I do trust you, and I know that Dan loves me, so I trust him too. But, there's always a little fear that my whole world is gonna drop out from under me, so you can see where I'm coming from."

Dan put his face close to Sindee's. "We will figure this out. I'm not going to break your heart, baby. That would only break mine too."

Sindee wrapped her arms around him and held him tight. She knew she was safe, even if just for this moment.

6

El Paso Police Department Detective Lamar Wampler had been on the force for fifteen years, but he'd never quite seen anything like this. A homeowner in a middle-class neighborhood called 911 because kids were congregating in a house that appeared to be recently abandoned. Detective Wampler mostly handled homicides, so he normally would never see a crime scene like kids trashing an abandoned property. The responding officers on the initial 911 call, however, found a large amount of blood on the garage floor. Kids may have trashed the rest of the house, but someone died on the garage floor, and that meant Detective Wampler got a call.

The case of that house got weird almost immediately for Detective Wampler. After a few hours of digging on the internet, he was no closer to an understanding. All of the things that should have been easy to learn about the house made no sense. The property title was in the name of a corporation that owned nothing else. It was clearly some kind of shell corporation. The utility bills were also in the name of the corporation, paid through auto drafts from bank accounts that had no other activity in the last six months. The neighbors all said they would occasionally see a car, maybe a couple of guys, but no one had met the residents of that house. Wampler then followed up by knocking on every door in the neighborhood until he had spoken to every resident. Nothing.

Wampler believed that sooner or later every crime scene reveals its story if he looked at it hard enough. He visited the house six times, spent hours combing the site, opening every cabinet door, searching every room, studying the pattern of blood splatter in the garage, and he still felt like he had only read part of the second-to-last chapter of a book. Wampler even spent two hours crawling through the attic with a flashlight and found nothing. It looked like he may have been the only person to have spent any time in the attic since the house was built. He was rewarded with the rare experience of having to drive thirty minutes to his house in clothes that were completely coated in dust and soaked with sweat. The air temperature in an average Texas attic is over one-hundred degrees by ten A.M. on a sunny day.

He was on his seventh visit to the crime scene when he decided to make his next two moves. He took out his cell phone and dialed.

"Crime Lab, Sargento," the voice answered.

"Hey, Sarge, how you doin'? It's Detective Wampler. Do you have someone you can loan me for a few days to do some fingerprint canvasing of a house?"

"Sure, how much of the house?"

Wampler tensed as he anticipated the reaction his next words would get. "Well, I'm going to need pretty much the entire house dusted."

Technician Sargento whistled. "The entire house? Everything?"

"Yeah, Sarge, I'm afraid so. We are absolutely nowhere with a crime scene that was almost certainly the location of a murder. Better give your guy a fifty-pound bag of fingerprint dust and a mop."

Sargento laughed. "Oh, we have some newer, high-tech stuff. When we get big areas, we have a sort of dust gun that blows a continuous stream of dust. Put a wide nozzle on it and you can cover a pretty big area with it. We also have UV lights that can show prints, as well."

"There's no electricity at the house, so if those devices don't have batteries, your tech is going to need a portable generator."

There was a slight pause before Sargento answered. "Oh boy. Okay. Well, whoever I send is not going to be happy about that. If they are using the duster, they have to wear a respirator, so they don't inhale the dust. They are going to be doing that in a house with no air conditioning? Okay. I'll send Porker. He likes fieldwork the most. He'll bitch the least."

"Tell him I'll supply a cooler with ice, water, and soda. I'd like to meet him here. Can you send him right away? It's 12605 Rancho Trail Drive, in El Paso city limits. I'm here now and will be for probably the rest of the day."

"I can do that. Send me the Crime Scene request on the computer when you can."

"Thanks, Sarge. Will do that probably late today. Take it easy." After hanging up, Wampler dug through his contacts for an FBI agent he had worked with in the past.

"Special Agent Miller."

"Hey, Glenn. It's Detective Wampler, EPPD." Wampler wasn't good with names, but he never had trouble remembering the name Glenn Miller.

"Hey, Detective. Whatcha working on? I'm assuming you are looking for a little federal collaboration."

Wampler went right into it. "And you would be right. I've got a crime scene, almost certainly a murder scene, and I haven't been able to get past zero point on it. I mean, I know almost nothing about it. Could you meet me here today?"

Miller said, "Well, oddly for me, I'm free right now. How fast can you get there?"

"I'm here now. The address is 12605 Rancho Trail Drive, City of El Paso limits."

Miller looked at the map on his phone, noted the ETA and said, "GPS says eighteen minutes. I will phone the address to our Internet and Cyber Division. See if they can dig deeper. Be there in fifteen."

7

IT guy was at Angelo's house doing his monthly routine maintenance on Angelo's computer and security systems. Angelo said, "You're usually pretty good at working and talking at the same time. If you can, how about an update while you're here.

IT guy thought about it for a moment. "Yeah, boss, I'm doing a virus scan on your desktop and laptop, so there's not much to do until they finish. I'm still going through the documents, paperwork, notebooks, and the filing cabinet stuff from the house. Imaging it, then organizing them on a computer in a way that they will be searchable. Optical character recognition software will allow you later to do a word search on the entire set of folders if you are looking for info about something specific. Manny has been working on the electronics, making inventories of what we have, checking model numbers, and getting detailed specifications on everything from the internet. We want to know the details of the machines, their firmware, software, and components to make sure there are no pitfalls or problems. It'll give us a good idea how to decide which machines to go after first."

The frustration was visible on Angelo's face. "Okay. I guess I'm just a little unhappy with the pace. But then, if you said you were done, I'd probably still think it took too long. You know me. If I'm not planning something, I feel like I'm stuck in the mud, and I can't plan without intel."

I better give him a realistic idea on how much longer this is going to take. "It's best to go slow with stuff like this, get educated first, then plan properly. I know you of all people can appreciate that. I can pick up the pace if there is some pressing reason. Just say the word, boss. But remember, we get one shot at all of this. I know you're frustrated now but imagine how you'd feel when I tell you that we made some mistake and wiped out a hard drive or fried some component. I'm treating this like it's intel that could be of huge importance to the organization. So far, I'm seeing nothing mind-blowing, or even newsworthy, about the equipment. But the data might be gold. The hardware is all pretty much off-the-shelf, so the actual makes and models don't tell us much about who could have been using them. But they clearly had their own IT guy, who was good, as the modifications seem pretty sophisticated. One thing that was of note, and this is really good, is that most of the access has already been done for us. Someone in that group lacked tech savvy to the point they created a small notebook labeled 'Passwords, etc.'" IT guy chuckled. "It really was filled with passwords and a lot of et cetera. That notebook is the other reason for getting educated first. Hacking the machines and the software hasn't been a problem so far. Once we get busy with the data, sifting through it will happen pretty quickly. Best guess? We'll be done with everything inside of seven days."

Angelo was listening, hanging on every word of the report. "You're right, you're right. Take your time. Sure, I'd like all the intel tomorrow, but it's more important that it's done right, with no mistakes that cause data loss or expose us. We still don't yet know what we are dealing with. Everything from El Paso is at the Barn, right?"

"Yeah, Manny is there now working on it."

* * *

The "Barn" was only known to a few members of the organization. Everyone knew about IT guy, but he and Angelo went to great lengths to keep IT guy's small house and workshop in the country classified information.

The property was a typical-looking Texas ranch. Small, rectangular, one-story house with a large front porch. It had a small, but real, barn. Behind that barn were four, long shipping containers arranged in a row that made them appear like one, big steel square.

Shipping containers were a pretty common sight in rural Texas, even ones like this that had electrical lines and air conditioners. People used them for all kinds of things, but anyone who looked closely at IT guy's "Barn" would know that his was a standout. IT guy bought an arc welder, then watched a dozen internet videos before welding the containers together and three of the doors shut. In fact, IT guy and Manny DeFilippo, his assistant, accomplished all of the work on their own that went into creating the Barn. After the containers were welded together, doorways were cut inside, connecting all four internally. The single outside door that opened was reinforced from the inside and secured with multiple locking systems. A large padlock was hung on the outside of the door as a decoy. It locked nothing.

The first container was a living area, with bunk beds, a kitchenette, couch, television, and refrigerator. It was designed to be enough of a living space that the Barn could be self-contained. The second container had a bathroom, complete with shower, and was used for storage of supplies and equipment. Lately, it was stacked with all of the El Paso material as well. There were times in the past when one or both of the men would spend the night in the Barn. With all the work Angelo wanted done immediately, that happened more often since the materials arrived. The third container was a shop with benches, tools, and diagnostic equipment. All non-sensitive work was done in the third container. IT guy and Manny paneled the walls in the first three containers for appearance purposes. The paneling in the fourth container was special, as the benches, tools, and diagnostics in that container were dedicated for work on anything they considered sensitive. The paneling went floor-to-ceiling, as well as the ceiling itself, and was signal-absorbent. No Bluetooth, Wi-Fi, cell phone, or any other signal entered or left the fourth container. It was the nerve center of the Barn.

Manny was in that last container at a bench. He just finished going through paper copies of specification and user information that they printed from the internet. He arranged the packets of papers in the order they would begin work on the electronic equipment. Standing behind Manny, IT guy said, "We'll start with the laptop from the office in El Paso, then the desktop from the same office. Probably both used by their guy in charge."

Manny had been crashing nights in the Barn; he'd spent the last three days there without seeing the sun. "That's enough for today," Manny responded to IT guy. "We'll start tomorrow. Gonna grab a couch and a beer."

8

The noise level in the meeting room had returned to near silence when the navy admiral caught Hatfield staring at the admiral's rank insignia.

"Major, you are probably wondering what the hell a navy admiral is doing in the room. You wouldn't believe who has taken an interest in the first, entirely intact, successfully captured mobile SAM missile site. Good thing it was in the damned desert. For a while there, more helo missions were flying personnel and equipment out there than were operating off of one of my carriers. We brought in bladders of fuel to give the site refueling capability for them. The army flew a hard shelter in on a Chinook, and a platoon to guard it day and night. Lights, generators, chow, guys from intel of every branch. Hell, even guys from Washington. If something from this action enables us to better find and destroy them, well, hell, son, you might have just saved a lot of lives all by yourself. Pilots, ground forces depending on close air support. We've even been able to tap into their air defense communication network."

All eyes in the room turned back to Hatfield. Clearly, he was being expected to make the next remarks, but he was nearly without words. Hatfield's head was spinning. As the U.S. forces decimated the Iraqi air defenses, Saddam Hussein scattered what was left that was mobile.

Jesus, that hadn't even occurred to me, Hatfield thought. "This is a bit overwhelming, I, uh—"

"Overwhelming?" An air force general cut him off with a laugh. "This from the main character of the story we all just heard!"

"Sirs, I was just doing my duty. Doing what any man in this room would have done."

More unexpected laughter erupted from everyone, except the marine general, who was groaning loudly at the ceiling. The laughter continued as the marine retrieved a U.S. twenty-dollar bill from his left breast pocket and handed it to the air force general on his left. The air force general tucked it into his own left breast pocket and nodded his head in exaggerated thanks to the marine. Hatfield's base commander provided the explanation. "Your colleague in the air force bet his colleague in the marines that that is exactly what you'd say. I will spare the marine the embarrassment of repeating what he thought would be said."

The marine general took a shot right back. "Maybe I should have the last laugh and make you a marine colonel right here and now. How about it, Major? Want a promotion in both rank and branch of service?"

"Sir, I thank you for your generous offer, but I prefer air force equipment. Besides, all my friends are here."

It was a good joke, and it drew laughs, but General McHugh noticed a few men checking their watches. All these men had commands of their own, so he brought the meeting back on track.

"Speaking of the men in this room, every one of them has a command of one type or another, so I'd like to bring us to the business at hand. I will get right to it, Major. I will be recommending you for the Congressional Medal of Honor."

The words hit Hatfield like a bolt of lightning.

General McHugh continued. "This situation is unusual in its widespread involvement with commands and branches of service as represented by the men in this room. There was only slight hesitation involving the bit about losing your radio, precipitating the heroic actions. However, everyone understands that combat is chaotic and dynamic, and that, well, shit happens. It wasn't through neglect or dereliction that your radio was lost, and *everyone* agrees that your actions in making up for that problem distinguished you, and I quote from the text of the CMH, 'conspicuously by gallantry and intrepidity at the risk of your life above and beyond the call of duty.' On that, there has been zero disagreement. The reason for this gathering is that all of these officers have inspected the SAM site personally and have made contributions to a classified briefing for need-to-know service members. Such as, airmen who could be asked to prosecute actions on future mobile SAM sites. Based on what they saw in the field, they have all asked to make contributions to your CMH nomination, so that it sees its way to completion as quickly as possible."

Hatfield scanned the room; they were all nodding in agreement with solemn expression. "Sirs. Thank you. This is... just... thank you."

General McHugh was beaming with pride and honor that one of his men was being so highly regarded. He stood, came to sharp attention, and in a reverse of the normal military protocol, General McHugh held a salute to a stunned Major Hatfield. Before Hatfield could react, the rest of the officers in the room repeated General McHugh's salute. Hatfield, with a lump in his throat, came to attention and returned the salute as perfectly as he could manage. General McHugh issued the "at ease" for the room.

The Marine General spoke. "Major? I'm General John Wilde. Your commanding officer is right; we all have places to be and things to attend to. However, I'm not leaving this room till I introduce myself and shake the hand of one heroic sombitch."

Major Hatfield took General Wilde's outstretched hand and shook it firmly. He then repeated that with every officer in the room as they filed out the door. In a few minutes' time, Major Hatfield was alone in the room with General McHugh.

"Dan. You have brought great honor to your squadron, your wing, your base, your service, and this country. I am going to put you on light duty while this CMH process sorts itself out. I can see it on your face already, Major, but you know how this works, and there will be no argument. You'll be flying back to the States soon enough where you will be able to name your next post. Seriously, anywhere you want to be. In the meantime, I need you to lay low from hazardous duty. Understood?"

9

Dan and Sindee slept in a bit, but only until Sindee woke first. On the mornings Dan woke first, he routinely woke Sindee with a cup of coffee. On the mornings Sindee woke first, she woke Dan in a way that was much faster and more stimulating than caffeine. That morning was completely typical, and Dan was completely awake when Sindee's effort was complete.

Dan breathed out. "Thanks, baby. You're my winning lotto ticket."

Dan really was like a surprise lotto win that he bought on a whim. Unexpected and the best thing that ever happened to him. Dan couldn't believe how much his life had changed in the short seven or so months since he gave his ex-wife, Sharon, the boot after finding her with his now-incarcerated — thanks to a little assistance from Angelo — ex-boss and ex-friend. Good riddance to both. Now, he had a good, strong, independent woman in his life who adored him and whom he adored. He couldn't help but smile when he looked at her.

Sindee gazed into his eyes. "My pleasure."

"I do, in fact, know that it was. Another thing that makes you one-in-a-million. Let's grab a coffee and sit at the table. We have a lot to discuss before this afternoon. Today is going to be a big day."

Sindee smiled her sexy smile. "You just lay there and enjoy that feeling I am responsible for. I'll be right back. She climbed out of bed and padded naked off to the closet. She returned to the bed less than two minutes later carrying men's pajama shorts and wearing a lace teddy with matching

G-string panties, stockings, and heels. "I call this 'business casual.' What do you think?"

"I think we need to sit on opposite sides of the table for this meeting."

Sindee laughed. "You have a short memory. You think a table is going to stop me?"

Dan sighed. "I remember. But I'd like to concentrate while we talk, and remembering the lunch show at Vincent's is not going to help."

. . .

Seated at opposite ends of the dining room table, cups of coffee in front of each of them, Dan and Sindee commenced their business meeting. Dan had his iPad in front of him for note-taking and the internet; Sindee had a pad of paper, and a cheap, ball-point pen that had "Crowne Plaza" written on the side. She wrote different titles at the top of the first five pages: Web, Maid for You, Airline, Business with Angelo, and Carleton. She thought that was a good order to go through their endeavors. Dan watched all of this. Sindee said, "Why don't I just take the notes, and you can take a picture of them when we're done with your iPad?"

Dan smiled. "Great idea, baby. I have a thought. Put Carleton's name on each page about an inch from the bottom, and then Mali's name an inch above that. Okay? I like the order you put those pages in, so let's start with the Web business."

Sindee looked at the time on her iPhone, then started jotting notes on the "Web" page. "Carleton and Mali are both supposed to get here about eleven, so we have an hour. Web is going well, and the viewers are still increasing. What I want Carleton to do is to organize my partners for shows, put together an actual budget for outfits and materials, work on sponsorship for the shows, and get a Sybian." *Just thinking about a Sybian makes me wet*, she thought.

"What's a Sybian?"

"It's the ultimate in sex toys, baby. Clients will love to watch."

He chuckled. "I'll trust you on that." Dan paused for a moment while he pondered. "I think the biggest issue is going to be time management. I also think we should give Mali and Carleton job titles and descriptions. Mali should be accounting, payroll, and business development, so let's call her our finance manager. Carleton can be our operations manager, as he'll be overseeing the general daily operations. How else can he help with the Web shows?"

"Well, I want to be able to separate myself from anything to do with operating the businesses. We let Carleton handle them all, and if he needs additional help, he can hire someone himself. I'd like him to organize the show schedule, line up the partners, and then just give the schedule to me. It's going to be the same with Maid for You. I just want him to handle all business. He is the business major; we shouldn't think too hard about this."

"Agree completely," Dan said. "I want to enjoy my life with you, and now we have the means to do so. Why don't we make one of the upstairs bedrooms an office for Mali and Carleton?"

Sindee nodded. "Carleton controls all of the scheduling, so if the noise from the web shows is distracting, he can just plan on being out of the office. Let's move on to Made for You. Pretty much everything I said about Web organization, we need him on with Made for You. Also, we need Carleton to come up with a system for buying supplies. The club had a service that dropped stuff off from time to time. Toilet paper, cleaning supplies, paper towels, all kinds of stuff. Otherwise, things are running smoothly, but it is just taking too much of my time."

Dan appeared slightly puzzled. "Now about this next page..."

"'Airline'? That's part of our businesses, as well, right? Is there anything you need or that might assist you with travel and organization? Also, I want to talk about going with you more on your overnights."

Dan thought about it for a moment. "I can't think of anything, really. I've got my system down pat, but I appreciate your thoughtfulness. As for the overnights, I'm going to put more thought into the overnight cities and how long the overnights are so we can do more of that. I'll research the best places to go. Hell, I'll even pay guys for a trip trade if I need to."

"Hint, I've always dreamed about Tahiti."

"Sure, but maybe we could make that an actual vacation. So... why the page on 'Business with Angelo'? We talked about this."

Sindee sighed. "No, lover, we have never really talked about this. I know Angelo is working on something, and he asked for my patience. That's what both of you are getting right now: my patience. But how can we plan long term? What will happen to me if something unplanned happens to you? You have my patience now, but it won't be forever; it can't be."

Dan reached across the table for her hands, and she offered them. "It won't be a moment longer than necessary. Angelo and I will work something out on this soon, I promise. I made a call to the attorney yesterday. He is drawing up a will, a trust, and arranging for life insurance on top of the insurance I already have with the airline."

Sindee nodded and thought, *I know it's something dangerous, probably not legal. They better come up with something fast.* Her face was uncharacteristically grim.

Dan could see his comment didn't assuage her concern, so he moved things along. "Okay, the last page is Carleton. We need Carleton's loyalty and his full attention, so I think he needs to feel like this is a real opportunity for him. Something beyond what he would be getting elsewhere. I was thinking we start him at ninety grand this first year, plus ten percent of any after-tax increase in profit he can show between now and twelve months from now. I'd like him to arrange for health insurance for any employees interested, and the same for 401ks. I'll match Carleton's 401k contributions at ten percent. Let's take the same approach with Mali. We should start her at something like seventy-five grand and same benefits. If you still want her in web shows, work out some kind of a cut from the web shows she does. We are going to need their loyalty. Only other thing I can think of is our taxes. Mali is a beautiful mathematician, but I want an accounting firm behind our taxes."

"I agree. She's always taken care of us girls with our taxes, but the tax law will be extremely complicated with all of the businesses and employee deductions."

Dan's eyes twinkled. "Spoken like a true businesswoman."

Sensing the meeting was over, Sindee stood up as Dan spoke his last few words. She walked around to Dan's side of the table, knelt down next to his chair, and slid her hand into Dan's pajama shorts. When she found what she was looking for, she said, "The only other business at hand is what's currently in my hand." Then just as she gave it a squeeze, the doorbell rang. The combination made them both jump and then they both laughed. Sindee slowly withdrew her hand from his shorts. "I think I better answer the door."

Dan looked her up and down. "Like that?"

"It's Mali or Carleton. Either way, it's okay. They've both seen me with much less on." As she padded toward the door, she could hear him laughing.

Opening the little window in the door, she saw that it was actually both of them. They had arrived simultaneously. They both gave her an enthusiastic greeting. Sindee closed the window and opened the door to a visible reaction from both of them. Mali flashed an open mouth smile, with clear desire on her face.

Carleton was a bit shocked. "Oh! I hope we didn't catch you at a bad time."

Sindee said, "In this house, I only have good times, sweetie, and what

would make you think I ever wear more than this when I'm home?"
Sindee stepped back and waved them in. The three walked together to
the back of the house; Carleton took in the house as he did.

"What a beautiful home. Sindee, that ensemble you're wearing makes
you look like a big piece of Christmas candy. You could be a model."

Sindee smiled at the sincere comment. "Aren't you a doll. Have a seat
in the living room."

They all sat down; the guys on the couch, Sindee on the loveseat, and
Mali on her lap.

. . .

Two hours later, with all the business discussed, everyone understood
their roles. Carleton suggested that they create a corporation, then put
everything in the corporation's name. Dan suggested the name: *Should
Be Smooth*. Dan explained, "That is what air traffic controllers tell pilots
all the time when the pilots ask whether there is going to be turbulence
ahead or at a different altitude, when they don't really know. But I think
it plays a few different ways." They all agreed.

Carleton stood and said, "How about Mali and I go to her work-
station so she can show me the books and schedules. I'll look around at
the office equipment and programs to see what additional furnishings,
equipment, and applications the office will need."

Dan held out a hand to pause the moment and left the living room for
his office. He returned a minute later with a ten-thousand-dollar bundle
of one-hundred-dollar bills. "Take this. Make the office nice, equip it
well, and plan for expansion. Part of your job is to make us rich, you and
Mali included, so this is where you start." Dan sat down on the couch as
Mali and Carleton left for the office.

Sindee climbed onto Dan's lap with a joyful smile. "Thank you, flyboy. This is gonna be great."

10

The drive over the rural Mexican road took just over an hour. But to Agent Eliazar and the junior agent he brought as backup, it seemed much longer. The country was beautiful; the road was anything but. The agents' four-wheel drive vehicle bounced for miles over the rough dirt road. Eliazar looked at the GPS for at least the fiftieth time; they were only a little closer than the last time he looked.

Eliazar was losing what little remained of his patience. "Fuck! It's like every time we get a stretch of thirty seconds of smooth road, we get hammered for ten minutes by holes in the road, or those damned ruts from water runoff. Now I know why they let us lead." He looked in the rear-view mirror at the four-wheel drive truck full of Mexican Federal Police — federales — who were sent as escort. It quickly became clear that the rough ride was the reason the Federales let the agents lead the way.

"Okay, we're getting close. GPS puts this place in the canyon ahead." Eliazar was navigating for the junior agent, who was driving. What they didn't know was that Mexico had just over two hundred thousand miles of roads, but only sixty thousand miles were paved. The road ahead had a sharp bend, then started a long descent into a deep canyon. The landscape abruptly changed from scrub desert to brush, and then trees. The canyon clearly had water running into it and through it. Eliazar appreciated how someone would want to build a house there. It was an oasis in the desert. The road wound back and forth until it reached the canyon floor, by which time the landscape was a rich green. They passed several large ponds, then drove over a bridge that crossed what barely passed for a river.

Eliazar said, "Finally, this is the turn coming up on the right." As they reached the turnoff from the road, Eliazar pointed it out, and the agent turned the car. The road immediately improved to one that was obviously routinely maintained. After about one hundred yards, they pulled up to a large, fortified gate that was wide open. Just inside the gate, on the side of the driveway, was a vehicle with three bullet holes in the windshield in a location that would not have been good for a person behind the steering wheel. The agent who was driving slowed so they could look at the vehicle, then proceeded further on the winding driveway, which eventually opened upon a wide, landscaped approach to a large hacienda. Eliazar whistled when he saw the spread in front of him. "And they say crime doesn't pay."

Eliazar saw immediately that things at the hacienda were not right. The neglected hedges and high grass were one sign. But the vehicle in the middle of the driveway with the same three bullet holes in the driver's side of the windshield was much more telling. The hacienda was enormous. They saw the wide-open front door as they parked in front of the house. The federales stopped right next to them and exited the truck immediately. Both agents exited their vehicle. Eliazar approached the front door first, with the junior agent right behind him, and six federales with rifles in tow. The door was intact, probably explained by the thick pool of dried blood at the side of the door. There were three bullet holes in the wall above the blood, at chest height from the floor. Eliazar looked back at his team to ensure they were ready to go into the house.

The eight men poured in and spread out rapidly; each man's gun tracked with his eyes as they all swept the room visually for threats. They stayed in their positions for almost a minute, waiting for Eliazar's orders. "I need three men on me as we sweep the downstairs. Then three men on my partner. You sweep the second floor. Questions?" The silence told Eliazar there were none. He said calmly, "Okay... go."

Eliazar watched the four men move tactically toward the sweeping spiral staircase to the second floor. He turned his attention to the first floor, and it was then that he noticed there was almost no furniture in the vast entryway and living space. There were smashed dishes on the floor near the kitchen, and an open, empty refrigerator. *This place has been stripped*, he thought. He advanced toward doors that led past the kitchen to other rooms. The men cleared each room; it was hard to tell how the rooms were originally used. One looked like a simple bedroom, another an office, but all had been left mostly empty. They worked their way around to the back of the house, to the multiple sliding doors that led to a large back porch. They swept the area quickly; it was also devoid of furnishings. The only thing Eliazar found was a broken drinking glass next to a large pool of dried blood.

Turning back toward the doors, Eliazar led the team into the house just in time to meet the second team descending the stairs. "We got empty rooms and a pool of blood on the back patio. Anything upstairs?"

His partner shook his head. "No boss, upstairs is the same, without the blood."

"Okay, we are leaving here in ten minutes. Now that we have secured the house, do a detailed and careful search of the second floor, I will do that down here." Eliazar didn't want to drive out there, over that road, for nothing. "I'm going to take a look at that office again. One hundred dollars to any man who finds anything of interest." After the ranking federale translated into Spanish, the federales all smiled, and moved in different directions. The sounds Eliazar heard as he reached the office doorway told him the men were searching the place vigorously now. Eliazar holstered his pistol as his eyes swept the room for any detail. What he saw was some very exquisite carpentry, with built-in bookcases and a desk that was built into the wall. All of it appeared to be as damaged as an angry person could manage with his bare hands. He searched the room thoroughly, looking for hidden spaces that an average person would miss. No such luck. But when he lifted up the heavy desktop, he discovered something on the floor.

A laptop. Smashed, probably worthless to whoever tossed this place. Our tech guys might be able to extract whatever is on the hard drive of this thing.

11

Dan's other phone rang, waking him up. It was Angelo. Right to the point as usual, Angelo said, "Regular time, regular place?"

"Sure, boss, of course." Dan had a hard time saying that. Sindee had also stirred at the sound of the cell phone, but a cell phone was not what she had in her hands.

"Did I wake you?" Angelo asked.

"Yeah, but you woke her too, so..." Dan just let that sentence trail off.

"Oh, good. She must have her hands full." *Click.*

Dan asked, "Baby? Angelo thinks you have your hands full. That true?"

"Mm-hm" was all she could manage.

. . .

Strolling into Vincent's, Sindee got attentive looks from all the restaurant patrons and from the bar too. She had her arm hooked on Dan's arm; when Dan felt her pull him closer to her, he knew that meant she noticed the attention, and that it was turning her on. He'd seen that look on her face many times. He looked at her and winked; she smiled at him in a way that would have turned most men into jelly. He smiled back.

"Captain Hatfield, Ms. Simpson, it is always such a pleasure when you grace my establishment with your company." As always, Vincent greeted them personally. And as always, Dan could hear the sincerity in his voice.

"Ms. Simpson, you are a vision. You never fail to turn the head of every man in my establishment."

Sindee let go of Dan's arm and stepped aside just enough to spin around slowly, giving Vincent a complete view of her white lace dress. Form fitting, with a low-cut top and plunging backline, ending a foot above the floor, revealing white boots. Dan admired his woman; every other man in the place did, as well. She leaned into Dan, kissing him on the lips. "I'm going to the bar to get a drink, lover. You go talk business with Angelo. I'm in the mood to give every man in this place a hard-on." With that, she sauntered toward the bar, making her way to a seat that the bartender had reserved for her. Just as she sat, she glanced back to see if Dan was still looking at her. He was.

Vincent held out his hand. "Mr. Genofi is already waiting. He's asked me to surprise you today with menu selections. I believe you will find them delightful." Vincent opened the large, mahogany doors for Dan, then closed them behind him.

. . .

Angelo relished the meetings with Sindee and Dan at Vincent's. His history with Sindee predated Dan; during the time when their lives crossed paths, and even since Dan appeared, she had given Angelo countless steamy memories. But it was more than that; he was really fond of her. With Dan, it was very similar. Angelo liked the way Dan dovetailed with his own thinking. He didn't have many people like that in his life. Angelo also truly admired Dan for his military history and job as a pilot. Just as he caught sight of Dan entering, Angelo was pondering whether he would rather be Dan or the Angelo he was.

"Captain Hatfield, good to see you," Angelo said warmly.

"Boss, I wouldn't miss a meeting here no matter what we were going to discuss. For some magical reason, Sindee plans her outfits and makeup for these meetings so that she can devastate the men out there and drive the two of us nuts."

Angelo sighed. "Your Sindee is as rare as an honest politician. Well, flyboy, trust me, I could talk about that beautiful woman all day, but let's get to business. The faster we get through this, the faster said bombshell joins us."

Dan said, "What have you got for me?"

"You have that first Houston overnight coming up in a few days, right? And you think you'll have no trouble getting more?"

Dan thought for a second. "I think we have about six flights a day to Houston Intercontinental. I could probably get one pretty quickly, anytime."

This was good news to Angelo. Hearing that the timetable he had in his head was possible, Angelo decided to present the op to Dan. "As I told you previously, Houston is my territory, and I've got that situation at the Silver Star Casino. Turns out that the old friend the casino president hired to be head of security is a real piece of shit. I won't go into all the details, but since our last talk, I also learned from my inside guy that the shithead's side hustle is trafficking underage girls from Mexico to a network of lowlifes around the U.S. My guy knows a helluva lot more than the casino head and head of security think he knows, thanks to IT guy working some magic in the casino."

"IT guy is a fucking wizard," Dan agreed. "He really fixed Sindee and me up doing all the work he did on the web business. Her shows are so much better than almost any other, thanks to the cameras, the angles, and the ability to frame the shots with a remote. I'll bet he worked in some kind of back door so he can watch them all."

Angelo laughed. "I doubt that. The only thing that gets IT guy off is IT. But I can attest personally as to the quality of Sindee's shows. I've taken in more than a few. But I digress. As you know, those two fuck sticks in the casino are planning on robbing the casino in a huge way, leaving my friend spinning in the wind in Houston. I think I mentioned that they're planning on pinning the robbery on him. I can tell you, good captain, that is not going to happen."

"Naturally." Dan nodded. "I feel like this is the part where I come in."

Angelo smiled. "Looks like their scheme is going down soon. Our plan is to split those two up before the robbery. You are going to take out the head of security. The head of the casino is not nearly as savvy or cautious as the security head. The op on the head of security is going to be tricky. The guy always carries a gun and wears lightweight body armor. I'm sending you on the op with a couple of guys who will get you in position, and then they will immediately handle the cleanup. This prick has a house in a suburb outside of Houston where he gathers the incoming underage girls before transferring them to buyers. He visits it regularly; as you know, what one does regularly also makes one vulnerable to schemers like me. The number-two in the casino gave us the details, and I've had him followed for a few weeks. He even occasionally brags to the number two about how he samples the new arrivals, personally. What an asshole."

"Agreed," Dan said with a disgusted look.

"One of my guys will be driving, and, with you in the car, he'll tail the asshole as he leaves that house. My driver will bump the guy, you get out, whack him, and the follow-up car pulls up. They handle cleanup; you don't need those details. Then they drive you back to the hotel. You'll get a delivery at your hotel as usual with needed items and last-minute instructions. Just get the details on your upcoming Houston overnights communicated through the usual channels as soon as you can. We have a pretty good idea when the robbery is going down, so let's get this done ASAP."

12

One of the things that Nico loved about Texas was the way someone could be driving through a residential neighborhood with the occasional commercial property, then in the next moment, the view through the windshield suddenly became rolling prairie, cattle, and grassland. Nico enjoyed that transition as his SUV bounced over the narrow, rural Texas roads that led to IT guy's ranch. *I can't decide if I love the drive or hate the distance. But Angelo wants an update; so, I get it, and that's that.* He made the turn onto the even smaller road that led to the ranch.

Nico turned his Cadillac Escalade onto the paved driveway that led to the back of the ranch. *I'm gonna retire someday and buy a place like this.* The long front porch that overlooked prairieland was especially appealing to Nico. He parked his SUV to the side of the house so he could still see the porch. He turned off the engine and paused for a moment as he pictured himself sitting in a rocking chair, with a glass of Italian red wine in his hand.

As he exited the SUV and turned toward the Barn, he was surprised to see IT guy had nearly made it all the way to the Escalade already. "If it isn't my favorite nerd. How are you?"

There was no change in IT guy's expression. "That is 'super-nerd' to you. You seemed surprised to see me. You didn't think you had to knock on the door, did you? I knew you were approaching when you were a half-mile from my driveway."

"Why does that not surprise me. But then, kid's stuff for a super-nerd, right?"

IT guy smiled. "I didn't tell you how, though. That really would impress you, but I'm not going to tell you. How about we talk in the house? We'll let Manny stay at it."

Nico nodded, and IT guy led the way up to the porch and into the front door. They got a few steps into the entryway, and IT guy said, "Can I get you anything?"

"No, thank you, I'm perfectly fine, and the boss really wants this report."

IT guy motioned toward the living room. "Okay, no problem. I'll grab a water, and we'll get right to it."

Nico headed toward the large leather couch while IT guy disappeared for a minute. When he reappeared, he had a bottle of chilled water in one hand, and a laptop in the other. "Okay, so the big question the boss wants to know is if it looks like we are going to get some solid intelligence? Will we be able to hack into the equipment? Then the next question will be: what do we know so far?"

Nico gave him a blank stare.

IT guy took a sip of water and sat the bottle on the coffee table as he started his report. "The short answer to the first question is yes, the paperwork and the equipment are going to tell us tons before we are done. So far, all of the equipment looks like we'll be able to extract the data. As for what we know right now, that has been slow-moving, but the pace is about to pick up considerably. We're on the verge of cracking the hard drives, the ones we didn't have the passwords to, and when we do, I believe a very clear picture of it all will take shape. There is one thing that is a bit off. We went through all the paper documents, catalogued them, grouped any that seemed related. But little of it seems to be any kind of official documents, reports to superiors, or operations documents.

That is odd, because everything else about this has the earmarks of an intelligence operation; the business documents, notes and contact lists all look like they are from some kind of intel op. We tried calling some of the numbers from an untraceable phone, but so far, none of the numbers are in service."

IT guy paused to take another sip of water. Nico slid forward on the couch and leaned in. This was beginning to get interesting. He knew that Angelo would want to hear every last detail.

IT guy continued, "We have also looked at the equipment from a pedigree standpoint, trying to figure out where they came from, tried running serial numbers, and preparing to power them up. The serial numbers were either not traceable — which is telling on its own — or they were traced to a batch of equipment sold to a company that is a CIA front, which tells us everything we'd need to know. Either way, we know the op was definitely CIA-backed. But when you combine what we know so far with the cash they found, the setup of the house, the house itself, and the people involved, it feels like a rogue op to me. We'll know for certain when we get into the electronics. There's also a good chance that it could've started as a legit op that turned into a lucrative side gig for the agents.

Nico took it all in, tried to paint a picture with all the information, and mentally prepared his report to Angelo. He nodded. "Keep working on it. I got a feeling that this is eventually going to be something good for us all. Just, Jesus, be careful. CIA, for Christ's sake. We wanna know, but we don't wanna square off with the CIA."

"No, we certainly do not. Fear not, Nico. Super-nerd is on it. We are being very careful, and very thorough. Now get out of here before Angelo starts wondering what's taking so long."

Nico was already halfway to the door as IT guy finished talking. "Thanks, brother," Nico called as he walked out. He was in the driver's seat of his Escalade a minute later. Alone in the car, he tried to sort it all out. *El Paso would make sense for some kind of a cross-border op. Could involve drugs, guns, trafficking people, coyotes, or a dozen other rackets that turn a buck. Hell, maybe a combination of a few. Juarez is just across the border, and it's the Wild West. No cartel owns Juarez, and it's a huge door into the U.S. Whatever, I gotta brief Angelo. We'll know everything when super-nerd starts nerding up that gear.*

. . .

Finally! My God, that has got to be some kind of record for number of prints at a scene. Technician Doug Porker found hundreds of prints in the house, and the processing of them was complete. "Processing" a crime scene involves multiple steps that begin with collection of evidence from the scene and ends with that evidence being analyzed. With a scene like an entire house that needed to be checked for fingerprints, the collection effort was extensive. If the collection yielded numerous prints, the analysis in the lab and on the computer was equally extensive. Porker started by setting up a generator; the scene would require electricity. He brought the lab to the scene in the form of a laptop that could run the prints through the Integrated Automated Fingerprint Identification System (IAFIS). Referred to as "afis," it has been maintained by the FBI since 1999. The request for processing submitted by Detective Wampler stated that the house was believed to be some kind of "ongoing criminal enterprise" conducted by three male occupants.

First, Porker wanted to get an idea of the size of his project. Removing the UV light from its case, he plugged it in and scanned the house, room by room, as he looked for concentrations of prints. He took notes in a paper notebook. When that step was complete, he put the light back in its case and opened another case that contained a piece of equipment that he considered a lifesaver for jobs like this. The traditional method for dusting prints was a fine dust, and a brush that looked like a makeup brush. The print was lightly coated with dust by spinning the brush so that the fine bristles lightly touched a surface containing a fingerprint. If done correctly, the dust transfers to the print, which can then be "lifted" using tape. The spinning motion took practice to master. From the case, he pulled out a handheld machine that looked like a weird hairdryer. *You're beautiful. I'll bet some poor bastard thought this up while brushing a big-ass house like this.*

Porker carefully loaded the machine with a supply of print dust, then set it down while he donned a hazmat suit. A full-face respirator was next, followed by gloves. *No A/C, it's hot, and I gotta wear this shit.* He went right to work with the duster, hitting the walls, door frames, windowsills, switch plates, plugs, cabinets, door handles, and pretty much everything else. It took numerous refills of the dust reservoir before Porker felt the job was complete. He walked out the front door, pulled off the respirator, and retrieved a bottle of water from the cooler he had placed on the front porch in anticipation of that exact moment. It took only a few seconds to empty the bottle.

The gloves came off next and he zipped open the suit just enough to retrieve his cell phone to check the wind speed. He had a formula from experience with the duster for clearing the house of the dust. Open the windows too much when the wind was high, and it could blow the dust off the prints, and the process would have to be repeated. The respirator and gloves went back on, and Porker re-entered the house to open the windows, and make the air in the house safe.

One hour later, Porker was at work lifting prints from the surfaces of the house. He had enough experience with prints to be able to tell that there were numerous duplicates. As he suspected, there were prints that came back with no record, and some that were attached to juveniles with records. The sizes all appeared to have been made by teenagers. He made little piles of like prints, and as he lifted more prints, it turned into seven large piles, with a few smaller ones. But nothing of significance appeared on the laptop. After hours of repeating this process, Porker wondered, *How is it that there are no prints showing up of the guys who worked here? Did they always wear gloves, did they sanitize it of prints from time to time, how is that possible?*

But, as he ran the last prints, he fought a serious case of discouragement. *Gotta be something I missed.* Walking into a downstairs bathroom, Porker realized he had dusted the outside of the vanity but failed to go through it previously. When he opened the under-sink cabinet doors, he stopped cold. There were three unmarked spray bottles, a stack of microfiber towels, and a stack of linen gloves. He picked up one of the gloves and examined it carefully. He saw no tags of any kind, but the elastic wrist and fine stitching told him they were not cheap. *Just like I would buy if I had to wear them all day. And I can smell the vinegar already, perfect for dissolving prints. So, there wasn't a viable print in this whole fucking house that I've found. All of those prints were from the neighborhood kids. No way those guys were in this house for a while and they didn't leave one print anywhere. I'm getting that UV back out and I'm gonna get creative.*

It was finally in an upstairs bedroom where he discovered more prints. Porker had been looking at everything from floor to ceiling. The print dust covered everything. What Porker spotted with the UV was a full hand-print on the ceiling next to a light fixture that must have needed a bulb change. It took Porker a few minutes to get the ladder from his van. He was excited; his hunch was that he'd found something. After carefully enhancing the prints with a brush, he lifted them. He then took the globe off the light and dusted the bulb. More prints, but duplicates of the prints from the ceiling. Porker ran them on the laptop. *Finally, something!* The prints were on file of a man arrested for DUI in California. It was old, but it was there.

Being thorough, Porker checked the lights and ceiling fans in the rest of the house but got nothing else. Satisfied he had completely processed the scene for fingerprints, Porker retrieved his cell phone from his pocket and found a contact. "Wampler? You owe me a beer. I just lifted and sifted through a gazillion prints, but I think I found something that might interest you. I'll text you, then I'm heading home. I'm covered in print dust and smell like a mountain goat."

13

It was a day off for Dan, and he had no set plans for his day or for Sindee. She had been unable to keep her hands to herself during the drive home from Vincent's, and Dan had trouble driving. When they got through the front door, and it closed behind them, Sindee said a single word: "Couch." While Dan sunk into the position he chose, the middle of the couch, Sindee reached behind her and slowly unzipped her lace dress. She made sure it slid to the floor slowly, revealing just as slowly the white lingerie she was wearing underneath: white corset, white G-string, white thigh-high stockings, and, of course, the boots. She smoothly sunk to her knees and started to work on getting Dan's jeans out of her way.

God, she moves like a cat, ohhh... as she went to work and stopped him from thinking.

Head leaned back and eyes closed for a few minutes, Dan was surprised to hear the sound of someone taking in a sharp breath to his right. He turned his head and opened his eyes to the sight of Mali, who clearly had been sitting there in the chair for a while and was busy herself. She had the look of having just peaked. Dan tapped Sindee on the shoulder; without even pausing what she was doing, she looked up at Dan's eyes, and made the "mm-hm" sound of approval.

◦ ◦ ◦

Sindee caught movement out of the corner of her eye, turned a little, and saw that Mali had just come down the stairs. Mali stopped and made eye contact with Sindee, who managed to continue what she was doing while nodding approval to Mali. The situation turned them both on even more, knowing that Dan had no idea Mali was there. Mali padded quietly over to Sindee, removed her own dress, and she then took a position on the matching chair. Sindee could see that Mali selected that seat because it offered her a great view of the action. Clearly, Mali chose a position that offered Sindee a display of what Mali was doing in the chair.

The previous conversations Sindee and Dan had about this situation swirled in Sindee's head as she continued to pleasure him. She knew that Dan was torn; Sindee told him when they discussed it that she wanted to occasionally play with a third person as a trio, but he told her he didn't want to complicate things. She also knew that the idea turned him on greatly; whenever they talked about it, the discussion always aroused him physically and it always ended with the two of them having passionate sex. But clearly it gave him pause because Dan had never taken the conversation to the action or even planning level. It remained a "discussion only" topic.

Sindee did not know that Mali was in the house. The garage is in the back, and Mali parks in the front. But the moment Sindee saw Mali standing there, mouth open, and toying with herself as she watched Sindee working on Dan, Sindee knew that the perfect opportunity had just presented itself.

No way Mali isn't going to be up for a threesome after seeing us, and the longer she sits in that chair, doing what she's doing, the more likely it's going to happen. When Dan sees her, he's going to lose it too. This is perfect.

Just then, Sindee heard Mali climax. It was a sound she'd heard many times before, and she knew that if she heard it, Dan did as well. Sindee looked up to see Dan staring intently at Mali and tapping Sindee on the shoulder. All of Sindee's attention was on Dan. She wanted to see his reaction when he realized that Sindee approved, and his fantasy was about to happen. "Mm-hm" was the noise she made.

Dan's face changed visibly as the realization sunk in. Sindee never lost eye contact as she climbed onto Dan's lap and put herself in the perfect position to ride him. Mali got up and came to Sindee's side, kissing her deeply. Sindee kept the rhythm slow; Dan was going to be on the edge as the situation unfolded. Sindee knew the way Dan breathed and the sounds that he made when he was ready; she was an expert in pleasing him. *He needs a distraction.* She thought. Sindee pointed to Mali's body, then to Dan's face. Mali understood completely, and deftly climbed onto the back of the couch, and sat on Dan's face. This went on for a few minutes, but soon it was too much for Sindee. She knew she was going to climax. She quickened her pace, matching it with Dan's peak, while he instinctively was doing the same with Mali. They all reached the finish line together.

. . .

Mali slid down the couch and cuddled up to Dan on the left side of his body. Sindee slid off of Dan and cuddled up to the right side of his body. In the middle was Dan Hatfield, whose head was spinning. His thoughts were not unlike the early nuclear weapon scientists watching the first successful test of an atomic weapon. It was a mix of "that was awesome" and the half-dread feeling of "how did history just change? Good or bad?" Dan loved Sindee, and he was fully aware of just how amazing and rare a woman she was.

How do I make her understand that I love her and want to be with her for the rest of my life, but at the same time I want her to experience all that turns her on — and me, as well? That I can experience a beautiful, sexual creature like Mali while knowing it doesn't threaten our relationship?

No one had really moved in several minutes, and Dan wondered if the girls had fallen asleep. Dan had certainly done his best to put them both to sleep, but he definitely hadn't been in charge of the scene that just unfolded. Dan felt some movement, but he was deep in thought and decided it was just one of the women stirring. That was until he felt lips, and then full-mouth, on him. He looked down to find Mali hard at work.

. . .

Sindee saw what Mali was doing, and that Dan appeared to be enjoying it thoroughly. Her thoughts wandered to the conversations they had had in the past when the topic of playing with a third person came up. Sindee knew that Dan had concerns, that he repeated that he loved the relationship they had and never wanted to threaten that.

How do I make him understand that I love him and want to be with him for the rest of my life, but at the same time I want him to experience all that turns him on — and me, as well? That I can be with him and a beautiful, sexual creature like Mali and know it will never threaten our relationship? Sindee rose to her knees on the couch, leaned in to Dan and kissed him deeply. She then put her lips next to Dan's ear and whispered, "Lover, we can do this whenever, with whoever, wherever you like. You are mine, always. I am yours, always. Nothing will ever change that. I want you to experience things that most men only dream about."

The pace of Dan's breathing quickened as Sindee whispered in his ear; Sindee noticed it. She had seen it many times. Leaning back to make eye contact, Sindee nodded to Dan her approval. She looked at Mali, because she knew Dan was about to explode, and watched.

. . .

Dan lay there recovering and playing back Sindee's words in his head. He realized he no longer feared damage to their relationship.

He said, "Okay, baby, I'm in. I'll follow you to the ends of the Earth and enjoy the trip any way you like. You're the best." Looking at Mali he said, "And you're pretty good too."

14

Bayan did good picking this place, thought Agent Eliazar. *Nothing fancy, but not a bad neighborhood. The kind that keeps to itself, mostly, and is working-class. It's on a cul-de-sac, so little traffic passes.* Eliazar went to the El Paso house to put eyes on it himself to see if he could find something that was missed. *There's got to be something. There's always something that didn't get spotted the first time around.*

The fact that very few cars were visible in any driveways made it obvious that most of the homeowners were at their jobs. Eliazar sat in his car for a half hour, just observing. The house had a few boarded-up windows in the front and police tape across the front door. Tape was also stretched across the garage door opening, even though the garage door was closed. He knew that since the police already investigated and processed the house, the chance of him finding something was low. But he guessed that the police didn't know exactly what they were investigating, or they would have torn that house apart.

As he looked down at his phone and checked email, Eliazar almost missed it. The face of a teenage boy peeked around the side of the house, then disappeared. *Okay, that's my in.*

He started the car, and drove the short distance to the house, backing the car into the driveway. Trunk popped, he walked to the back of the car and looked over the contents of the trunk. *Wear black pants and a white shirt, and with a few accessories, you can make yourself look like anything from an accountant to a warfighter.* Eliazar selected a baseball cap, and a light jacket, both labeled in bold yellow: "POLICE." Already under his shirt was flexible body armor, a pistol rig, and two extra magazines for his handgun. Fishing through the equipment in the trunk, Eliazar selected an overly large flashlight. *No one calls the cops on the cops.*

Knowing it was better to make entry out of sight, he walked around the side of the house to the back. The back door of the house was obviously forced open, which made Eliazar's job easier. As he approached, he heard what sounded like three or four kids, laughing and joking. Just inside the door was a dining area, but the house was surprisingly dark. He selected the flashlight as a prop; it was now a tool.

"This is the police! Anyone in the house needs to come to the back door. Now!" Eliazar shouted in his best "cop" voice. Four boys, none older than eighteen, slowly gathered in the dining area with Eliazar. He stood there and panned the flashlight back and forth over the boys for almost a minute in silence. That was deliberate; the longer they stood there, the more uncomfortable the boys appeared.

Eliazar broke the silence. "I don't give a shit what you guys are doing here today. I need information about this house. What do you know about this place? Do any of you live nearby?" When he asked the second question, he saw three of the boys look at the fourth. Illuminating that boy with his flashlight, Eliazar said, "Talk."

"Uh, well, I live next door, and like, I saw the three dudes who lived here sometimes. I saw two of them come and go, like, a lot. The third dude I saw every once in a while. Then, one day, like, about seven or so months ago, a box truck backs up to the garage. We'd seen trucks go there sometimes, no big deal. So, like, when it was, like, a week later with the garage door open, and no cars and no guys, me and my friends snuck into the house through the garage one night. The place was, like, all fucked up. Looked like someone had emptied and trashed the place. We been hanging out here ever since. Except for, like, a couple days the cops were here. Sorry, officer, we just been hanging out. We didn't do any, like, damages."

Eliazar had heard enough. "Okay, thanks, now fuck off, all of you. Don't come back." The four of them visibly relaxed when they found out they weren't in trouble. Eliazar shined his flashlight on the back door and the four of them hustled out of it. Now alone, he panned his flashlight around to get a good look at the place. It really had been cleaned out, but then he knew that an op house wouldn't have had much in it in the first place. Papers scattered about, broken dishes, pieces of clothing; really nothing of value, and all of it in plain sight.

If it was significant, the cops would have taken it.

As he walked through the house, all he found was more of the same: a tremendous amount of fingerprint dust and numerous rectangular clean spots on the walls where prints had been lifted. *If the guys were following the glove and cleaning protocols, the police won't find any prints that are of interest to them.* Eliazar took a closer look at the doors and fixtures and noted that the processor had been very thorough in his search for prints. *Jesus, there's lift marks on the fucking ceiling. This guy was good, but the agents must have been careful. If they'd found any significant prints, we'd have heard already.*

After a sweep of the second floor, Eliazar descended the stairs, sweeping his flashlight as he did. He almost missed it.

I gotta think like a spook. If this was my op house, I'd have some kind of hidden room or safe room. Wait...

He started carefully examining the built-in bookcase in the hallway adjacent to the stairs. Letting out a slow whistle, Eliazar knew he found something that he would notice that the police would not. The bookcase was actually a disguise for a door.

Jackpot. This is going to be good.

He spent a few minutes looking for the door release but gave up. The crowbar from the trunk was on his mind as he went out the back door. Eliazar fought the urge to run and made himself walk to his car in a stride that told anyone looking that he was in charge. As his hand found the crowbar, he thought, *Oh yeah. This is going to be good.*

15

Years prior, when Dan and Sharon were house hunting during their move to the Dallas/Fort Worth area, they looked at dozens of properties. With every house, Sharon complained it was "too small" or "not close enough to shopping" or "lacked curb appeal." Dan would have bought half of the houses they looked at. But when he walked through the last house and saw the huge, double shower in the master bathroom, he was sold. Dan was pleasantly surprised to hear Sharon say that the house was "perfect." In the years that passed, his fantasy of having Sharon wash him from head to toe, though concentrating on halfway in between, never happened. That was his last real thought as Sindee washed him from head to toe and was on her knees, concentrating on halfway in between.

. . .

Half of the master bathroom was designed as the woman's "side" of the bathroom; it was complete with makeup desk, cabinets above, and multiple mirrors. It took Sindee just a few seconds to wrap her body in a towel, wrap her hair in another, and pad over to the seat at the desk. Dan got to the doorway to the bedroom and saw all of his clothing laid out neatly on the bed. *Sharon would have never done this for me. Sindee must have done it while I was standing there, waiting for the water to get warm before we showered.*

"Sweetheart, thank you," he said, smiling at the bed, then smiling at her. She returned his smile with one full of love. "It's so easy to treat you like a queen, because you treat me like a king. I love you."

"I love you too, and likewise. Give me twenty minutes or so to get all dolled up, and I'll show you a few reasons why it's good to be the king."

Dan walked over to Sindee's chair, where she was already skillfully applying makeup. He slid his towel to the floor. "I'm sure you will. I'm looking forward to it."

Sindee looked him up and down, and said with a sexy smile, "I can see that."

◇ ◇ ◇

True to her word, looking like a naked Miss Universe, Sindee crawled into bed next to Dan. The anticipation nearly gave Dan a heart attack, but he managed. What Sindee did next brought him even closer to an emergency room.

After, Sindee sprawled across the bed and watched Dan dress very slowly for work. It wasn't that he was putting on a show, although to Sindee, watching him put on the uniform always turned her on. Her arousal was obvious by what she was doing with her hands. "Seeing you put that on makes me absolutely wet."

The comment at any other time would have reduced any normal man to a pile of ashes. But for Dan, it only made the hard situation harder. For years, he enjoyed and was proud of being a pilot and a captain. He would check himself in the mirror before he left to make sure his uniform was perfect. The sight in the mirror always caused him to smile proudly. But his mirror now was Sindee, who checked him head-to-toe before he left, making sure "her captain" was perfectly appointed. It was her last gesture before he walked out the door, and it displayed how proud of and in love with him she was. He never got this love from Sharon. But now, putting on the uniform meant time away from Sindee; in Dan's mind, he had catch-up to play. For the first time in his career, the symbol of that which he felt born to do, caused him dread. The uniform meant time away from a woman he had only ever dreamed about.

He decided to make light of the situation and not burden Sindee with it. "You know, since money isn't an issue anymore, I've been able to drop a few trips and spend more time at home. But just occasionally, every once in a while, I gotta be a pilot. What you're doing right now is really making it hard to go to work."

Sindee smiled and said, "Flyboy, you could have stopped at 'making it hard.' I know exactly what I'm doing. Now, let me look you over." Sindee rolled out of bed, strutted over to Dan and looked him up and down. She adjusted his tie, buttoned his uniform jacket, retouched his hair with her right hand, and placed his uniform hat on his head carefully. She nodded, and the two walked wordlessly to the back door. Standing in the doorway completely naked, Sindee gave Dan a long kiss, which he returned. A few "goodbyes" and "I love yous" later, and Dan dragged his bags toward the garage, the truck, and then the airport.

As he drove, he tried to mentally put on his captain hat. Thoughts occurred to him, such as remembering the need to communicate his Houston overnights through the travel agency website. *I'll do that on a crew lounge computer when I get there.* But try as he could, Dan still daydreamed about Sindee as he boarded the employee parking lot bus.

16

Major Hatfield was given the position of Base Safety Officer. His heart sank when he was informed of General McHugh's decision. Hatfield stood in the doorway of his new office, surveyed the scene, and he realized it was worse than he feared. His large L-shaped desk nearly filled the room. On it was a computer to the right, a large pile of paperwork and folders on the left, and an empty space in the middle where the new Base Safety Officer would work. Dan realized, *this could not be any more different than what I'm used to, what I was born to do.* Dan's normal office was way more cramped; it was a cockpit, control stick in his right hand, throttle in his left, and an airspeed indicator showing at least three hundred knots.

He ambled behind the desk and slid into his government-issue desk chair; he immediately wished he'd brought some kind of seat cushion with him. *I just went from being shot down as a combat pilot to being the Base Safety Officer. This is some kind of full-circle irony bullshit.* Pilots tend to think, review, replay, and overanalyze previous flight situations. This job was going to give Hatfield a lot of time to think about his last week. He leaned back in his chair, blew out a heavy sigh, and proceeded to not start his work as Base Safety Officer due to a complete lack of motivation. Hatfield's eyes closed for about ten seconds when there was a knock at the door.

Dan sighed again and reluctantly said, "Come in."

An Air Force lieutenant with a tentative look on his face entered the office, came to attention in front of Hatfield's desk, and held a salute. Hatfield stood and returned the salute as the lieutenant spoke. "I'm your aide, sir, Lieutenant Kyle Kane. Permission to speak freely, sir?"

Oh. This job comes with my own aide. I just met him, and he already wants to speak freely. Maybe I'll have a little fun with him. With a serious look on his face, Hatfield replied, "Granted."

"Sir, I heard about what happened in the desert, and I just wanted to say I'm honored to be working with you. I was hoping to ask you a few questions about your mission—"

"Lieutenant, the details of my last several days in this combat area are classified, and you know that." Hatfield purposefully twisted his face and cut him off with an agitated voice. "Simply asking me for additional details is a violation of information security, something I take very seriously. In fact, I'm going to need the source of any details you think you may have heard about something that may or may not have taken place."

Lieutenant Kane had started his conversation with Hatfield wearing a small smile that appeared to be holding back a larger smile. But now that smile was gone, and with each passing moment that Hatfield dressed him down, Kane seemed to lose an inch of height. Panic wrecked his face; his mouth moved a few times, but no sound came out.

Hatfield let the silence hang for a few seconds before he let Kane off the hook. Suddenly laughing, Hatfield said, "Lieutenant, I'm just fucking with you. Breathe, Kane, Jesus you look like you're ready to fall over. All the details of what happened in the desert will be coming out soon, and so I have no problem telling you the story, just between you and me. It is under an informational classification. I don't even remember why, other than Command said they want to be able to release the story officially at a later time."

At the command to breathe, Kane took in a deep breath that he clearly needed, blowing it out in obvious relief. The smile returned to his face. "Christ, sir, you about stopped my heart. I'm glad you have a sense of humor, sir, you'd be surprised how many people in this building were never issued one by the air force."

"Or maybe they had a sense of humor until the air force removed it as an unnecessary part. That is one of the reasons I've always avoided this building, Kane. Hell, I'm a pilot. We don't take anything seriously. We are going to get along just fine for the minimum amount of time I am marooned on this desk." Hatfield pointed at the stack of folders and paperwork and said, "Speaking of getting along. Perhaps you could clue me in on what the fuck I'm supposed to be doing here and what the hell I'm supposed to do with all that."

"You're in good hands, sir. You're the sixth different Base Safety Officer I've worked with. It seems that Command uses the Base Safety Officer position like the gym teacher of the base. When they have someone they don't know what to do with, they put them in this office. The job for you, sir, is a lot of reading reports, signing forms, and signing letters I will mostly be writing for you. Maybe the occasional visit to the location of one of the reports you read. I'll do the heavy lifting for you, sir. I'll make you look good. Can I get you a cup of coffee or have the mess hall send something over?"

Hatfield was as relieved as he was impressed. "Thank you, Lieutenant, sounds like you have a real handle on this. Coffee, yes, with two packets of that fake creamer shit that changes the color of, but sadly not the flavor of, our coffee. Mess hall delivers to the Command building, really? I can assure you, they don't deliver to the flightline."

Kane smiled. "Anything for the Base Safety Officer."

∘ ∘ ∘

Major Hatfield was now alone in his new office, it was late afternoon, and it had been an eventful day. He liked and appreciated Lieutenant

Kane. He spent most of the day acquainting Hatfield with his new duties and procedures in a polished way that showed he had done it before. By Kane's count, this was his sixth time doing it. But Hatfield knew that, sooner or later, his door would close, he'd be alone in that office with not much to do, and his mind would be left to wander.

It had only been a few days since ejecting from his jet, but Dan had replayed the entire movie in his head numerous times. Each time he analyzed the various scenes, he would slow some of them down, add some what-ifs, and analyze it again. Other than dropping the radio in the darkness, Hatfield found no other things he would have done differently.

Hatfield's motivation for all the analysis was due in large part to his pilot DNA. Every segment of aviation in history learned from their mistakes, and this was no different. But what Hatfield knew, and few others did, was that an announcement about the Congressional Medal of Honor was going to happen, and when it did, the plan was to roll out the entire story in *Stars and Stripes*. Publicity was a foregone conclusion. Hatfield knew the Air Force would try to get as much recruiting mileage out of his story as they could.

Thinking about the desert, for Hatfield, was much like repeatedly watching a thriller from a theater seat, only to be yanked back into the reality that it actually happened to him. He found it dizzying at times. One thing he pondered every time was the question of remorse. He killed those men, and that fact seemed as if it was just another detail. He knew that he may have been shot down by them, and for certain that they wanted to either capture and torture him or just kill him. They would have celebrated shooting down any rescue aircraft with their SAMs or that anti-aircraft battery. They certainly intended to kill Americans or others coalition forces.

Many times, new Base Safety Officer Major Hatfield replayed the events. Never once did he feel any remorse for killing those Iraqi soldiers.

The more he ruminated on it, the more his feelings turned into satisfaction for having won. But so far, he kept those feelings to himself. The U.S. Air Force taught airmen to kill the enemy. But they didn't teach them to like it. Dan's childhood taught him that, and the air force gave him the opportunity to relive those feelings. Unfortunately for the Iraqis he crossed paths with, when they shot Major Hatfield down, they presented him with an opportunity, too.

17

There were few casinos in Texas, and the ones that did exist were almost all of dubious beginnings. The common denominator was that the land a casino was situated on had to be outside the normal purview of Texas or even federal law, and that most often meant land owned by a tribe of Native Americans. But it took more than that. Casinos were big business, involving big cash, and in many parts of that often-conservative state, they represented vice and immorality. Building a casino in Texas was an uphill battle that few had fought successfully.

The Silver Star Casino and Resort was one of the exceptions. It was planned entirely before it was built and financed completely prior to the moving of a single stone. The land was mostly tribal, and what little land that wasn't, was acquired before the plans were announced. It was the grand vision of the tribal leader of the 1980s and 1990s, who patiently put all of the building blocks for the casino in place before announcing it to the tribe. It was an endeavor that was ready to go. The plan was met with enthusiasm by the tribe members, and with mixed reactions by the very few people who lived near the site in that rural Texas landscape. It was completed in less than a year, and the money was flowing in every day after the opening. It was all going according to plan, right up to the moment the mastermind collapsed from a heart attack and died in his office.

No one saw that coming, and the power vacuum left at the heart of the new tribal endeavor caused much division. After months of discussion, and at times, argument, the tribal council decided the best course of action would be to hire someone familiar with the operation of a casino to do just that. The council contacted other tribal casinos around the country and asked for recommendations. They needed a captain to take charge of the ship, quickly. They understood that a casino run properly is like a big press that prints money. Run improperly, it's just a bottomless hole money is shoveled into, never to be seen again.

The other problem, largely unspoken, was that of the Mob. The American Mafia looked upon casinos as an industry belonging to them. The Native American tribes were free to open casinos on their own land, of course. But the Mafia thought of them more as subcontractors than independent business owners. The land the Silver Star was built on may have been tribal, but the concrete delivery, construction materials, delivery drivers, liquor wholesale, and a myriad of other businesses, are controlled, influenced, or outright owned by the Mafia. Just to build, and then continue to operate the Silver Star, required shaking hands with the Mob, and putting cash in the Mob's hands at the same time. In the case of the Silver Star, it required a relationship with Angelo Genofi.

Michael Grim heard about the Silver Star's dilemma from a friend in Angelo's outfit, Nico Hamretti. They grew up together in New Jersey, parted ways after high school, but kept in touch and were still friends. Nico was delivering a load of rare wines to the Silver Star that the tribal leader requested for high rollers when he heard the news about the man that was supposed to sign for the shipment. Nico immediately thought of Grim; he walked quickly to the parking lot and dialed Grim's number as he exited the door. While Nico found his way to Texas after high school, Grim ended up in Vegas, where he quickly gained a reputation for being ruthless. He worked his way up to the number two position at his casino in Las Vegas, but there was no way he was going to rise any higher in any Vegas casino. Grim had two things working against him. His first problem was his name, and the history that went with it. He was born

Michelangelo Grimaldi, a surname that was well known by the City of Bayonne Police Department for the numerous entanglements his father and brothers had with them over five decades. Grim managed to cover his tracks enough that the LVPD didn't connect the dots. But he knew that before he could be a casino head, the Nevada Gaming Commission would complete a deep background check of him that would expose him, and kill all job possibilities.

Even without that hurdle, Grim put the second nail in his own coffin. The casino president took only a few days off a month, and on those days, Grim was left in charge. On those "sanity days," as the president called them, Grim was sole authority; the president was not to be disturbed unless the casino was burning to the ground. It was on one of those days that security informed Grim they had a drunk in the "cell." The man created a disturbance at a bar on the casino floor. Then the drunk broke the jaw of one of his guards, who had responded to the call from the bartender. By the time Grim got to the holding facility deep in the casino basement they called the "cell," the guards had tuned up the drunk pretty good. He was bloody and babbling about how he was going to kill them all. Grim took it as the rambling of an angry drunk and was considering going easy on the man — until he spit in Grim's face. "Show him the desert" is what Grim told his head of security as he wiped bloody spit off his face. Grim ordered the murder and burial in the Nevada desert of a made man in the Mob who was there on an unannounced vacation. The Chicago Family made inquisitions, but the disposition of their man was never solved. The president of Grim's casino put two and two together, so he owned Grim.

When Grim heard about the leaderless casino in the Houston area of Texas, he made a few phone calls, and within a week, he was in. The tribe thought they were lucky to find a guy who was so high up in a Vegas casino to step in and run theirs.

. . .

Another of Grim's high school friends made his way to Texas. Danny Justini was known to be proud of his Italian heritage. He told friends in Texas it gave him street cred in a state not known for its large Italian population, and Justini had the actual street cred to back it up. Justini's brashness and his sadistic propensity to violence got him labeled a loose cannon, one that put the organization at risk in New Jersey. It was his banishment by the operation in Jersey that had him on a bus to Texas, somewhere that felt just far enough away. After some inquiries, Justini tracked down his old friend Grim in Houston.

Soon after taking the position of casino President, Grim brought him on as the Silver Star head of security, a position Justini ran with an enthusiastic ruthlessness that built his reputation quickly. He enjoyed the cautious looks from the employees, and how they all made way for him when he strolled the casino floor. But as much as it stroked his ego, Justini knew that, much like Grim in Vegas, he had reached the pinnacle with his position as the security head. His past would never allow him to gain a senior management position in the casino. He was head of security for several years when he had an idea that he thought would set him up for life. He spent the next two years putting it all together.

The casino was successfully run by Grim and the tribal leadership was happy. Grim's life changed direction the day Justini walked into his office, shut the door behind him, and said, "We need to talk about something." The door, and the serious look on Justini's face told Grim the conversation would be unusual. Justini took a seat in front of Grim's desk, and, after a long pause, asked the question, "Do you want to run this casino for the rest of your life until you fucking die on the floor of this office, like the last fucking guy did, or would you rather retire in a few months with millions in the bank?"

Grim laughed. "What do you think?"

Justini noticed the smile leaving Grim's face slowly, as Grim realized that the question wasn't rhetorical; it was asked for a reason. Justini knew this was the pivotal moment, the point of no return, and the reason why he waited so long to bring Grim in on the plan. He knew Grim needed to be in to make it work, but he didn't want to give Grim too long to think about it.

Grim said, "Danny, I've been looking at all the angles on this place since the day I took this office. I can't find a good way to score off this casino other than my paycheck. What are you thinking?"

Justini took in a deep breath and blew it out. "Okay, Mikey, I've been working on this for a few years, and I got all the pieces in place, all the details worked, all the angles covered. I'm just going to give you the plan and we can talk details after if you like. You gotta be in this, but your vice president doesn't. He is a boy scout and we need to keep him in the dark. He's going to be the fall guy."

Grim leaned in, so Justini continued.

"Silver Star has a Saturday coming up that will be our score. Armored car picks up Saturday night, well, Sunday morning really, and in it will be a week's worth of deposits, plus we got three concerts that week, and the yearly Texas Hold 'Em tournament. I'm guessing there will be more than thirty million dollars in that armored car. I got a crew of guys who will be working that armored car. They are my guys, took a while to get them in, but nobody likes working Saturday nights, and everyone knows the casino bags are heavy. So, the new guys get that shift, my guys. I got it worked out so we transfer the money to a box truck on a property of mine outside Houston city limits, whack the armored car crew, point the robbery at your vice president, then drive the truck to Mexico. I got a cartel down there willing to wash all the money for two million. You and I split it fifty-fifty, then head our separate ways."

"You got a Mexican cartel to agree to wash the money?" Grim's head was spinning.

"Yeah, well, two actually. I had one lined up, and they just disappeared about six months ago. It took a little doing, but once I got the right guy on the phone, they were all too happy to take a two-million-dollar fee."

It was Grim's turn to take in a deep breath. Justini could see that Grim was sold, but knowing Grim the way he did, Justini also knew that he was about to get dozens of questions about the details.

. . .

The back porch of the large and lavish Mexican hacienda had a beautiful view. An obviously wealthy man in a chair, cigar in one hand and glass of tequila in the other, was taking in the view. There was a man standing off to the side, scanning the horizon the way someone tasked with the personal protection of an asset would. He asked, "What are you planning, Jefe."

The seated man took a long pull on his cigar, then paused before blowing the smoke out. After a small sip of his tequila, he said, "Well, we have two gringos who want to bring me a truck filled with American dollars, and they want to give a little bit of it to me to work for them. Like I am the money exchange at the airport? No. I think I will take it all and dispose of them while they are still warm."

18

The door to the hidden room under the stairs was no ordinary door. Eliazar discovered the hard way that in addition to being beautifully crafted in its stealth, it was hard engineered in its security. He made a mess of the craftsmanship, was soaked with sweat, out of breath, and still stared at a closed door. It took Eliazar over half an hour just to confirm that the door swung out and not in. He was a man not easily defeated; he wouldn't have gotten as far as he did if he was. With a loud yell of anger, he jammed the crowbar hard into the thin crack between the door and the frame. His rage was rewarded not so much by the door, but by the door frame. It showed a wider crack, which allowed the crowbar to gain purchase. *That's it, that's how I'm getting in. Work on the frame, not the door. It's only a matter of time now, you bastard.*

Once he worked a sizable gap between the door and the frame, Eliazar stopped to take a look with a flashlight. *Fuck.* Clearly visible were four metal rods, about an inch in diameter each, protruding from the door into the frame. *Well, not insurmountable. I'll simply tear the vertical door frame out in pieces. God, I hope they didn't put them in the top and at the floor too.* Eliazar understood that there are two kinds of locks in the world: locks that keep you honest, and locks that keep you out. The locks on the front door of the house are designed to keep you honest. Anyone could kick them in. This door had a locking system designed to keep everyone out. But that encouraged him. *The more design that went into this door, the more important the contents it protected.*

Next time bring a cordless saw and metal blade, Mario. I'd have been done an hour ago. The vertical frame was defeated and all four metal rods fully exposed. Eliazar hooked the crowbar into the door and gave a hard pull. Much to his relief and satisfaction, the door opened. There were no vertical rods at the top, or into the floor. He opened the door roughly; he took out his anger on the now inert barrier. Examining the inside of the door, he saw the geared mechanism that extended the pins into the frame. He couldn't tell how it was activated, and he didn't care. He was in. But what did intrigue him was the level of sophistication. This wasn't homeowner level, or even drug cartel level of sophistication. This had intelligence agency written all over it.

That level of sophistication warranted a high level of caution. Eliazar decided to take a hard look at the room from the doorway, before entering the room. He started with the doorway and the floor immediately inside, carefully inspecting with his flashlight. When he was certain there were no anti-personnel or intrusion detection devices, he scanned the ceiling for cameras. None.

Finally looking upon the contents of the room, it became clear that this space was a panic room. There were sleeping bags, bottles of water, boxes of food bars, and buckets with lids. Hanging on the wall were three sets of body armor, three AR-15's, a big shelf with three Glocks, and a copious amount of ammunition for the firearms. *The body armor, the weapons, and the ammo: all of that goes with me.*

The flashlight beam shined on an item on the floor in the corner. Eliazar froze as he noticed it. *Oh, what do we have here?* A big smile slowly stretched across his face. *That's a server, and I'd bet my Corvette that it was set up as the backup for everything. That's what I'd do.* In the dark of the panic room, Eliazar nodded, knowing he had found something significant.

He grabbed a sleeping bag, loaded the weapons, ammo, and body armor into it. It was heavier than he expected. Eliazar was unsure if he'd be able to heft it to the car over his shoulder with the server under his other arm. He wanted to make one trip to the car. There's no way to know how many eyes were on him when he loaded the bag into the trunk, so he wanted to do it once, then exit. Setting the bag and the server inside the back door, he made one more sweep of the house to make sure he didn't miss anything. Satisfied after his sweep, he lifted the server and then swung the heavy bag onto his back. *Oh my God, you're not in high school anymore, Mario.*

· · ·

Alberto Vaca was a name that was known to the CIA. The Agency keeps a vast, searchable database of "assets," and Vaca's name was listed as a "computer/cyber specialist." But that vastly understated Vaca's qualifications. Just a few years after graduating from Stanford University with a master's degree in computer science, he left his job at Google to open a shop in his hometown of El Paso. Ironically, the El Paso operation of John Bayan was supposed to call on Vaca if they needed help. Eliazar knew this, because when he searched the database, it was Vaca's name that came up. Just a week prior, Eliazar brought Vaca the laptop he recovered from Mexico. Now he was in Vaca's shop with the server.

"Okay, Mario, first things first. The laptop was completely recoverable. It is an off-the-shelf, standard laptop that was easily hacked, and all the information on it is available. From the pictures, document names, email addresses, emails themselves, at first glance it appears to have belonged to the head of the Villareal Cartel. The weak level of security, the appearance of the desktop, the lack of any kind of password protection, and the applications installed all point to the owner being in his fifties and certain that he was the only one to have access to it. A laptop, routinely used by the owner, is a goldmine of informa—"

"Alberto, remember what I told you about that laptop," Eliazar snapped, "and the information on it. Probably ninety-five percent of the information is harmless bullshit, but there is almost certainly stuff on there that is highly classified. Your job is to open the doors, and I will go through them all."

"And that's what I did, Mario. I didn't go digging through the hard drive, didn't read a single email. But I've seen enough computers to give me a good idea who the owner was just looking at file names and email subjects. In this case, it doesn't hurt that I grew up in Juarez before my mother could get me to El Paso. I don't just speak Spanish; I speak Juarez Spanish. Anyway, the laptop is ready to go. Be careful. If you believe there's classified info on it, also be aware that there is zero security on it. Anyone powering it up can look at anything on it. So... what's this hardware you brought today?"

Patting the server that Eliazar had put on the counter that separated the two men, he said, "This is also a question mark. If it is what I think it is, it's a backup drive for a few other computers that we were not able to acquire. Consider the security level of the information on this to be much higher than the laptop, so please be careful with this. What's on it could be extremely important. I would just like you to migrate everything on the server to a portable hard drive, if possible. But for right now, I'd like you to try to power it up and give me a quick assessment of what you see."

"Sure thing. You want me to operate carefully, so it's going to take a little while. You might want to have a seat, or go next door to the diner, grab a Coke or a coffee."

Eliazar shrugged his shoulders, surveyed the three chairs in the sparse waiting area, and chose the one that appeared to be the most comfortable. As he settled into the chair, disappointed by the feel of it, he watched Vaca disappear into the back of the shop, carrying the server. Eliazar thought about all of the things he could do on his phone while he waited, and then decided to just close his eyes and take a break.

. . .

Almost forty minutes later, Vaca tapped on Eliazar's shoulder to wake him. Eliazar fell asleep almost as soon as he closed his eyes, and it took a moment for him to get his bearings. Rubbing his eyes, he said, "Okay, where are we on the server?"

"Alright. I looked up the specs and it is, in fact, a proxy server, with massive storage, designed to operate autonomously, networked to several devices. I was able to, to... what?"

Eliazar was staring at Vaca, taking in the report, spoken in a language Vaca was excited about, and Eliazar was not. During the first sentence, Eliazar was already losing patience, which showed in his expression, and his shaking head. He paused for a second and said, "I don't need to know what the circuit boards taste like if dipped in ranch dressing. I just need to understand what the damn thing did, what kind of information is stored on it, and what kind of actionable intelligence we can harvest from it."

Chuckling, Vaca took a breath, and started over. "Okay, it was designed by their computer tech to be sort of a gateway through which all information flowed on all the devices they had connected to the Wi-Fi in the house, so to speak. All the devices also backed up regularly to this server, a function their geek programmed them to do. In general, we have nearly perfect copies of the hard drives on two laptops and two desktops, even though we don't have the machines themselves. Well, we don't, do we?"

"No, the house was stripped. This server was hidden. Even the crime scene investigators from El Paso P.D. missed it. Impressive really. What about their phones? Did any of the phone data go through the server?" Eliazar could see from the look on Vaca's face that he was dying to hear how it was concealed. *No, he doesn't need to know that. Better that he doesn't know.*

Continuing his report, Vaca said, "No, no phone data that I could see. They probably didn't use any cell phones for long periods of time before rotating to a new one. Anyway, I have a portable drive that I have migrated all the data to, and all the files are stored in a way that they can be easily accessed, and even searched. That was also courtesy of their computer nerd. You can take it with you today. My charge for everything so far is just under a grand. Do you want a bill?"

Reaching into his pocket, Eliazar retrieved an envelope. "I'll be leaving here today with everything. You've done good work, we will think of you in the future, but this should take care of you for now." Handing the envelope to Vaca, the pair turned toward the shop, where all the machines and the drive were loaded neatly into a cardboard box. *I may actually have something for Langley in this box. This was definitely worth the six-hour drive from Del Rio.*

. . .

A minute after Eliazar left, Vaca opened the envelope and counted twenty, one-hundred-dollar bills. *Yeah, that takes care of me just fine.*

19

Dan planned to arrive at his flight's gate twenty minutes early. He wanted to spend time at the computer emailing his Houston overnight information to the travel agency. The job could be done in a few minutes by copying and pasting his trip data into an email and then formatting it into a request for the agency. He knew that. He also knew that the second he walked behind the gate and positioned himself behind a computer, a parade of passengers with questions would line up in front of him. It never ceased to amaze Dan that he could stand behind any gate at any airport, wearing a pilot's uniform complete with captain hat, and in less than a minute, a passenger would walk up to him holding their ticket out in front of them. Dan didn't mind trying to help people and helped many with the questions he could handle. He nearly always made the decision to arrive early at the gate instead of going out of his way to the pilot lounge, a place free from the queries of lost passengers.

Even at a distance, Dan recognized the familiar face of Mike Chelsea, who arrived at the gate even before he had, and was chatting with the attractive gate agent behind the counter. *Well, now I can trade answering passengers' questions for banter with Mike. Nice to be flying with him again.* The app on Dan's phone told him on the way to the airport that his First Officer assigned to the three-day trip was still Chelsea. Even though the two of them were supposed to fly together the entire month, Mike had "dropped" his last two trips. Dropping a trip was just putting it into the daily list of flying that had not been assigned to a captain or first officer, in Mike's case. Then Mike was free to "pick up" any trip in that same list. It could be used to get time off that was needed, or to add to a pilot's month and make extra money. Dan looked forward to hearing Mike's explanation.

"Well, if it isn't First Officer, uh, what's your name again?" The line Dan delivered got exactly the reaction he thought it would when Mike turned around to the familiar voice.

"It's First Officer Chelsea, Captain Hatfield. You may remember me as the FO that taught you how to land an airplane."

Dan laughed. "I don't know how I managed to survive decades as a U.S. Air Force combat pilot, then airline captain, without the expert instruction that could only be provided by a newbie Blue Sky first officer."

Mike shot him a wry smile. "That's what I keep telling everyone, but they insist we give you one last chance in the cockpit. Fingers crossed you finally get the hang of it this time."

Dan and Mike shook hands as they shared a laugh. Dan asked, "So where the hell have you been lately? Dropped the last couple of trips and didn't even text."

"Yeah, been flying my ass off. Toni has this idea that it would be great to buy a boat. I'm a city kid; I know exactly shit about boats, so we don't even know what we're getting yet, but I know it's going to be expensive. I can't decide whether to get something we can party on, like a pontoon boat, or something we could ski with and get around the lake fast. I visited a few marinas. I think we have it narrowed down to Lake Lewisville; there's a good place there."

Dan listened to the excited rambling of his younger first officer before weighing in. "Boats aren't the worst idea for younger couples like you and Toni, but they are holes in the water you pour money into. They say the same thing about boats that they do about airplanes: two best days of owning one are the day you buy it, and the day you sell it. As far as what to get, I think I know you well enough that you'll be doing more partying than skiing on boats. Get a pontoon."

"That's what I'm talking about. That's what I told Toni."

Dan motioned to the jet bridge door. "Shall we? We can talk about boats for the next three days."

. . .

The flight from Dallas-Fort Worth to Phoenix was uneventful. They were assigned to keep the same airplane leaving Phoenix for Los Angeles International. More often than not, a crew will fly an airplane into a hub only to be assigned a different aircraft at a different gate for their next leg. Dan was aware of some of the reasons that aircraft were shuffled around like so many pieces on a chessboard and was also aware that there were hundreds of other reasons he knew nothing about. His job was to move the metal assigned to him where they wanted it to go and when they wanted it there.

Pilots had enough to be concerned about with their duties to the operation of Blue Sky. With the complexity of aircraft like the Boeing 737, pilots needed to maintain very high levels of technical proficiency, both in knowledge, and flying skill. But the greatest tool in the pilot's toolbox was decision-making; the skill a pilot is really paid to possess. A study was conducted years ago that estimated a pilot makes over ten-thousand decisions on a single flight. Dan, Mike, and every other pilot understood well that some decisions were more important than others, and that occasionally, a poor decision could kill every person aboard.

. . .

"*Blue Sky 4277, SoCal approach. Cross GAATE intersection at five thousand feet. You are cleared for the ILS Runway 25 Left approach to LA; contact Los Angeles tower at GIGII on 120.95. Have a great day.*"

"SoCal, Blue Sky 4277. GAATE at five, tower at GIGII. Good day to you."

To the untrained observer, the relief in Mike's voice on the radio would be imperceptible. But it was there and Dan heard it in his headphones. Every pilot loved to be switching to tower at the end of a long day. Dan smiled a little at the recognition of a feeling he had as well.

At the GIGII intersection, Mike pushed the "Talk" button on the radio he just tuned to 120.95 megahertz and spoke, *"LA Tower, Blue Sky 4277 is GIGII inbound on the ILS 25 Left."*

"Blue Sky 4277, LA Tower. Runway 25 Left, cleared to land."

"Blue Sky 4277, cleared to land." A moment after saying that on the radio, Mike said out loud to Dan, "Check out the airplane in front of us. We have maybe two-and-a-half miles between us and them, but we are closing the distance."

"Yeah, I was just noticing that. We are going to slow..."

"Blue Sky 4277, LA Tower. Slow to your final approach speed."

Dan pulled the engine thrust levers back to the idle stops and slowed the aircraft to its minimum approach speed. Both pilots were looking mostly at the Traffic Collision Avoidance System (TCAS) to see if the distance was still narrowing between them and the aircraft ahead. It was, and in his head, Dan rehearsed the "go around" procedure, the maneuver for rejecting the approach to landing and transitioning to a climb away from the airport. *TOGA thrust, flaps 15 degrees, positive rate of climb, gear up.* As Dan's aircraft was on a half-mile final, with the aircraft ahead of them still on the runway, everyone involved in the arrival of Blue Sky 4277 realized they weren't going to be able to land.

The tower controller spoke: *"Blue Sky 4277, go around, comply with the published missed approach instructions."*

As though he did it every day, Dan flew the maneuver he just reviewed in his thoughts, a maneuver that he'd executed in the aircraft many times, and in the simulator many more. He was "hand flying" the maneuver; he guided the aircraft on the complicated missed approach procedure without the autopilot, while Chelsea changed the aircraft's configuration on Dan's commands. It was when Dan called for the flaps to be retracted from fifteen degrees to five degrees that he knew something was wrong. Mike moved the flap handle, and immediately Dan felt the aircraft want to turn to the left on its own.

"Mike, check the flap position indicator. Something doesn't feel right."

There was a pause while Mike studied the gage, making sure he saw what he saw. "We have a flap asymmetry. Right wing flaps are at fifteen degrees, left flaps are just under ten."

"Okay, Mike, get out the Quick Reference Handbook procedures for a Flap Asymmetry. I'll handle the radios." FO Chelsea took his iPad in hand to look up the procedure while Dan pressed his talk button on the airplane's control yoke in his hands.

"*Mayday, mayday, mayday. LA Tower, Blue Sky 4277 is declaring an emergency. We have a flight control issue and will need vectors out over the ocean while we handle it. We would like the emergency vehicles on standby for landing.*"

"*Blue Sky 4277, LA, understand declaring emergency. Turn left heading two two zero degrees, climb and maintain three thousand feet if able. When able, say souls on board and how much fuel you have.*"

Captain Hatfield ignored the questions for the moment as he listened to FO Chelsea work his way through the emergency procedures, approach speed calculation, landing distance calculation, and then the normal checklists for landing. Chelsea then vocalized what they both knew. "So, boss, this is basically a normal landing at a higher speed because the flaps are stuck where they are, and the rolling tendency of the airplane that you have under control. Winds are light, and the runway at LA is long, so kid's stuff, right?"

"All true. Plus, if I remember correctly, you taught me how to land an airplane." They both had a good laugh, remembering the conversation in DFW before the trip started. Captain Hatfield maneuvered the aircraft to a visual approach to Runway 25 Left at LAX. With all of the emergency checklists, normal checklists, and cabin communications with the flight attendants and passengers completed, there was nothing left but to land the plane. As they descended on a final approach about a mile from the runway, Dan and Mike spotted something in the air just to their left, something they recognized was a drone hovering just south of the final approach for Runway 25 Left. It passed just to the left of Dan's cockpit window. Dan put it out of his mind and executed a perfect landing. As the aircraft rolled to a stop, the airport emergency vehicles converged on it.

Dan said on the radio, "*Fire commander, this is the captain of the emergency aircraft. Can you please inspect the wheels and brakes with your heat gun?*"

"*Captain, this is the fire commander, stand by.*"

In the next few minutes, the emergency vehicles slowly circled the aircraft, inspecting the wheel brakes carefully with very expensive, Forward-Looking Infrared heat measuring equipment mounted on top of the fire vehicle. With the flaps in less than a landing position, a much higher landing speed was required, and there was a danger of the brakes overheating. Overheated brakes carry the risk of exploding tires.

"*Captain, this is the fire commander. Wheels and brakes appear to be normal levels of heat and you are safe to taxi to the gate. We will follow you in.*"

"*Blue Sky 4277, Los Angeles Tower. The alley to your gate is being held clear for you. You are cleared to cross Runway 25 Right and cleared to taxi Gate 71.*"

"*LA Tower, 4277, cleared to cross 25 Right and cleared to taxi to 71.*" Captain Hatfield took his left thumb off the transmit button and put that hand on the steering tiller. He moved the thrust levers forward slowly, and started to taxi the aircraft to the gate with the emergency vehicles close behind. While taxiing across Runway 25 Right, Dan caught sight of the drone again, pointing it out to Mike. Shaking his head, Mike started to say something, but was stopped by Dan putting his finger to his lips. Dan knew, and was reminding Mike, that a review of the Cockpit Voice Recorder was always a possibility when an emergency was declared on a flight. Mike understood and nodded his head. They had been pilots long enough to know that first they finish the flight, then discuss everything later over a beer. The drone was visible to them both all the way to the gate before it disappeared.

Dan wondered, *what the fuck was that all about?*

. . .

Captain Hatfield stood in the cockpit doorway, said goodbye to all the passengers, many of whom thanked him for a safe handling of the emergency. One of the last passengers to leave the aircraft was a twentysomething man dressed in grunge with an equally grunge female companion in tow.

As Hatfield thanked them, the man spoke up. "Hey, are you gonna tell us what really happened?"

With a smile, Hatfield said, "Sir, I've been doing this for a long time. I have never lied on the PA informing the passengers, and I never will."

Just as Hatfield finished saying that, the flight attendant in the galley next to him spoke up. "We were all very lucky today to have such a skilled and experienced crew. Days like today are rare, and your pilots handled it like they were grilling steaks."

The pair looked at the flight attendant, back to the captain, then walked wordlessly off the aircraft. Dan just shook his head. *Unbelievable.*

20

The pair were nearly swallowed up by the big living room sofa; Mali was completely wrapped up in Sindee's arms. Sindee just put on a racy movie on the TV, as she was always looking for inspiration for her online shows with her favorite partner. Mali had suggested that if they watch a movie together, it would help them brainstorm about their show. They knew they wouldn't make it to the middle of the movie without acting out at least some part of what they were watching.

Mali was paying casual attention to her phone's social media feeds while Sindee paid casual attention to Mali's nipples. Something on one of her accounts caught Mali's eye. It was a story about a young actor with a substantial social media following. It seemed he boarded a flight to Los Angeles and was pissed off because he was unable to sit in first class. Instead, he was given a seat in the very back of the aircraft, something that he found even more demeaning. On top of all that, he said the pilot screwed up the approach to landing in LAX, endangered all the passengers, and then lied to the passengers about some kind of flight control problem in order to cover up his mistake. He posted that the captain even made the fire trucks come out to the plane, which made no sense to him. "Why would you need fire trucks if it was flight controls — WTAF? Lying!" he posted.

Attached to the post was a video of his encounter with the captain, captioned, "Captain says he never lies." Mali got caught up in the movie for a few minutes, as the scene in the movie turned her on just as much as what Sindee was doing to her. When the movie slowed down, she looked at her phone, and clicked the Play button on the screen. She looked at the first ten seconds of the video, and her eyes got wide.

"Oh my God, Sindee, isn't that Dan?"

Mali played it a few more times for Sindee, but they both knew after the first time it was Dan. Watching it over and over again had an effect on Mali. "Look how in control he is, standing there in that uniform like the captain of a battleship. Just listening to him talk sets my pussy on fire, then makes me wet enough to drown out the flames."

Sindee let out a deep breath. "Holy shit. He's probably busy right now, so I'll let him..."

Just then Sindee's phone rang, and the caller ID showed it was Dan.

"I've had an eventful day, sweetheart. We had to abort our landing in LAX, and then had a flap emergency flying around the airport making another approach."

"Wow, sounds like it was eventful, but I think I know something about your day that you don't."

Sindee could hear the puzzlement in Dan's voice, which made her amused. She enjoyed teasing him in many ways. "Uh, what are you talking about?"

"Remember that guy you talked to after the flight? The guy you told you never lie to the passengers, never will?"

"Okay, baby, you're freaking me out. Of course, I remember him. How the hell do you know about him?" Dan's voice was now an octave higher, and Sindee loved it.

Sindee decided to let Dan off the hook. "That guy is an actor; a guy who has a pretty large social media following. He posted a short video of the encounter he had with you. Give me a sec. I'll text you a link. Your face and your voice are clear in the video. Clear enough that watching the video several times brought Mali to a boil. He even said in the video that your name is 'Hatfeld.'"

There was a pause. Then Dan said, "Well, he got the name wrong, but not wrong enough. I wish he hadn't done that. Nothing good ever comes from getting social media famous. But I didn't do anything wrong. I'm sure I'll get a call from a chief pilot, but I think all he is going to want is a debrief of the situation."

Sindee smiled. "Come home, baby. I want to debrief the captain too." They both laughed. "Where are you now?"

"I'm in a hotel van right now, but I can't wait to get to the hotel room and call you. And when I get home after this trip, we will debrief each other."

. . .

Under normal circumstances, Angelo never discussed business details over the phone, on any phone. These weren't normal circumstances, and the conversation Angelo was having with the men he sent to Houston for surveillance didn't include anything incriminating. Still, it made Angelo uncomfortable.

Angelo spoke. "Okay, tell me what you have so far, and when we are done, I'll have another phone number for you to call. This conversation burns this phone."

"Okay, boss, here's what we have. We've been alternating following Justini and Grim since we got here a few days ago. It's only been three days, but they both seem to have their routines. Justini has a house on the outside of town, the one he uses for human trafficking. We saw an exchange where they brought in a bunch of girls with a box truck, and then they loaded them into the house. It was at night. A few hours later a different truck showed up and took the girls out. The girls looked under-age and drugged. It's a transfer house. That looks like the best place for them to transfer the money from the armored car the night of the boost. Maybe not, but that looks most likely. With the right assets, it's a great place for us to intercept at their transfer. We know the route Justini took there and back, and when you map it out, it's the only probable route to take. This Justini is a real piece of shit, boss. Girls? I got a daughter, boss. I can't wait to take this motherfucker down."

Angelo interrupted, uncomfortable with where the conversation was going. "Let's not get ahead of ourselves. You are there for surveillance and forming a plan. What do you have so far in the way of plan execution? I only want to go through this once on the phone."

"Okay, boss. So far, he has gone to that house every night. Once he had another guy with him, but the other two nights he was alone. To do this, I think we need two cars, the three of us, and the guy you are sending down. We'll put your guy and a driver in the bump car. The second car is for security and to take his car out if he tries to drive off. We'll have tow trucks on standby, and we have a great place picked out to make it all happen. His car is a five hundred series Benz, so he's gonna be pissed when we tune up his bumper. Boss, I like your plan that we send the Benz to Mexico so it gets "found" by someone later, make it look like a carjacking gone bad. You can bet that Benz has some kind of locator, so my guy is going to drive it across the border that night. The bump car gets crushed, and if the security car gets involved in any way, it goes away too. We have the cleanup worked out too. It'll be one of the standard ways, but best if I don't say."

Angelo stepped in. "Yeah, don't say, you can tell me later. Sounds airtight. I like it all."

"I learned from the best, boss. No doubt."

Angelo thought for a moment, then moved to the next subject. "Okay, and what about their op? What do we know about how they are going to pull off the heist?"

"Well, we already know it's going to be a boost of the armored car, but we know nothing about the actual method. These guys don't seem like they'd be able to pull off some kind of full tactical assault. I think we're looking at an inside job. That is more their background, and they've had enough time to maybe put together a few inside guys at the armored car company. I have no idea what they are planning to do with all that cash, but they won't get a chance to do anything with it."

Angelo leaned back in his lavish office chair, pleased with what he heard. "Okay, boys, top notch. Excellent work. Stay there, keep a low profile, and keep doing what you're doing. I'll be sending you resources and my guy. I'll text a new phone number. When you hang up, wipe and trash that phone." *Click.*

21

The amount of data was dizzying. Eliazar compared the laptop data with what was on the portable drive from the server for almost two days, and a clear picture was emerging. He was now fully certain that the El Paso operation was completely rogue and unsanctioned. CIA knew they were there, but they were falsifying their work to their superiors to make it look like they were making actual inroads into Mexican Cartel activity. He also got an idea of how much bank they were making, and he knew what bank they were putting it in. The more he understood about the El Paso op, the more difficult it was to suppress the question of what he was going to do with all the info he had. When Eliazar discovered the folder with the specific bank account and bank website login information, he pushed his chair back from the desk and sighed heavily.

I gotta wrap my brain around this before I go any further. I got two ways I can go here. If I turn all this stuff in, I have no move I can make with this information. It'll be embarrassing for the upper level, so there's half a chance they will hang it on my neck and sink me with it. Even if it went well for me, it's still something they can't really own. It'll be classified, boxed up, and buried. The other way to go is to cash in their chips. Whoever took them down took them all the way down. They took out the Villareal Cartel first. That's really all that the supervisor knows. I'm the only guy who knows what they were doing, how they were doing it, and how they were paid. But for sure, if I take one step down that road, I'm committed to go the distance and no half measures. The only hole in this is who has the rest of the computer equipment that was in the house? The backup server was backing up the other computers. The kids said everything was gone when they broke in. Whoever burned down this op must have taken everything with them. I'm gonna have to decide soon. The moment I move that money, I have committed an overt act, and I'll have no choice but to go all the way. If whoever took the computers finds those accounts, they will move that money instantly.

Pondering the situation, Eliazar knew that he was approaching a place where the direction of his life would change significantly — permanently. He went back to pouring through all the computer data. He wanted to make sure he fully understood his situation before he took that next step. *If I can't find any more holes in this deal, I know which way I'm leaning. But the big question is, what is the step after that? Do I take the money and go buy an island somewhere? If I run, they will come looking for me. How long before they find me? No, there will be time later to retire and get fat on tequila sunrises and tacos. If this looks like I can make it airtight, I'll take the money and keep working as if nothing happened.*

*   *   *

Seated at a table covered in computer equipment, Manny and IT guy discussed what to do with the hardware in front of them. Angelo tasked the pair with inspecting and squeezing every bit of intel out of the computers that they could get. Manny and IT guy were meticulous, precise computer experts who knew that they might get one shot at information that was very important to their boss. What Angelo hadn't told them was where the computers came from, and who their previous owners were. Or even any idea what might be on them. The pair knew a potential cyberspace minefield when they saw one, and this was it.

IT guy paused for a moment, gathering his thoughts, then said, "Okay, so we both agree, we need to plan all the steps first before we make a move. The research we need to do, what order we will inspect them in, everything. Then come up with specific plans for each piece of hardware before we do a thing to it. In order to be able to do any of that, we need to know what we have first. I think we should research the hardware and components of the hardware first. I'll take the desktop; you take the laptop. Catalog the components and research them on the net. We will prepare reports on the computers, then the plan for each, and the plan for everything."

Manny nodded. "Sounds good. The laptop should take me less time than that desktop will. Maybe an hour. I'll organize a plan for the components and an overall strategy so we have something on paper to discuss."

"Sounds great, Manny. Let's get to it." IT guy glanced over at the desktop he was going to dissect and thought, *Let's dance.*

. . .

Manny carefully opened the laptop, recorded the specifics of the components, and downloaded the specifications for each. Then he sat in front of his own laptop and prepared a short report about the laptop, components, and a plan for powering up and inspecting the data on it. An hour-and-a-half into his work, he was ready to start formulating the overall plan. It didn't take him long to create the plan, compile everything into a single document, and print it.

Manny hit the ENTER button to print the document, but didn't move, as he knew it would take a while to print. He looked over at IT guy's bench, where IT guy was working on the desktop. *I'm not going to interrupt him with this report. He's in the zone; I don't want to ruin his concentration.*

. . .

Finally, thought IT guy as he hit the ENTER button to print his own report that described and cataloged the desktop. "I'm printing the report covering the desktop. Let's take a break, you can show me what you put together, and after we have it all worked out, we will get right to the desktop.

The pair worked together well, and after a short discussion that took the amount of time needed to drink a cola, they had a plan. IT guy suggested, "We should work together from here until we finish both machines. Two sets of eyes and two brains every second we are working on them."

Manny nodded. "Yeah, that would be wise."

They worked together to get the desktop completely connected to peripherals and the power cord. IT guy said, "Okay, let's take a step back before I finger the power button. Look at the big picture, make sure we got everything right." Both men retraced their steps mentally. After a minute, they made eye contact and each nodded to the other. *So many different ways this could go. Time to find out.*

IT guy put his finger on the power button, and before depressing it, made eye contact again with Manny. With no hint of hesitation from Manny visible, IT guy pushed and released the power button on the desktop. They barely breathed as the desktop booted up in a completely normal fashion. Both breathed a sigh of relief when it appeared that the desktop computer was fully-functional. That relief lasted mere seconds for IT guy; as he surveyed the desktop screen, what he saw looked like a mess. "If the hard drive looks anything like this desktop screen, we have a lot of work to do on this thing."

22

"*Fort Worth Center, this is Blue Sky 617 at flight level three three zero, and the ride is smooth.*"

"*Blue Sky 617, Fort Worth Center. The ride at three three zero has been reported smooth ahead. Below flight level two four zero in the descent has been reported light to moderate turbulence.*"

"*Fort Worth, Blue Sky 617. Thanks for the head's up.*"

It was Mike Chelsea talking on the radio. Dan was the flying pilot; with the autopilot on, there wasn't much to do. He thought about the call he got on his cell phone less than a minute after walking into his hotel room the night before. It was the chief pilot on duty, and he wanted to know if Dan had anything to add regarding the video of him that was trending on social media. After Dan said no, the chief gave him a little speech about social media, corporate image, and even texting with friends about work incidents. That while Dan didn't know he was being recorded, in these times you should always assume you are. Dan let the chief know that he agreed completely with the speech, even if it sounded as if it had been delivered numerous times.

A low profile was definitely in everyone's best interest. Dan was sure that Angelo would agree completely. Thinking about the turbulence in the descent, he pushed the PA button on his audio control panel and said, "Flight attendants, please prepare for landing." Hearing the prerecorded announcement about preparation for landing meant to Dan that they heard his announcement, and they would be safely seated by the time they were in turbulence.

Mike smiled at Dan and said, "Have I told you enough times today that your girlfriend is hot like the fucking Sun?"

"Jesus, Mike. This again?" Dan knew Mike was again referring to the dinner he and Sindee had with Mike and Toni at Del Frisco a few weeks prior. Dan wanted the Chelseas to meet Sindee, and Del Frisco was Dan's favorite place to get a steak dinner done right. When Dan told Sindee about the dinner, he noted the sexy smirk she wore as she said it sounded like a great idea. He took one look at her outfit and knew she was doing her best to look like eye candy on Dan's arm. Mike kept asking Dan who Sindee really was, in a humorous way, and they all had laughs.

"So, you've finally accepted that she is, in fact, my girlfriend?"

Mike said, "Yeah, I guess I understand. She must be a very generous and sympathetic type, you know, taking on a charity case like you." They laughed, and then Mike sighed. "I didn't tell you this: I paid a pretty hefty price for all that once I got home. Hell, not even that far. Toni started blowing me shit in the car. She took the whole dinner and the conversation as me downgrading Toni every time I made a joke."

"Well, you did lay it on pretty thick."

"How could I not? Sindee is, on a scale from one to ten, at least a fifteen. I don't know how you even leave for work."

The webcam shows were still a secret. Dan hadn't told Mike about them in more of an effort to keep a low profile. Dan wasn't concerned about how Mike would feel about them. He was pretty certain he knew exactly how Mike would feel about the shows.

. . .

The approach, landing, and taxi to the gate were routine. As soon as he brought the airplane to a stop at their assigned jet bridge, Dan set the parking brake, and said what he always said to his first officers. "As soon as we get the checklist done, grab your stuff, and head out. I'll finish putting the airplane to bed."

"Thanks, boss. You get paid the big bucks, right?" Mike joked.

As soon as Mike was off the flight deck, Dan stood in the doorway, thanking the passengers as they left the aircraft. Captain Hatfield watched all the passengers, and then the four flight attendants, exit his airplane. Finally alone, he shut the airplane's electrical system down completely, and walked onto the jet bridge with his bags in tow.

On the way to the employee parking shuttle bus, he sent a quick text to Sindee. "Headed to the truck. Be home in a half hour. Can't wait, baby."

. . .

Reading the text on her phone, Sindee's smile grew. She was looking forward to her man coming home, and she wanted Dan to know he was missed. Sitting on the counter of the kitchen was a bowl of ice, a whiskey tumbler glass, and bottle of scotch. Hair and makeup took the better part of an hour, even though she intended to completely wreck both in the following two hours. Completing Sindee's "Welcome Home" was a lace full-body stocking and red, four-inch heels. She checked her look in the full-length mirror in the master bedroom closet. She held her phone out to take a selfie to hurry Dan home, but the phone buzzed. It was Angelo.

"Hey, big guy, how are you?" she purred.

"I'm good, darling. What are you up to?" Sindee could hear the smile in his voice.

Sindee moved in for the kill. "Well, my man is coming home right now. When he walks in, he's going to find me laying on the bed, covered in lace, in heels, and warming up for him."

Angelo sucked in a breath. "Oh my God, sweetheart, that is a picture that is affecting me."

"I know it is, but you called me, big guy. How can I help you?"

"Your man has a few days off from flying. If you two don't have plans tomorrow, I'd love to see you for lunch. Regular place, regular time." Angelo was asking, but Sindee knew that when Angelo asked, you didn't say no.

"No problem, big guy, we'll be there. I'll tell him all about it before I spend the next two hours draining every ounce of energy out of him. I may have to remind him later."

Angelo said, "Baby, thank you, but I gotta hang up now or I won't be able to concentrate for the rest of the afternoon. See you tomorrow." *Click.*

. . .

Angelo disconnected the call and placed the phone on his desk in its proper location with the other phones. "Jesus Christ, that woman is a white-hot flame. That was Sindee."

Nico was in the office. "Boss. Oh my God, I caught one of her Web shows a few days ago. That Asian broad was on there with her. She's amazing, both of them are. You need to be home alone to watch one of those shows."

Angelo was losing his patience. He had a busy day, and was already thinking of his next phone call, but was having great difficulty getting Sindee out of his head. "Yeah. Dan is on his way home right now, and he is one lucky motherfucker." *Speaking of Dan's future plans...* Angelo selected the correct phone for his next call and dialed his guys doing surveillance in Houston. The people Angelo called usually picked up by the second ring. "My guy confirmed he will be in your area on the date we already talked about. That gives you some time to put everything together."

"Boss, it's already set. All assets are in place, the guys all know their jobs, and we've been gaming it all out, practicing. We are ready. This is fuckin' big, boss. Fuckin' huge, and we are going to execute for you. We are not going to let you down."

Angelo was pleased. "That's what I like to hear. This'll chop up into huge pieces. We do this, and no one can ever talk about it again, but I'm gonna make sure everyone gets a big enough split that they'll want to keep their mouths shut. We will talk details in person. Good work, I'm counting on you. I'll call you morning of to check in." *Click.*

23

The ride home from the airport, as always, was an exercise on autopilot. Several times in Dan's career, he intended to stop somewhere on the way home from the airport, only to realize he'd forgotten when he was turning into the alley behind his home. This day was a bit different. He had a serious desire to go home because he had a good idea what was waiting for him, and he was daydreaming about it. He knew he had a woman that was actually waiting for him, looking forward to him coming home. It was something he hadn't felt in years. There was a long period of time in the past when he actually dreaded coming home. But no longer. The thought of Sindee and the deep love they felt for each other had Dan setting the cruise control for a speed over the speed limit.

At times, the contrast of his fortune with Sindee reminded him of the difficult years with Sharon. Dan understood how providential it was to be able to quickly rid his life of Sharon, then share his life so quickly with a woman who loved and honored him. As he pulled into his subdivision, the last conversation he had with Sharon was playing in his head. *Fuck her. I know Sindee is home right now waiting for me and is going to welcome me home in a way that shows me she missed me. Something Sharon never did, even back when she allegedly loved me. I don't think she even knew how to love.*

He pushed the garage door button and parked his truck in the garage. Sindee's car, with the Maid for You logo, was parked in the spot where Sharon's BMW used to sit. That put a smile on Dan's face.

As he dragged his bags through the back door of the house, he noticed with a smile that his heart rate was up. It wasn't from the luggage; it was excitement of coming home. He didn't call out for Sindee; he knew where she would be, and he wasn't disappointed. Reclining on the bed, smiling broadly, and looking like a work of erotic art, Sindee growled with the confidence of someone who knew what the next hour would be like.

"My queen."

"My king." Sindee gracefully slipped off the bed and sauntered to Dan, who appeared to be using every last ounce of strength to play along patiently instead of running to her, scooping her off her feet, and throwing her onto the bed. Of all the feelings Sindee inspired in Dan, it surprised him to realize that contentment was the strongest. It wrapped him in a bubble of love and trust that he'd never experienced before and superseded even the lustiest of desires.

Sindee reached Dan and put two hands on his belt. He would feel many things over the next hour, but at the end of it as they lay in bed arm in arm, it would be the contentment that stuck with him the longest.

. . .

Breathing hard, Dan laid in bed next to Sindee. *I run five miles on the treadmill, and I don't breathe this hard this long.* Sindee was lying next to him, stroking him casually.

"So, tell me what happened in L.A. I heard you screwed up a landing and then endangered everyone's lives. Then lied about it." Sindee teased, knowing she was poking the ego of a pilot who knew she was joking.

Dan explained. "Air traffic control put us behind a slower plane, and they screwed up the spacing. I had to abandon the approach. We call it a 'go around.' We climb, fly another approach, and land. The flaps were down at a landing setting, but when we tried bringing them back up to an approach setting, one of them didn't come up. When that happens, the plane doesn't want to fly right. The airplane will want to turn on its own and I have to manually control it to fly wings level." Sindee started stroking him faster as he told the story, causing Dan to have difficulty finishing the story. "I declared an emergency, flew the approach with the flaps we had, and landed. The landing was faster than normal because I didn't have the flaps to slow us down, so we asked the firetrucks to come to the plane and make sure the brakes were not overheated, which could cause the tires to blow. My God, baby, you have me all worked up again."

Sindee only picked up the pace. "Well, I found the story exciting. I thought it would be nice if you did too. By the way, we aren't the only one's excited. Mali watched the video of you on the internet about a dozen times. She said that watching you, all in control, talking to that man... I'm quoting her: 'he sets my pussy on fire, and then makes it so wet it drowns the flames.'"

Dan could see the look on Sindee's face change, as if she thought of something she wanted to talk about. She had also slowed her pace; she was now teasing him while they talked. She said, "Lover, we know each other's histories well, so I know you may be nervous about this topic, but I wanted to ask you a question. The time Mali walked in on us and we all had fun together... baby, that was very hot, and I know you enjoyed it. It kinda felt like a spontaneous thing. Do you think that if we set some ground rules, it would be okay if you, Mali, and I could play sometimes? I don't mean other people, just her, and just occasionally. Is that something we can do? Does that scare you?"

"Fuck yes, it does. I'm afraid the two of you would kill me, and the mortician wouldn't be able to get the smile off my face. Baby, we do know each other, and I know that your heart is one hundred percent mine. I'm not afraid of anyone coming in between us. Okay, that came out wrong. I mean, I'm not afraid anyone is going to affect our relationship. I love you, and I know you love me."

Sindee smiled big. "I do love you, baby, and I know we will have some epic times with her. I've explained to Mali why we couldn't before, and she understood. I was thinking we should surprise her."

Dan nodded, Sindee smiled, and then the talking stopped while Sindee finished the task at hand.

• • •

The office of the Head of Security was deep inside the Silver Star Casino building. The windowless room was more like a big, well-appointed cave, complete with a wall covered in monitors fed by cameras all over the casino. The man behind the desk, Danny Justini, was on his cell phone. "Thanks for the update. If anything changes, let me know. Otherwise, we need to limit communications until the night of the operation. Keep the rest of the crew cool. Business as usual. Later."

Justini disconnected the call and leaned into his office chair, one chosen for its comfort, as he often spent many hours in that chair. The rest of the office was furnished with the same goal of making the office his comfortable refuge, a place where he could, and often did, spend entire days. Even nights were possible; there was an attached full bathroom with shower, wardrobe full of clothing, and a couch that was more like a bed. During his time occupying that office, he'd had hundreds of meals, drinks, and women delivered to him. Leaning all the way back in his chair, Justini reminisced about the many experiences he had in the office, only now he was doing it through the lens of knowing his life was about to change directions drastically.

He looked around the office that he had transformed into a working apartment. *Hard to believe that soon I'll be walking away from all this. My whole life really. Good riddance. We pull this off, I'll buy a life most guys only dream of. I am gonna miss that transfer house, though. But I'm guessing fifteen mil in the bank — well, thirty mil after I knock off that knucklehead*

Grim — will go a long way toward upgrading my life in Thailand. Couple short months, I'll have a killer condo north of Lumphini Park in Bangkok, make connections with the locals, and go back to having a different girl to fuck every day of the year.

His eyes found the backpack sitting on the floor at the end of the couch. That was his only luggage for his flight from America, and to his new life. *I'll buy anything I want in Bangkok. I'm walking away from all of it with only a couple changes of clothes and a bathroom kit. And thirty mil.* That put a smile on his face.

Just then, his desk phone rang, and he saw the extension was Grimaldi's. "Hey, Grim, what's up?"

"Just checking in, making sure everything is in place, everyone on your end has their assignments." Grimaldi sounded upbeat to Justini.

"Spoke with the lead on the car crew a little while ago. Everything is a go. Where are we on moving the money? Is all that set?"

Grim said, "That's a done deal. All goes as planned, and in a few days, you and I will be crossing the Mexican border in a box truck full of cash.

24

While Major Hatfield spent two weeks adding Base Safety Officer to his list of accomplishments, many things were going on behind the scenes of which he was completely unaware. His story was, in fact, given the low level of classification, For Official Use Only. That level was intended to restrict dissemination of information that was not classified as Confidential or Secret. The story was getting around the base by word of mouth, and it reached the reporter pool almost immediately.

One of the first in the pool to hear it was the man who was listening for any whisper of a story he was sitting on exclusively. He was nervous that it was no longer just his story. *Stars and Stripes* reporter Miguel Volpe recognized the story when a few details were related to him by another reporter. The FOUO classification made the servicemen in the know hesitant about talking to reporters, but not to each other, and some of the reporters were beginning to piece the story together.

After a few of them asked the Base Information Officer about it, he called a meeting of the reporter pool. To Miguel's slight relief, the BIO explained to the pool that dissemination of any part of the story was prohibited, and violations would have consequences. He added that all details of the story would be released as soon as possible. After the meeting, Volpe went straight to Dan. Volpe had been keeping track of Dan and knew about his appointment as Base Safety Officer.

Hatfield recognized Volpe the moment he walked into the office. He also noticed that Volpe shut the door behind him and didn't look happy.

"Major, you promised me the exclusive, and I sat on the story before the military locked it down. Who is going to be the actual outlet that breaks your story?" There was almost panic in his voice. "I've promised my boss a huge story. I'm going to look like an idiot if I don't break it."

"Relax, Miguel. I can't tell you why the information is being restricted, but I can tell you that my whole story will be released after a few things happen. I also can't talk about those things, but I can say that the plan Command has for the story is that it is our story, an air force story, and they want it coming out in *Stars and Stripes* first."

Volpe visibly relaxed and took a seat in one of the two chairs in front of the desk. "Major, you wouldn't happen to have any of that Dewar's in the office, would you? I could use a drink. I thought my career was over."

"Miguel, you know how hard that stuff is to get here in Saudi. A guy would have to know someone who works in the Officer's Club. A guy like, say, my good friend Captain Swordfield, who is the O-Club supply officer." As he spoke, Hatfield opened the largest drawer of his desk and retrieved a bottle of the very scotch they were discussing. "I'm afraid all I have is coffee cups in the office. My apologies to Mr. Dewar. Miguel, can I buy you a drink?"

. . .

Miguel Volpe did, in fact, have a lot to worry about. Major Hatfield promised him the story, but Hatfield was not actually in charge of the plan for releasing it. The first issue was the information that was harvested from the combat and capture of the mobile SAM site. Numerous meetings were required in order to produce a detailed report from the collection of investigators. An unofficial deadline of two weeks was established by the officer in charge of the forensic examination of the incident and the site. Everyone had different opinions regarding what information should be classified and what would be disseminated in the press release.

Many were focused on what could actually be released; almost no one was concerned with how it would be released. Luckily for Miguel, the story had a person looking over it who wanted it to be told the right way when the time came.

Major General John Wilde was the marine corps general who listened to Major Hatfield's briefing of the command-level officers. He understood the recruiting potential that stories like Hatfield's story had. Wilde had no doubt that Hatfield's CMH process would go quickly and without any issues. So far, everyone who read the account was sold. That process would culminate with a ceremony at the White House, where a proud President of the United States would place the Congressional Medal of Honor, suspended on its blue ribbon, around the neck of Major Dan Hatfield, USAF.

Wilde felt that the story would most appropriately be disseminated first by *Stars and Stripes* in a multi-day cover story, then after a few days, *Stars and Stripes* would allow other outlets to pick it up. The *Stars and Stripes* article would be timed to go out a week before the White House Ceremony, which would also be announced that day. Hatfield would be free to give interviews after that, coordinated by someone in the Air Force Pentagon Information Office.

. . .

Major Hatfield's phone rang at his desk. *That's odd*, he thought. The phone didn't ring all the way through to Hatfield often; calls were handled by Lieutenant Kane first, and he usually handled them without Hatfield's involvement. When Kane told Hatfield that that is how the office worked, Hatfield's words were, "That's good, because only one of us knows what the fuck he's doing, and it's not me."

He picked up the phone. "BSO Major Hatfield."

"Major Hatfield, it's General Wilde. Do you remember me from your briefing?"

"Sir. Of course I do, sir. How are you?"

The General sounded upbeat. "Well, Major, I wanted to give you a call and bring you up to speed on some of the plans for when the investigation is complete. Do you have a few minutes you can spare from your busy day as the BSO?"

Hatfield laughed. "My day is not that busy, but I suspect you knew that already, sir. Does the Corps treat the BSO office like the gym teacher as well, sir?"

Wilde laughed hard, a confirmation that the Corps was similar. "That's very funny, mostly because it's very true, Major. Well, I do only have a few minutes, so here is the quick version. Your CMH jacket is moving smoothly through the process, should be done soon. We are going to release the story about a week before the White House ceremony and release the info about that ceremony at the same time. You can coordinate your interview schedule with the Pentagon for after the ceremony. We want miles of coverage out of this. Hell, write a book and do a Netflix movie, like everyone else. And oh, by the way, my idea was to release the story in *Stars and Stripes* first, then everyone else can have it."

Oh my God, I never officially cleared my plan with Miguel with anyone. Wilde thinks it's his idea. "General, I have a friend who is a *Stars and Stripes* reporter. With your permission, sir, I'd like him to be the guy to write it. He is here on base, and I could start him working on it now so it will be ready to go."

"Major, that sounds like a helluva plan. Send me an email with his name and contact information just so I have it and can pass it to the Pentagon Info Office. Nice job, Major. See to it that the article is multipart and ready to go as soon as possible. You just took something off my to-do list."

Relieved, Hatfield responded. "Will do, sir, consider it done. I will send you that email, then contact the reporter."

"Roger, Major. I'll be in touch." *Click*

25

To a meticulous planner, unknowns cause anxiety. Angelo was in his office, struggling to deal with unknowns of his own. He was mentally rehearsing and ruminating over the Houston operation. Angelo couldn't find a single angle not covered or detail not completely planned. To him, it was like he already had the money. But El Paso was a different matter. El Paso bothered him because it was full of unknowns. Several times in the last hour, Angelo picked up a cell phone, only to put it back down without placing a call.

I wish they'd hurry up with those fucking computers. He knew many of the unknowns would be blanks that got filled in when Manny and IT guy were done with their work at the Barn. But he also knew it was concentration work they were doing, and every phone call he made asking for an update only broke that concentration and prolonged the process. Loose ends were Angelo's kryptonite.

"Fuck it." He said out loud. *I got Houston in front of me, and it needs my full attention. El Paso can wait. There's no connection between the two, so El Paso's got no effect on Houston, no overlap. I need to concentrate on the short-term and get Houston handled. El Paso is long-term, so by the time Houston is handled, I'm sure I'll have details from the Barn.*

* * *

In his Del Rio, Texas, home, Mario Eliazar struggled to decide the direction in which his life was going to go. In his mind, it was coming down to the downside risk versus the upside potential. *If I bring what I found to Tuber, I'm basically just getting myself out of a hole, then dropping a huge problem in his lap at the same time. There's no credit or recognition there. Worst case is they hang this around my neck. There's no upside potential there and a lot of downside risk. I go the other direction, the upside potential is life-changing, but the downside risk involves prison time — or even death. Either chained to a desk working for a guy who sees me as a pain in the ass, or a well-paid life in the field working with a Mexican cartel that I need to keep happy, or else I end up in an oil drum full of acid.*

He pushed his desk chair back and turned to look out the window at another hot, dry South Texas afternoon. His mind wandered back to the time when he first joined the CIA. Just out of college, Eliazar had several job offers, but none that sounded as exciting as the CIA. He smiled, remembering the fact that it was a spy movie that made him make up his mind. As he watched the movie, he pictured himself as the lead character, a CIA field agent, and by the closing credits, he was sold.

His happiest days at the CIA were the first day, when he was processed in, and the day he was made a field agent right after training. But it was all downhill from there. No one would make a movie out of his exploits working in the field, and there didn't seem to be any potential for that to improve. Then one day, he found himself neck deep in his current situation. When his thoughts returned to that present moment in his office, he began gaming out his new path.

I've got everything in front of me, except my out. If I'm going to disappear, I'm going to need time to carefully set up my plan for doing so. When I disappear, the CIA is going to come looking for me. My out plan is going to have to be rock solid. Fuckin' Bayan. I thought we were friends. Sure, I can recreate his situation, especially if I'm starting with his bank accounts to do it. I need to pitch a new operation to Tuber, one that is modeled after Bayan's. He was making regular reports to Tuber and taking credit for busts that happened using info fed to him by Villareal. The op Bayan was running looked and felt to Tuber like it was being legitimately run. The only thing Bayan wasn't reporting was his conspiracy with one cartel, and the money he was making. I have basically two tasks here: I need to identify a cartel to pitch, and I need to write the whole thing up as an op proposal for Tuber and his superiors. Recreate Bayan's gravy train, put away a pile of cash to retire with, make preparations to disappear forever, and keep working the op until I can. That's a plan. Okay. Fuck it. I'm in.

Eliazar recalled that Bayan's op was named Crossbow. He looked at the Scottish sword hanging on his wall, a gift from a fellow agent who was sent to Scotland years ago on an op involving terrorists setting up camp in the northern part of the U.K. *Claymore, I'll name it Claymore.* He turned his chair to face his desktop computer and began typing out the proposal.

26

There was an exasperation in Sindee's voice Dan rarely heard as she related the recent near disaster at a Maid for You client's house. "It seems that one of our entertainment staff went to the home of a client that only gets his house cleaned. When she was let in, she asked him what he wanted, and he told her he wanted 'the full service' and to 'start in the office.' Well, she goes to the office, takes off her scrubs, under which is a sexy lace ensemble. He walks in the office and laughs his ass off. Turns out, he's gay, and they both had a good laugh."

Dan asked, "So what happened next?"

"The dancer asked the client if he wanted her to put her clothes back on, and he told her no. He told her, with a big smile, that having her clean the house like that was decadent, that he loved the idea, and if she did a good job, he would have her back every week. Then he asked if Maid for You employed any men."

Dan laughed. "I think we need to stick to the present business model. So, what went wrong? How was that possible?"

"Carleton is doing a great job organizing everything, but I think we may have screwed up on priorities and threw him too many tasks right away. Clearly, we need him to drop what he's doing and make our structure and scheduling foolproof."

"Yeah, baby, I see your point, and I think you're right on the money. Why don't you, Mali, and Carleton do a top-down assessment of Maid for You. We don't want missteps to create some kind of attention; we need to keep a low profile. That could have gone very differently, and we can't afford to have anything that blows back on the club. I haven't pissed Angelo off yet, and I would like to keep it that way."

"A top-down assessment? In my world, that means Mali and I have a meeting with our tits out." They both chuckled.

"It means you need to look at how everything in Maid for You is organized. Everything. Change anything where an error is possible and make it foolproof, so nothing like this can happen again. It sounds like we are okay on this one, but that was luck. Let's make sure it was the last time."

Sindee thought about it for a second. "You're right, lover. But that meeting with Mali might be with our tits out anyway. I don't think Carleton will mind." She giggled, then purred in his ear. "Where are you tonight?"

"I have another half hour here on the ground before my flight to Houston. That's my overnight tonight."

Sindee imagined meeting him at his hotel. "How is the hotel there? I could meet you and give you a top-down assessment."

"It is the long overnight hotel downtown. The Statesman Hotel. It's pretty nice, but it's Houston, so not that great of an overnight. Next week, I overnight in Colorado at Eagle Vail. It's beautiful. Let's plan on you going with me there."

She squealed with excitement. "That sounds great, flyboy. Call me tonight when you climb into bed. I want to tuck you in."

° ° °

Dan put his phone in his pocket and went about the process of getting the airplane ready for the short flight from the DFW airport to Houston Intercontinental. He hoped the rest of his trip would be nice and uneventful after the emergency he had on the last trip. He knew that the key to an easy flight as short as the Houston flight was preparing as much as possible on the ground before pushing back from the gate. A check of the weather showed him that afternoon thunderstorms were inconveniently placed on some of the arrival corridors used by Houston ATC for aircraft inbound to Intercontinental. That added even more challenge to an already challenging flight.

The F.O. on this trip was not new to the aircraft or the company. He was, however, a recent transfer from the New York domicile and had little experience flying into Intercontinental. Captain Hatfield made the decision to have the F.O. fly the plane, while Hatfield handled the checklists and radios. That knocked the new-to-Texas challenge down to nothing.

A little over two hours later, Dan had gotten his wish of an uneventful flight into Houston. They were on the van to the hotel. The F.O. told Dan he was looking forward to a couple of beers at the hotel, but Dan told the F.O. he had some work to do on the computer and bowed out.

Dan got to his room and was changing out of his uniform when the knock he was expecting sounded on his door. Looking through the peephole, Dan saw a guy in an Amazon uniform, hat, and mask. He had two boxes in his hands. Dan opened the door, wordlessly took the boxes, closed the door, and put them on the bed. Both were labeled to appear as Amazon orders, Amazon logos on the boxes, and taped heavily. Dan tore the first box open and found that it contained a pistol with threaded barrel, suppressor, two fully-loaded pistol magazines, and a leg holster. When he opened the second box, he found a single page of printed instructions, baseball cap, face mask, reversable shirt, roll of one-hundred-dollar bills with a rubber band, a large plastic garbage bag, and black gloves. As was usual, at the top of the instructions it stated, "Read these instructions carefully, then destroy them completely."

The instructions detailed the op. "This op will take place on a rural road north of Houston. Start by completing the work with your pistol. Properly load the weapon and make it ready. Place the pistol, the suppressor, and the holster in the box they came in, you will carry that to the car. Dress with the provided items, shirt light-colored side out, and keep your gloves in your pocket until you are in the transport car. Once inside, put the gloves on, then the seatbelt. When you exit your hotel room, turn left and take the stairwell at the end of the hall. A car will pick you up at the stairwell exit door at 8:30 P.M. You will be in a car with one other man, the driver. Your driver will take you to a location where you will wait until the driver is signaled to intercept the target vehicle, a high-end Mercedes sedan, black in color. Change the shirt so it is now dark side out. The holster will allow you to add the suppressor to the barrel while still in the holster. Put the holster on and be prepared. Your target will have just left a country house and will be driving in the direction of Houston. Your driver is going to bump the target car at an intersection as they leave a highway. Your driver will get out first, a beer in hand, acting drunk to distract the driver of the bumped car. You then get out of the passenger side of the car, beer in left hand, acting the same, and as you walk between the cars, appear to stumble, getting up with gun drawn from holster. Shoot him multiple times. You will then get in the car with your driver, who will drive you back to the hotel. Reverse your shirt on the way back to light side out. Your involvement at that point is over. Please read these notes carefully and mentally prepare carefully. The target is in charge of security for a large casino. He is careful and methodical. He is usually armed and may be wearing concealed body armor. He needs to be taken down quickly and overwhelmingly. Do not underestimate this man, do not hesitate, do not give him time to reach for his pistol. He will be on edge when he gets out of his car. Re-read these instructions, then destroy them. Mental preparation is extremely important in this op."

Dan looked at the time on the face of his cell phone: 4:47 P.M. *That leaves me plenty of time.* He pictured the scene playing out several times in his head, gaming the op out, and looked for ways it could go bad. *Gotta remember, this asshole could be wearing light body armor.*

Satisfied with his initial preparation, he continued reading. "As always, watch, wallet, cell phone all stay in the room. There's two thousand dollars in cash in case money is needed for something; keep it if not needed. After you get back to the room, unload your weapon, remove the suppressor, place all items back in the boxes, put everything in the plastic bag, and the items will be picked up. Make sure to wash your hands thoroughly."

Dan went through the situation again and identified the key factors: distraction by the driver, the timing of him exiting the vehicle, selling the situation of them being drunk and therefore less of a threat to the target, and how the target would be focusing on the situation.

At first, the target will see the driver as the initial threat. When I get out, I become a threat, so I have to sell the stumble, making me less of a threat so the focus will go back on the driver. The right-side leg holster will conceal the pistol from the target's view. Nice, Angelo. The setup, the equipment, the instructions all had his signature all over them. Biggest key, though, is going to be emptying that pistol mag into the target rapidly, getting at least one head shot.

27

There was a nervousness in Angelo's voice that was born from the magnitude of what was about to happen. Angelo was usually a cool customer. But the execution of many details needed to be perfect in the next twelve hours, and he wanted to make sure all of his planning was going smoothly.

He phoned his guy in Houston. "Okay, so are we all set for tonight? My guy will come through, don't worry. He's a pro."

"I'm sure he is, boss. You wouldn't work with anything less. Everything is a go. Everyone knows their jobs, and we have timing planned accurately. We are not going to let you down, boss."

Angelo nodded. "Sounds good. You know how I feel about talking details over the phone, so you know the deal. After this conversation, destroy your phone and go to a backup. I have the numbers. Now, is the hole ready?"

"Yeah, boss. All of that is good to go, ready to be filled and disappeared. The crew stayed up most of the night getting it ready. They think it's just some rush job. They have no idea. When they return to the site on Monday, they are going to find it filled-in and levelled, ready for the concrete pour. Where it's at, they're gonna pour a huge concrete slab; they're putting up some of those enormous warehouses that are going up all over Texas. That truck won't get found for a hundred years."

Angelo paused, thinking through what he was just told. When he was satisfied that that part of the plan was in place, he went through another aspect. "Good work. These guards are going to be armed, probably a single Glock apiece, nine-millimeter, or a forty-caliber Smith. How are you going in?"

"Yeah, boss. Each of us will be strapped with a suppressed Glock, and three of us with suppressed AR-15's. One guy with night vision goggles and a scoped rifle that is a sweet setup. He knows what he is doing with it, in case we need to reach out and touch someone far away. Like you planned, boss, they need to load the cash in the box truck, lose their utility belts and change into their getaway clothes. We let them do all that, and then move in. We take everything, and the bodies, throw them in the back of the armored car, then everyone knows their tasks to finish. All the evidence gets buried in the armored car."

Again, Angelo paused. When he was satisfied that all the planning was tight, he nodded. "You've done a great job, so far. All that's left is to execute. Go over the whole plan with your guys one more time. Everyone's lives are going to change if we pull this off. Remember to destroy that phone." *Click*

Surveying his row of cell phones on the desk, Angelo selected a different one and dialed his friend, Silver Star Casino vice president. "Andy, listen. All is going well in Houston and that first thing is going to happen tonight. You might want to meet with some friends or something. It might be good if you were around people who know you. You get me?"

On the other end of the call, "I understand. I already have a plan tonight to meet for a long business dinner in a very public place."

"The second thing is this weekend, so get ready for a promotion." *Click*

* * *

Sindee was on an emotional roller coaster; her thoughts bounced between two, intense extremes. Earlier, she envisioned a way for the two of them to give Mali the good news that the three of them were going to play together. But it was impossible for Sindee to think about it without fantasizing scenes in her head, and after several of those movies played in her mind, she was deeply aroused. She wanted to share that arousal with Dan, but he wasn't picking up his phone. That worried her.

He always answers when he sees it's me. One or two calls? Ten minutes even? Maybe. I've been calling for over an hour now with no answer. I don't like this.

For the first time, Sindee put serious thought into what it could possibly be that Dan is doing for Angelo. Sindee knew Dan wasn't supposed to talk about it, and that it was probably best that she didn't know. But she wanted to know. Needed to know. She needed to know that when Dan told her she had nothing to worry about, he was being truthful and not just placating her. Still, the more she thought about it, the more she realized that the mystery of it, the thought of Dan doing something secret and possibly dangerous, also turned her on.

We are going to have to talk about this.

. . .

Sitting in his home office in Del Rio, Texas, Eliazar stared at his computer screen, deep in thought. He wanted to wrap his brain around the proposal he was about to create before he started typing.

If I'm going to sell Claymore to the directors, it has to be a whole package with an endgame that at least sounds good. A goal. But that goal needs to be broad enough that it can never really be accomplished. Something along the lines of "significantly interdict the flow of drugs through differing border sectors of the shared southern border with Mexico."

The actual endgame, of course, was Eliazar piling up wealth, then disappearing.

The first step was moving all the money he'd identified in the offshore accounts to different offshore accounts of his own, then quickly closing the original accounts. The next step was to contact and establish a relationship with a cartel he intended to partner with. After some research, it was the Serpiente cartel, which looked to him like the best bet. Eliazar knew that while the southern border of the United States was porous along its entire length, there were two major areas of the border with a significant flow of drugs. To the west, the extensive border area roughly from El Paso to San Diego; and to the east, there was the border area from Laredo to the Gulf of Mexico.

The Serpiente Cartel owned the eastern area, and also the Texas border from the Gulf of Mexico to most of the way to El Paso. They ran everything into the United States that was illegal, but most importantly, they were the cartel that seized the Villareal fentanyl facility north of Mexico City. It was the biggest fentanyl facility of any of the cartels, conveniently located near the Pacific Ocean ports where the imported Chinese chemicals landed.

Yes, I'll definitely target Serpiente to hook up with. El Paso is burned, and my house in Del Rio is in the middle of the eastern area. Eliazar took the mouse in hand, placed the cursor over an icon on the desktop, and double-clicked it to open. It was a classified report with detailed drug trafficking intelligence, organized by the different cartels and different border regions. He knew his pitch of Claymore needed some real intel in it to make it tasty enough for the directors to bite. He wasn't selling a concept; he wanted to be selling something real.

28

Using his reverse timetable method, Dan planned his meeting with the transport car perfectly, and met it behind the hotel exactly at 8:30 P.M. The driver didn't leave right away; he seemed to know that Dan had a task to do. Dan retrieved the gloves from his pocket and put them on before putting on his seatbelt. Both men had studied the instructions; so, without a word spoken, both men knew the other had studied them carefully. The driver took in a deep breath, which Dan noticed, before he put the car in drive, and the two left the parking lot.

A few minutes after they drove away from the hotel, they entered a highway that headed north. As was the case in the previous ops, no words were spoken, so Dan had no way to know, even after a half hour, whether or not they were even close to their destination. Dan realized it was probably better that way.

If I knew how far away we were, there would be anticipation. Anticipation would bring stress, and stress is the enemy of concentration. Like I say in the airplane; stay cool, do the job.

Dan knew this was going to be a hard target, a guy who was always on his guard, and not someone who would go down easily. He spent the rest of the ride gaming out the op, brainstorming ways that it could possibly go wrong, and what he would do in each situation.

After forty-five minutes of driving, they pulled off the highway. The driver took the first left after the exit, which took them under the highway, where he made another left turn and pulled off to the side. The driver turned off the lights but kept the engine running. During the drive, Dan turned his shirt inside out and strapped on the holster with the pistol inside. With the car stopped on the shoulder of the road, he retrieved the suppressor from his pocket, and feeling down his holster to the bottom, he threaded the suppressor to the small part of exposed barrel. He checked and the holster felt secure. Even so, Dan gave the adjustment strap one more little pull, making the holster tight to his thigh. Dan felt ready.

The driver reached behind Dan's seat and picked up a paper bag from the floor. From the bag, the driver pulled out two cans of beer and an expensive-looking two-way radio. He placed the two beer cans in the center console cupholders, then switched on the radio. It responded with a splash of static that let both men know it was on and working. The noise reminded Dan of the rescue radio he lost in the Iraqi desert years prior.

Dan picked up one of the beer cans to look at it, and the driver touched the top of the can and wagged a finger at the can. It took Dan a moment to realize the nearly unbelievable irony of the situation. Open carry of a firearm was legal in Texas; open container of an alcoholic beverage was not. Also illegal in Texas was shooting someone, regardless of how much he deserved it.

The radio crackled. A man's voice broke through the silence. "Two to One, arrived."

The driver responded with a terse, "One, two."

Dan noticed the driver visibly relax in his seat after he spoke on the radio. *That has got to mean that the target has arrived at the transfer house. That's where they are going to locate and tail him.*

. . .

The single occupant of a black Mercedes S550 pulled the car onto the long dirt driveway that rose from the road below to the small house at the top. The driver of that sedan was Danny Justini, who was making his regular visit to the transfer house used in his human trafficking operation. He saw the box truck from the road; it indicated that the day's shipment of humans had already arrived.

I've been looking forward to a piece of Mexican ass all day. I hope there's some cute ones tonight. He parked his Benz in front of the house and hurried to the front door of the house. Sitting next to the door was the single guard that stayed at the house, a man whose name Justini didn't think was important enough to remember. Justini had set the house up so that a single guard was all that was required. All the other doors and windows were sealed, and at this stop in their journey, the girls had everything they needed in the house. There was plenty of food and drink, a working kitchen, working bathroom, soap, and towels. Most importantly, there were a lot of beds. Most of the girls chose to lay down, since they had all been given a small dose of fentanyl.

Justini walked in. Every girl in the house who could see the door, slowly turned her head in his direction.

Okay, yeah, they all look like their brains have been slowed down just enough to have a little fun. When Justini scanned the room to make his selection, he saw mostly fear in the eyes of the girls. His head stopped as he caught sight of something different in the back of the room; it was a look of defiance. She was older than most, looked to be about twenty years old, but he could see why she was brought there; she was beautiful. *She's got a little too much spring in her step. She needs another dose.*

Justini went to the cupboard that he knew contained the small pills all the girls were supposed to get when they arrived. She must have spit hers out. He took two out of the container and picked up a bottle of water. He slowly walked over to her. He set the pills and the water bottle on the small table she was standing next to. He slowly pulled a pistol from a holster in the small of his back and raised it to her head. With a look of defeat, the girl put both pills in her mouth and chased them down with water.

In ten minutes, she'll be much more agreeable.

. . .

Justini walked out the front door of the transfer house an hour later feeling like he had his whole world under control. *Soon, it's going to be so much better.* He was daydreaming about millions of dollars and much better scenery, when he pushed the start button on the dashboard of his Benz. He put it in drive, spinning the wheels on the dirt yard, and giggled knowing he was pissing off the guard on the front porch with the cloud of dust he just created. In a few minutes, he was on the highway, headed for Houston.

. . .

Dan heard the radio crackle again. The driver sat straight up in his seat when he heard the noise, even more so at the sound of the voice.

"Two to One, outbound, point A," the voice on the radio said.

Again terse, the driver responded, "One to Two, copy." The driver put his finger on his watch, then held up three fingers followed by a zero gesture. Dan thought briefly if that was thirty minutes or thirty seconds. When the driver turned on the headlights, Dan knew it meant thirty seconds.

Dan felt time slow down to a crawl. With that heightened level of awareness, of tension, each second felt like an hour. He knew there was one direction for his life right now; his path was laid out before him with meticulous precision. *The target's path has been laid out too, and he has no idea.* Dan checked his holster one more time, pulling on the strap to make it just a bit tighter.

Go time.

29

The driver stared at his watch; the seconds ticked away. He suddenly put the car in drive without looking away from his watch.

They've got this planned to the fucking second, Dan thought just as the thirty seconds had elapsed and the driver pulled out onto the road. He moved the car up the highway on-ramp and entered the highway. Dan looked ahead, then behind, and could see no cars. *Was their timing off?* They went past two exits. More cars were on the highway now, but Dan didn't see any Mercedes sedan. Then he saw headlights behind them, coming up fast. The driver tapped on the beer cans, and Dan rightly interpreted it was time to open them; the driver nodding as he did so.

Of course, the target would be flying in that car. My driver is doing the speed limit, and there's an exit a half mile ahead. This is one of those math problems from grade school I said I'd never use in life. The ones that start with a train leaving a station at two P.M. traveling at sixty miles an hour. By doing their math, they were actually going to follow a car that was coming up from behind.

The driver already had his right turn signal on when the Mercedes passed them and exited right in front of them, with no turn signal. There was a traffic light at the bottom of the off-ramp. Dan wondered what they would do if the target ran the light. He didn't have to wonder for long as the driver pulled up behind the Mercedes, and stopped about two feet too late, bumping the Benz with just enough force that everyone would know there was damage. Dan and the driver both saw the backup light briefly flash, signaling to them that the target put his car in park. Dan's car was already parked.

As the door opened on the Benz, the driver of Dan's car opened his door, grabbed a beer, and exited the car, slamming the door hard.

Justini shouted in a fury, "What the fuck! Are you fucking drunk!"

The driver, slurring his words, said, "Aw, man I'm fuckin' sorry." The two men met at the rear wheel of the Mercedes just as Dan exited the passenger side of his car, beer in his left hand. The target was pushing on the driver's chest as the two of them continued a heated conversation that Dan wasn't listening to.

When Dan got between the two car bumpers, he stumbled to his knees and said, "Oh fuck, I dropped my beer."

Dan heard the target yell, "Get the fuck out of my way so I can see the damage to my car!" The target had both hands on the driver's chest, pushing him backward. Dan had drawn his pistol from the holster and was holding it at the ready, aimed where the target's chest would appear. When the target came into view, Dan fired rapidly, working the rounds up the target's chest and finally to his face as he unloaded his pistol on the man.

The target briefly had a look of horrified surprise on his face before three of Dan's bullets changed the shape of his face forever. Dan stood and walked to the target, making sure the target was down, and he was. But something wasn't right.

Why did I hear a gunshot with the suppressor? Why did I hear one of my shots? The driver, on Dan's left, stumbled to the ground, holding his chest. Dan looked back at the target and saw the small Glock, still in the target's right hand. With only the light of the headlights, the driver didn't see the gun in the target's hand. From Dan's point of view, the gun was invisible, buried in the driver's chest by the right hand of the target. Dan knew from his military training that the location of the wound was bad.

He holstered his gun, ran to the car, and retrieved the radio. "Two this is One. Need you here, now." Two had positioned themselves on the other side of the highway so that they could be there quickly. Dan had just started first aid on the driver when they pulled up.

Two men got out of the car and looked at Dan, dumbfounded. It took a moment for Dan to realize that they were waiting for him to give the orders. Dan thought for a few seconds. "Whoever is driving the Mercedes, get in it and go. Whoever is driving the target for disposal, get him in the trunk and get ready to go. My driver is shot, so..." As he said "my driver," he turned back to look and realized that his driver had died. Dan drew in a lungful of air and blew it out. "Whoever is driving the target for disposal, take my driver too. I'll drive myself to the hotel. This car will be in the hotel lot, key under the driver's seat. Go!"

With that, they sprang into action. The two men from Car Two loaded both bodies in the trunk of Car Two. One man climbed into the driver's seat and sped away. The other man climbed into the Mercedes and did the same. Dan was a bit slower, but he hit the highway not far behind the other two.

Dan spent the drive analyzing and reanalyzing the scene, how it played out, and whether or not he was to blame for the death of a man who worked beside him, that he never actually met. This was not one of the possibilities he anticipated. Still, he could not get out from under the feeling that a man was lost, and it might be his fault.

. . .

Sipping on a glass of Port, Angelo stared at the row of phones on his desk and waited to hear from Houston with great anticipation. When one finally rang, he answered. "Yeah?"

"Boss, it went off and we got it done. Cleanup is done, and I believe we are clean. But, boss, we lost one of the crew."

Angelo paused; the words hit him like a hard punch to the gut. "Who?"

"Boss, you always tell us, not on phones…"

Angelo angrily interrupted. "You don't think I know that? I'm asking because I need to know!" In a way, to Angelo, it didn't matter who. All of them were men he trusted, men he liked, men he knew he could count on, and men he was going to make wealthy with this one job. Now one wasn't coming home.

"It was Mikey, boss."

Angelo thought, *Oh, fuck. Mikey.* "What did you do?"

"We took him to the same place we took the target."

"Why?"

"Boss. Your guy told us to." Angelo's mind was racing, and it took him a few seconds to reply.

"Okay, stick to the rest of the plan, and I'll talk to you when you get here. You all did fine, and I think my guy made the only call that could have been made. Destroy that phone, go to another backup. We'll talk face-to-face when you get back." *Click*

30

Not knowing Houston very well, and without a cell phone in his possession, Dan pulled off the highway when he got downtown and used a hundred-dollar bill to get directions to the hotel. The money provided in the op package was all Benjamins, and at that price, Dan didn't have to ask more than one person for directions to the Statesman.

The nature of a pilot is to always reflect on a flight, think about what could have been done better, and understand why mistakes were made. An emergency during a flight was dissected with very precise tools. A man died on this op, a team member, and still Dan tried to decide if it was at all his fault. He finally concluded that he did nothing wrong.

If only the driver had said something, warned me somehow. But he said nothing. Maybe he didn't see the gun either. In his mind's eye, Dan saw the gun laying on the ground, still in the right hand of the target. It was compact; one of those small-framed Glocks that fit in your hand.

The Statesman sign was large and well-lit; Dan saw it from blocks away. Thinking what the most appropriate place to leave it would be, Dan parked the car just outside the stairwell door he had exited, in the same location he got in the car. Deep in thought, Dan almost exited the car wearing the leg holster and suppressed pistol. He stopped himself at the last second, reached into the back seat, and retrieved the box he had carried into the car. He took the suppressor off the pistol first, gun still strapped to his leg. The holster came off next. With the gun, holster, suppressor, extra magazine, and pistol in the box, and car key under the driver's seat, he exited the car. Dan entered his hotel room just over two minutes later and collapsed onto his bed. He knew that the knock on the door would happen soon. So, after a few moments, Dan got himself out of bed, and put all the clothes back in the box, to get ready for pickup.

The knock on the door happened just as Dan put the boxes into the plastic bag. Dan hesitated for a second, mentally running over the list, and the instructions, making sure everything was done as instructed. A second knock let Dan know his time was up. Bag in hand, Dan looked through the peephole and saw a man in the uniform of a hotel employee. He opened the door and wordlessly handed the man the garbage bag. As he closed the door, Dan knew his involvement in the op was over, but he still anticipated having a serious conversation with Angelo. How serious, he didn't know.

. . .

Car Two pulled up in front of a funeral home in North Houston. Even at that late hour, there was an old man waiting for their arrival at the back of the building. The driver of Two rolled down his window and said to the man, "I've got a double. We have to wait for the pickup package."

Almost a half hour passed before another car pulled up. On the back seat was a plastic bag with two boxes inside. Both bodies were taken from the trunk of Two and loaded onto a gurney, along with the plastic bag. The gurney was rolled inside through the wide back door and up to a cremation oven. The owner of the funeral home set the oven to its highest heat setting, approximately 1,600-degrees Fahrenheit. In a few hours, everything in the oven would be reduced to ash, except the gun parts. They would be deformed by the heat, unusable to anyone trying to obtain a ballistic match from the barrel. All DNA evidence was gone. The contents of the oven, twenty pounds of ash and steel, was left in the trunk of

Two. Both cars were delivered to the scrap yard on the Northside area of Houston, and the op was tied off clean.

. . .

Sindee had just climbed into bed when her phone rang with Dan's caller ID. She anticipated his call, and when she saw it was Dan, she picked up a large vibrating wand from the nightstand with her left hand as she answered the phone with her right. "Hey, baby!"

Dan replied, "Hi, sweetheart."

Something in his voice sounded off. "Everything okay?"

"It's been kind of a difficult evening, baby. I just wanted to hear your voice."

Now she was concerned. Sindee put down the wand and rolled over on the bed face down, setting the phone down in front of her face. "Tell me what happened."

"I wish I could, babe, I just can't." There was a long pause before either spoke.

Sindee only ever used Dan's name when it was something serious. "Dan, I don't know how much longer I can do this. I'm not sure I want to know what's going on, and you've told me it's for my protection, and I believe you. But how are we going to keep doing this? How long will our relationship be able to go on like this? I heard something the other day in a movie, and I confirmed it's true. If I was your wife, I could never be forced to testify against you in any court."

There was another long pause before Dan spoke. "It's true. That is very interesting, and something that hadn't occurred to me. Lover, I promise you when I get home tomorrow, we will talk about everything. Angelo is going to want to speak to me first, so please be patient enough to let that happen. But after, you and I will get a room someplace nice, order room service, and talk everything out."

Sindee whispered into the phone. "Baby, when you and I get a room, we will do much more than talk."

Dan's voice suddenly perked up. "Pack a nice bag, pick someplace nice, and I will pick you up after I see Angelo." After a long pause, Dan asked, "That sound good?"

"Yes, flyboy, sounds good. I'll pack right now. Tomorrow, I'll head to the hotel on my own. I'll be waiting for you, then neither of us will do much talking for an hour or so. You need to get some sleep now, baby, you're gonna need it. Wanna know what I'm doing right now?" Sindee rolled over onto her back. Her left hand immediately found what it was reaching for on the bed.

31

When it came to phones, Michael Grim was the polar opposite of Angelo. Grim's approach was to soundproof his office in the Silver Star, then have it regularly swept for listening devices. Justini swore to him he had equipment that could determine if his phone line was compromised, and that he checked both of their offices regularly. But Grim was unable to get hold of Justini this morning, and he was fielding a call from the guy in Mexico who would be paid well to launder Grim's cash.

Staring at his speakerphone, Grim said, "I've been calling him all morning. His personal and his work phone both go straight to voice mail. Location is enabled on his work phone, but it's off. I've been calling since he didn't show for work. My guy at Houston P.D. ran the plate number, and the computer says his car crossed over the border into Juarez just after three in the morning today. It's a Mercedes S550 he bought this year, new. Definitely a car worth jacking and driving to Mexico. No way Justini would take off like this. Especially not now."

The voice on the speakerphone asked slowly, "Are we still on for tomorrow night?"

Grim said, "Of course, of course." *And it looks like my cut just got much bigger.* "There's no reason not to go. The armored car crew all have their outs planned. They'll leave the transfer point with their cuts and disappear. My plan is in place for after we meet in Mexico. It would be ideal if you could provide us with an armed escort from the border to your hacienda."

. . .

On the other end of the phone was Eduardo Gaston Mendoza, also known as EGM. He was the boss of the Serpiente Cartel. At the moment of the phone call, he was relaxing on the veranda behind his large hacienda, a cigar in one hand and cell phone in the other. EGM went to great lengths to keep his identity a secret from anyone who didn't need to know who he was and his connection to Serpiente. This phone call was no different. He had go-betweens who dealt with Grim. But he placed this call as one, last personal follow-up with the man in Texas who was going to deliver a truck filled with cash to be laundered.

"An escort to the house, yes, I can arrange that. You'll be protected all the way here. Keep me informed. Adios, my friend." Mendoza hit the red button on his phone, ending the call. Mendoza turned to the other man on his veranda, his number-two man, Javier Mora. "Grim thinks an armed escort from the border to here is a good idea. I agree. I will have men of mine, with guns, meet him at the border." They both laughed.

Mora got the nickname "Sombra," or Shadow, from Mendoza when he brought him on. Mora, however, gave it a more sinister slant with the ruthless way he ran the day-to-day operation of Serpiente. He gained Mendoza's complete trust over the years, so when Mendoza had situations that he felt were going south, it was his Shadow that Mendoza always turned to.

"Mí Sombra, hermano, I need you to go to Houston right now, put eyes on that armored car and make sure all goes as planned tomorrow night. They are going to have to transfer the money to a different truck to bring to us. Be a tail on the armored car to the location they transfer the cash, and then follow the truck to the border. That money is mine as soon as they steal it. I want nothing to go wrong."

"You got it, jefe. I'll leave in less than an hour. I should take some weapons. A man to help me drive might be a good idea too."

"No, hermano," Mendoza said. "I know it is a twelve-hour drive, but I'd like you to go alone. I want to keep this between you and me. Take a smuggle car with Texas plates, and yes, whatever weapons you think you'll need. That is our money. Bring it home."

. . .

One of the phones on Angelo's desk chirped a text notifier. Picking it up, he saw it was a text from Dan that read, "I'll be at your place about two."

Dan's smart, Angelo thought. *He knows I'll want to talk to him in person as soon as he gets in town.* Angelo set the phone down and turned his attention to IT guy, who was seated in front of Angelo's desk. "So where are we at with the computers?"

"We've gone through everything, boss. I think we have the big picture. The El Paso op was definitely CIA, and we know for certain they were working rogue for Villareal. The Cartel was paying them to help get their drugs, mostly cocaine and fentanyl, across the border, while sabotaging the efforts of other cartels. We found evidence that it was becoming known by the other cartels that the success of Villareal was artificial, but none suspected what was really going on. The Juarez area used to be contested territory, but Villareal was becoming stronger, dominating the area, and had become the primary importer in that border area."

"It definitely went to their heads," Angelo said, "and that is why Villareal thought they could move in on El Paso."

"We have quite a bit in the way of contact information south of the border, the structure of the cartels, territories, cartel activity, locations, etc. A pile of information, boss. Question is, what do we do with it all?"

Angelo took it all in, nodding. "First, great work you and Manny are doing, it will not go unrewarded. Yes, that is the million-dollar question. What do we do with all this?" The gears in Angelo's head started spinning.

"Boss?" IT guy asked.

"I'm going to put some thought to that, but you guys did great work for me on this. I'm not going to forget about it."

"Boss, there's something else I didn't want to bring up until I knew we had control, and I only closed that loop this morning. You're gonna love this. We identified seven accounts in the Caymans, we have all the information necessary to transfer the money out of them and into our accounts. The total is just a shade over eleven million. Most of the accounts are definitely personal accounts that the CIA crew set up for themselves. The money in those accounts is from the cartel, and I'm positive the CIA didn't know about them, and probably still doesn't. But I can't be certain about two of them; they might be CIA-funded accounts, maybe operating money for the crew. In the accounts I'm sure were personal, there's about nine point seven million, with the rest in the other two."

Angelo didn't need to think long on this. "Take every penny in the accounts we are sure have dirty money, leave the other two. But let's do that right now, before someone else finds it."

"I'll call Manny on the way back to the Barn and have him set everything up."

Angelo said, "Do it. You and Manny get a cut of anything you can wash through our laundering accounts that we get into our hands clean."

32

"I just parked the airplane in DFW. I'll be in the truck in a half hour, and in front of Angelo a half hour after that. I don't know how long the meeting will go, baby, but it's Angelo, so you know it's going to go as long as he needs it to. After that, I am all yours."

Sindee said, "I'll be all yours as well, lover. Whatever you want, as long as we talk later."

"I promised, baby, and I'll keep that promise."

Sindee's voice took on that smokey sexuality that told Dan everything he needed to know about how she was feeling. "I will, too, and I want you to know that right now, my body misses you very much. Keep that in mind; maybe it'll put a spring in your step." Dan huffed into the phone. "You know it will. I'm gonna hang up now so I can get off this plane. Text me the name and address of the hotel. Are you there already?"

"I got here an hour ago. The room is ready, my look is ready, and I'm getting my body ready right now." Sindee's last words came out with a heavy breath.

"I love you, baby. Gotta go. I will hurry."

"I love you too, flyboy. Please do."

With a goodbye, Dan hung up the phone, and quickly completed the Parking checklist for his aircraft. Then he did something that was very uncharacteristic for Captain Hatfield. While the passengers were still getting off the airplane, he darted from the cockpit, bags in tow, and hurried up the jet bridge. Dan was missing Sindee so much, he skipped his usual routine of thanking his departing passengers.

. . .

Special Agent Glenn Miller of the FBI decided to take a second look at the house in El Paso. To him, the house was a loose end, an odd one completely without explanation. Miller was meticulous, a quality that suited his job as an FBI Special Agent, but that quality worked against him when an investigation stalled. The house in El Paso made absolutely no sense to Miller. Whoever lived in that house, and whatever it was they were doing, had tracks that were too well covered for it to be some kind of criminal operation, even for the Mob.

The financials were dug into by the Financial Crimes Division, and they made no inroads at all identifying who actually paid the utilities, the taxes, or anything else. The closing on the sale of the house was a cash purchase, conducted entirely online, with electronically signed documents. Cyber Crimes looked at the pictures of the house and believed that it contained sophisticated electronic installations. Interviews of the neighbors revealed little; what was seen did not at all support the idea of a drug cartel setting up an operation in El Paso.

Miller's hunch kept coming back to an intelligence operation, but CIA isn't sanctioned to operate within the United States. It didn't mean they weren't behind this or that they never operated within the United States. But to be legitimate, they would have been required to have the cooperation of local law enforcement. El Paso P.D. had no idea what was going on.

All of this was going through his mind as he stepped through the back door of the house, with pistol in one hand and flashlight in the other. The house was empty. Miller thought, *you always miss something.* Then he noticed the forced open door under the stairs. *What the hell?*

Miller walked down the hall to the previously hidden door and shined his flashlight inside the opening. *This was definitely something we missed that someone else found. Kids maybe? Would teenagers have been smart enough to even look for it? And if it wasn't them, then who?*

Miller entered the hidden room, looking around methodically with his flashlight. There was no graffiti, no vandalism, and there were numerous items that were stored in the room that all appeared to be in order. *No, not kids.* Scanning his flashlight around the small room carefully, he saw holes in the wall in one corner. *Looks like some kind of electronic equipment was there. It's gone now.* Miller took cell phone pictures of everything he could see, then left the secret room. He was moving to the front of the house where the office was when his cell phone rang.

"Special Agent Miller? This is Greg White from the Crime Scene Analysis office of the El Paso Police Department. I was told to call you if we had a hit of any kind with regard to a crime scene you were brought in on in El Paso."

"Yeah, I'm actually standing in that crime scene right now. What do you have?"

"I have something small. Some of the prints taken from the scene come back to one person who has a small record on the NCIS. He was fingerprinted from a DUI stop in San Francisco about twenty years ago. Searches of the internet revealed that this guy probably graduated with a computer science degree about that same time from San Francisco State University. But otherwise, he's invisible on all other networks. It appears that he, or others, have scrubbed all evidence of his life from the internet. From any net."

There was a pause, and Miller felt like the technician was waiting for him to fill in some blanks. Finally, Miller spoke. "Okay, thank you, please email me everything you have. Oh, and make sure you read in Detective Wampler on this."

"Will do. Good day."

• • •

Miller sat in his office, looking at an email that he felt certain the technician sent less than a minute after they spoke on the phone. He opened the attachment. It was pretty much exactly what White described. An arrest record for David Arrowwood for Driving Under the Influence. His breathalyzer blow during the arrest was one-point-three; he was hammered. His address, phone number, and his student status at SFSU were in the report, along with the person he called to bail him out of jail.

Twenty years ago. Jesus this is thin.

Miller opened the phone app on his cell and dialed the number. To his surprise, a woman answered. "Is this Sarah Ito?"

"Yes?"

Miller was surprised again. "This is Special Agent Glenn Miller of the FBI. I want to ask you a few questions. Is this a good time?"

"Of course."

Miller asked, "Do you have any interaction with students from SFSU?"

"Yes, I run a small apartment building that I purchased thirty years ago. My husband was SFPD, and he was killed in the line of duty. I used the life insurance money to buy the building."

"I'm sorry for your loss. This is a long shot, but do you remember a male student from about twenty years ago named David Arrowwood?"

After a short pause, she answered, "Why yes, I absolutely do. Why do you ask about him? Is everything okay?"

Miller continued. "Can you tell me what you remember about him?"

"He kept mostly to himself; his major was in computers. He was very smart and very handsome. This is embarrassing, but I was attracted to him, and when he came home from a party drunk one night, we had a thing. It became a fairly regular relationship and lasted about a year. We both knew he was graduating, and someone was going to hire him, most likely not in San Francisco. When he passed his last exams, he and some friends got pretty drunk. He got arrested for DUI and called me to bail him out. Not long after was graduation, and then he moved out."

"Do you know where he went?"

Ito said cheerfully, "Oh yeah, I do. I always knew someone would recruit him; he was so smart. He went to Langley, Virginia. The CIA hired him."

Miller was pleasantly surprised one more time. "Thank you, Ms. Ito, you were very helpful."

"Is David in trouble?"

"Oh no, Ms. Ito. We just need his help."

33

Lieutenant General Taylor Hawkins stared at the email on his computer desktop and sighed. *Well, it was only a matter of time. The guy's a pilot, for Christ's sake, and we clipped his wings. BSO must be hell.* Hawkins had the Base Commander's extension memorized, having called it so many times. He picked up the desk phone and dialed.

"Commander McHugh's office."

"This is General Hawkins for the Commander."

"The General is in. Standby one, sir, I will put you through."

General McHugh picked up his phone. "General McHugh."

"Stacy, it's Taylor Hawkins."

"Taylor, how's the wing?"

Hawkins began the hard part of the conversation. "Operations are fine, General, I'm calling you about Major Hatfield. I knew that sooner or later he'd be requesting a meeting, and it isn't rocket science guessing why he wants to see me. He's been in that office for almost two weeks. I've known Dan since he arrived here. He's a pilot. He lives and breathes it. I'm sure he's going nuts in that office. I agree that he needs to stay there. The reason I'm calling is I was hoping you've heard something so that I might be able to give him an idea of his parole date."

"Yeah, Taylor, I guess that was easy enough to see coming. As a matter of fact, I called the Pentagon early yesterday morning. The Congressional Liaison for Award Affairs updated them. In keeping with the plan, the vote was taken confidentially and the award for Major Hatfield was approved. Of course, the vote results will be released with the story in *Stars and Stripes*, but it was unanimous. My order for Major Hatfield is to begin packing. He will be on a flight for the States in less than forty-eight hours. Tell him that comes from me, and I will get him written orders in a few hours."

"Okay, Stacy, that's great news. I'll tell him, and I'm sure he'll be glad to hear it. Did you want me to share all of that with him? That his CMH Citation went through? Usually, that would be your prerogative."

General McHugh thought for a moment and replied. "No, Taylor, I believe you should be the one to do it. He's your boy, a pilot in your wing. This is once-in-a-lifetime. Let him know but remind him that that information isn't public until we make it public."

"General, thank you, sir. It'll be an honor. I'm heading over to his office right now."

* * *

Major Hatfield was sitting behind his desk, telling his story, and answering the questions of Miguel Volpe, being recorded on two different recorders set in front of him on the desk. Volpe also took notes, which Hatfield assumed were the questions that came to Volpe's mind as Hatfield spoke. It was their fourth session like this; they had spent hours with Volpe collecting every detail and every viewpoint he could. Hatfield was deep in thought and trying to be precise in his answer when someone knocked confidently on his door and shook him back to reality. The sight of the man walking through the door surprised Hatfield.

At the sight of Lieutenant General Hawkins, Hatfield stood quickly at attention and held a salute. Hawkins returned the salute. Hatfield said, "General, when I sent the email requesting a meeting, I was just trying to schedule one at your convenience in your office. There was no need to..."

Hawkins cut him off. "Major Hatfield, I make my own schedule, and

I'll meet who and where I choose." Dan nodded, and Hawkins continued. "I wanted to meet with you today to discuss a few things. Did I interrupt?"

Volpe stood and offered his hand. "Miguel Volpe, *Stars and Stripes*. Twenty-two years, army and air force. Medically discharged. Pleased to meet you, General."

Hawkins took his hand and shook it firmly. "Thank you for your service, sir. Volpe? Volpe. You were Air Force Pararescue, right?"

Proudly, Volpe spoke the motto of the Pararescue, "That others may live, sir."

Hatfield injected, "Major General Wilde of the Marine Corps called me to inform me that information release would be through *Stars and Stripes*. I suggested I get started with Miguel, a friend, and the general authorized it. We were just working on getting the articles put together."

"Articles?" Hawkins asked as he took a seat.

Hatfield explained. "Yes, sir. General Wilde suggested a multi-part series of articles covering a few days. But sir, the reason I requested a meeting with you was to discuss my present situation. If I could speak freely, sir, this office job could be done so much better by someone else, and being grounded is very difficult for me. I understand the reasoning, but I just wanted to put in my formal request to be restored to flight status. I've been medically cleared. You could give me low-risk missions. I just want to do what I was trained to do."

Hawkins listened to Hatfield's plea, then spoke. "Dan, we have plenty of pilots. We have very few heroes, and like it or not, that is what you are. Your story will inspire, and so it needs to be told. It needs to have a happy ending, so you need to come home to America. You've earned it."

Hatfield opened his mouth to respond, but General Hawkins cut him off by raising his finger in the air. Hawkins paused for a few seconds, then said, "Okay, I think I have the right two people in the room I need to talk to and share some news with that I think you are going to like, Major. Let me start by reminding you that anything discussed here today stays between us until you are authorized to speak on the subject." General Hawkins stared down the two men.

Hatfield and Volpe nodded an affirmative.

"Wilde briefed you on the plan, Major, and I'm sure you briefed Volpe, who would be a person with a need-to-know, so that's fine. What you don't know is that the event we have been waiting to happen, to launch the dissemination of the story has just happened. Major Hatfield, it is one of the highest honors of my life to inform you that you have been awarded the Congressional Medal of Honor, ceremony to be conducted at the White House at a date about a week from today. It will be conducted by the President himself. General McHugh has asked me to inform you that he is ordering you stateside, to begin packing immediately, and that you will be on air transport within forty-eight hours. Written orders will be delivered today. Congratulations, Major."

Hawkins rose, and for the second time in his life, Hatfield received the salute of a superior officer. Hatfield returned the salute.

Volpe said, "Good Lord, Dan. The CMH? Congratulations. Jesus, in the history of Pararescue, we have only one CMH. Well, I've heard the story now several times, and you sure as hell deserve it. General, would you join us in a toast."

The question appeared to surprise the general, who up until now had assumed there was coffee in the coffee cups in front of each man. As the smile spread across Hawkins's face, it was matched by Volpe and Hatfield. "On a day like this, at a time such as this? Absolutely. What are we drinking, gentlemen?"

Hatfield retrieved the bottle of Dewar's from his desk, along with a third coffee cup. He poured a healthy shot of scotch into it and offered it to the general.

Hawkins made the toast. "To Major Dan Hatfield. A warfighter in the air and on the land. A warrior truly deserving of the Nation's highest honor, whom I've had the privilege and honor to have had in my command. To Hatfield!"

. . .

With Volpe in tow, Hatfield strolled back to the part of the base that contained officers' quarters. Volpe wanted to take in the scene of Hatfield packing and saying his goodbyes to his fellow airmen. What Volpe guessed was that before Hatfield could even get back to his quarters, much of the camp would have heard he was leaving. The scene of Hatfield packing while half the base filed into his quarters and wished him farewell was something that Volpe felt would be a good addition to his articles. He knew that the actual ceremony in Washington, D.C. would be a part of the story that would tell itself as video when it occurred. The warm camaraderie of this evening, of a combat unit sending off a member of which they were very proud, was something Volpe very much wanted to be a witness of, and to document for the country they were defending.

It turned out that Volpe underestimated the response. At first, it was just the other pilots in the long, rectangular tent, asking what was going on when they saw Hatfield packing up. Then, airmen filed into the quarters one or two at a time, saying they heard Hatfield was leaving, and wanted to wish him well. As the group grew, the cloth partitions between the pilots' individual areas were taken down, creating one big room that filled up with groups of four or five at a time. Volpe took notes and a few pictures.

Everyone is wishing Dan well, but no one is leaving, like they're waiting for something. Holy shit, they're waiting to hear Dan tell the story. Of course.

Volpe was torn about his next move. Hatfield was quartered in one of the biggest tents on the base, and it was now full. Volpe wanted to capture the scene of Major Hatfield relating his story to his fellow airmen, and he knew they really wanted to hear it. That was obvious by the looks on their faces and the fact that not a single person had left. Making up his mind, Volpe climbed onto a chair and made the announcement.

"Attention! Can I please have everyone's attention?" Silence fell about the room; there were at least one hundred faces looking at Volpe in anticipation. "Who here would like to hear the story of Major Dan Hatfield's shootdown and desert rescue?" There was only a half-second of silence before the room erupted in cheers and whistles. After a minute, Volpe held out his hands and the room slowly returned to silence. He turned to Hatfield. When they made eye contact, Hatfield nodded and laughed. When he traded places with Volpe on the chair, the airmen erupted into cheers again. The noise attracted even more airmen; their number grew by at least twenty more before the crowd quieted down enough for Hatfield to begin. Volpe stood next to him, holding the recorder that would capture the tale.

34

Angelo saw Dan's pickup make the turn into his driveway, and slow as it approached the gate. Before Dan could push the intercom button, Angelo had already selected the front gate to "Open." Looking at the computer monitor, Angelo clearly saw a look on Dan's face that was of a man being called to the carpet. *I'm finally going to get the story, but why does he look like he's bringing me bad news I don't already know?*

The sound of the back door opening, and then close, and the warm greeting Dan had for Maria carried to the office. She was busy cleaning up the late lunch she had served Angelo, singing quietly to herself when Dan opened the door. She offered him a cup of coffee, which he politely refused. The alligator boots Dan preferred to fly in made his steps audible throughout the first floor of the house as he crossed the wood floor of the kitchen to the hall leading to the office. *I can actually hear in the way those boots touch the floor that Dan's step is missing his usual swagger,* Angelo thought.

Angelo rose from his desk at the sight of Dan and extended his hand. Dan looked at the hand, then Angelo's eye before shaking it firmly. "Tell me what happened. Just start from the beginning, Dan."

"Everything was going like clockwork, it was perfect, all the way through the driver bumping the back of the target vehicle. My driver gets out first, gets the attention of the target. I get out next, and boss, I've replayed this in my head a hundred times. As I get between the cars, I see the target with both hands on my driver's chest, cursing him, saying he wants to see the back of his car. I stumble like I'm supposed to, come up off the ground with my weapon at ready. The target still has both hands on the driver's chest. I unload the weapon on the target, stitching him from navel to forehead. I could see the body armor stopping the chest shots, but he was shocked and falling backward. Last three rounds were to the face. As he falls backward, I know he's down but I can't figure out at first why I heard one of my shots. Then I see the small Glock in his right hand. I turned, but my driver took one in the chest. I knew it was bad as soon as I saw where he got hit. I tried to help, but he didn't make it. Like I said, I've replayed this a hundred times. I know his hands were empty when I went down. When I came back up, I wasn't looking at his hands, I was concentrating on taking him out. Why the driver didn't say anything, I don't know. The target had to have drawn that Glock when I was on the ground. Why didn't he warn me?"

Angelo held up his hand. "Okay, Dan, that's enough. I know everything else. Listen, you were in combat, and I'm going to guess that you've lost friends before."

Dan nodded.

"You couldn't blame yourself when another pilot took a wrong turn or made a mistake that cost him. It doesn't sound to me like you should be taking any blame here. Put it out of your head. Mikey knew what was going to happen when you got to your feet. Why he chose to just stand there, I don't know. But it's not your fault. Where are you going after we finish?"

Angelo could see that Dan's mind was still on that rural Houston highway, and his question snapped Dan back to the present. "Uh, well, Sindee is waiting for me in a hotel room so we can blow off some steam, talk about a few things."

Nodding at what sounded to him to be a good thing, Angelo spoke. "That's perfect, Dan. We're done here. Get outta here; go meet up with Sindee. I'll be calling a meeting at Vincent's soon for the Houston crew.

I'll let you know. Dan, bad things happen. We don't have to like them, but we move on. You did well."

Dan stood, nodded, and without another word spoken, walked toward the back door of the house. *That stride already sounds more confident. If I was meeting Sindee, that stride would be faster.*

. . .

It was after 2:30 P.M. when IT guy got back to the Barn; Manny was working diligently. "So, Manny, where are we now with the accounts?"

"Right after you called, I moved all five target accounts, the ones we talked about, into five new accounts, then I moved all five into one of the laundering accounts. Then I moved it through a crypto transaction, which I cashed into three new accounts in a different bank. Now it is all sitting in one account in a third bank, Banco Mundial, a Brazilian bank with a physical facility in Georgetown, Grand Cayman. It's clean as a whistle. Now we just need to find out what Angelo wants to do with the cash. If he wants to chop it up, I can set up more accounts at Mundial, or move it anywhere he wants."

"The boss said he is going to take care of us for all the work and for grabbing this money. Good work, Manny." IT guy took out his cell phone and dialed Angelo. "Boss, we are done with all that we talked about in the office today. We got it, cleaned it, now we just need direction for what you want to do with it."

IT guy could hear the excitement in Angelos's voice. "That is great news! Plan on bringing a laptop to my place day after tomorrow. We will finalize things." *Click*

Manny heard the voice of Angelo even though he was six feet from IT guy. *I grabbed and washed nine-point-seven mil today for Angelo. The boss will take care of us well, he always does. But this? This is huge.* As soon as IT guy put down his phone, Manny asked, "So, what did he say?"

IT guy sighed. "He said to bring a laptop to his office day after tomorrow to put the money to bed. We're gonna get our cut of nine-point-seven mil, brother."

* * *

Eliazar sat in his office, staring at his computer; the late afternoon sun leaked in the window behind him. He'd spent hours writing up the outline and pitch for Claymore. Several more hours were spent citing and sourcing data that he used to give the pitch the numbers it needed to make it look well-researched. Since he was CIA, he already knew much of the general data, but reports deserve specific numbers, locations, and names, when possible. Eliazar knew the drill. Deliver an idea to the directors that makes them confident it will make them look good later. Between his access to CIA intel, and the Bayan server, he had all the information he needed to sell Claymore. His sources also gave him the intel to make Claymore work.

Writing reports and proposals was simply time spent at the computer. Eliazar knew he had not crossed any lines yet, but he also knew that he was standing in front of one, and a decision had to be made. It was time for his first "overt act." Mario Eliazar decided it was time for Mario to take care of Mario.

He opened a folder on his computer desktop screen, double-clicked an icon, and a banking website opened in his browser. The Falcon Bank of Kuwait has a physical location in the Cayman Islands, with account services available online. Accounts managed by the webpage dedicated to that location were then subject to the financial and accounting laws of the Cayman Islands. Any money deposited into one of their accounts was effectively put into a safe that only the account holder had the combination to.

Or if, like the El Paso crew, the account holder was dumb enough to have all of his accounts set up for auto-login on his browser, anyone with access to his computer would have access to the money. In Eliazar's case, access to the backup drive of the account holder was enough. He executed the steps necessary to access the seven Cayman bank accounts he had identified from the drives and was fully prepared to take that first step and cross the big line.

The bank accounts screen popped open — Mario stared dumb-founded at the computer screen. It wasn't possible. He double-checked to make sure they were the right accounts. Triple-checked. Quadru-ple-checked. But every time he saw the same results: the account balances were wrong. Five of the seven accounts showed zero balances.

What in the actual fuck!?

The two remaining accounts with money in them were the ones Elia-zar suspected were CIA-owned accounts. Accounts set up to fund the El Paso op, government money. He had the capability to confirm whether those accounts belonged to CIA, but then his inquiry into those accounts would be recorded by the CIA. If he moved money out of those accounts and they were CIA, he would be arrested when the CIA went to reclaim the money.

Fuuuuuck!

What is my play here? Did the El Paso crew have another member that I don't know about that still had access to the money? The CIA didn't know about those accounts; they haven't even policed up their own money yet.

"Motherfucker!" He yelled. But then he had an idea. *I'm going to pitch this as part of Claymore. I'd then be free to inquire about any accounts attached to Crossbow. If only one of the two turns out to be opera-tional, I am then free to empty the other. If they are both CIA operational accounts, they can both be re-budgeted to Claymore. Either way, I won't be pitching something new. I'm already funded and allegedly conducting the same operation.*

Eliazar knew that he needed to put the finishing touches on Claymore and move soon if he was going to grab those accounts before someone else did. And if someone did grab a CIA-funded account, he'd be free to go after them, and then maybe he'd find out who liquidated El Paso.

35

Sindee stood in front of Dan wearing knee-length black boots, a leather-strapped garment that covered nothing, and perfectly appointed makeup. Sindee was a vision, almost unreal in her beauty and sexuality. She certainly never disappointed.

The first hint Dan got that he was in for a good time was the knowing smirk from the guy at the front desk when Dan asked for a key to the room she had reserved. Clearly, Sindee left an impression on the clerk, enough that he remembered the room number. Dan boarded the elevator of the upscale, downtown Dallas hotel and pressed the top button.

When he exited the elevator, he noticed that there were not many room numbers on the sign, and the room numbers had an "S" in front of them. The floor was comprised entirely of suites. Many travelers liked suites; they were larger, had more of a feeling of actual living space, and allowed for the traveler to have guests or meetings. Sindee liked a suite because it offered a more delicious variety of sexual situations than were possible in a regular hotel room. Dan loved Sindee deeply and was committed to her completely. But he also loved the raw sexuality of her, and the way she expressed her love with Dan through sex, without inhibition or hesitation. He knew Sindee was a rare woman, a rare lover, and that he was a lucky man.

Knowing all that, he still was not completely prepared for what he saw when he opened the door to the suite. He was yet again blown away by the pure sexuality she displayed, and she was all Dan's.

Sindee walked up to Dan, and while he still had a hand on his bag, she dropped his pants and sank to her knees.

. . .

The two lovers were in each other's arms, laying on sheets that were damp for a number of reasons, and both slowly catching their breath.

How did Dan become such a good lover? How does he know exactly how to wreck me in bed? He's only really been with one woman in his life? She decided to start their discussion from that direction.

"How is it possible that you are able to keep up with me? You and I both know, I'm no amateur. But you, flyboy, you don't just keep up, you are able to just wreck my body. You light me up like a pinball machine. Sex has dominated my life since I got a driver's license. You've had basically one woman in your life and your full-time day job involves airplanes. How is this possible?" Her face and voice displayed true appreciation.

Dan smirked. "Baby, I told you, you get the benefit of the pilot personality. We like to master the tasks we choose to do. I have been gaining skill in the area of horizontal arts my whole life, and you get the benefit of all the studying I've been doing."

Waiving a hand over her body, Sindee said, "Studying, huh? This university would give you a Ph.D. for your studies, Professor Flyboy. You put the 'stud' in 'studying.'" She reached down and started to lightly fondle him, and Dan sucked in a breath as she did. "Well, lover," she purred, "I could talk all day about the sounds you make me make, but I have some questions for you, some other stuff I want to talk about."

Dan held up a finger. "If I could, I have two questions for you first. One, as much as I love what you are doing, can you please stop? The way you do that pretty much shuts down all activity in the big head. If you want meaningful conversation, we need to put that wonderful activity of yours on hold for a few minutes."

Sindee pouted a little as she brought her hands up to her nipples and started fondling them.

Dan chuckled. "Not better."

Sindee pouted again. "Okay, okay. What is the second question?"

Dan paused as the smile melted from his face. "Will you marry me?"

Sindee's mouth opened in true surprise, which bordered on shock. She mentioned marriage to Dan, of course, but she was used to being the one in control. Dan was asking her a real-life question that had long-term consequences, and yet, she knew what her answer would be the second he asked the question.

Sindee's voice was nearly a shout. "Absolutely I will, flyboy, I love you so much!" They hugged tightly for a long time, whispering "I love you" over and over to each other.

Dan created space between them and made eye contact. "Okay, we can move to your questions, but I want to say, be careful what you ask. Make sure it's a question you want the answer to. After we get home, you're coming with me to the office so we can shop for an engagement ring. You have a fifty-thousand-dollar budget."

"Oh my God, really?" Dan just nodded. The joy of the thought of ring shopping faded quickly. Sindee felt the seriousness of the questions she had in mind. "Okay, you're doing work for Angelo? Is the work you do dangerous?"

Dan's face was serious now. "It has some danger in it, yes, but the operations we do, ops for short, are meticulously planned, and the danger is low."

"I'm guessing it is illegal?"

"Yes," Dan replied.

Sindee paused for a moment, taking in what Dan said, unsure whether or not to ask the next question. She decided she needed to know everything even before he arrived at the hotel room, but now that the moment arrived, she hesitated. She pulled in a breath, held it for a second, and asked the next question with it. "Do you hurt people?"

Dan nodded. "And worse. The ops are actually hits, but they are only people who deserve it."

"Something happened last night, I could hear it in your voice. Was that an op? What happened?"

He explained. "Yes, it was an op. When I say 'deserve,' Houston was a good example. The guy was a real piece of shit who, up until last night, was operating a human trafficking operation, most of them underage girls. He traveled to a transfer house outside of Houston nearly nightly, raping at least one of the girls there every time he visited. Every hit has been taking out the garbage."

"But I heard something in your voice I'm not sure I've ever heard. What happened? What was it?"

Dan paused for a moment, unprepared for whatever reaction she might have. "When I shot him, he had just gotten out of his car. We didn't see the small gun in his hand. He pulled the trigger as he fell. The shot hit someone I was there with. The round caught him in the chest. He died before we could even get him in the car. Baby, I know this is all pretty shocking, but I don't take ops involving people who don't make the world a better place by their leaving it abruptly. I've only been on a handful of ops, I can quit any time, and I can choose whether or not I'll do a job for Angelo. Tell me what you are thinking, sweetheart."

Sindee took in another breath and held it a second before speaking. "Is that everything?" Dan nodded. Sindee thought for a second, and then nodded also. "Well, I am surprised but not shocked, and if they are child rapists or worse, fuck them. I'm just worried that something could happen to you, or you end up in prison."

"I completely understand, sweetheart, and I'm relieved. In at least one version of this conversation I imagined, you ran from the room screaming."

She went back to fondling him. "Baby, I'll be screaming in a little while, I'm sure, but I won't be using my legs to run."

36

Javier Mora arrived in Houston with very little time to spare. His boss, EGM, wanted him to oversee the armored car robbery, but the guy who had planned it was gone now, probably dead. Mora couldn't just ask the other guy involved, Michael Grim, what the plan was or the location of where they were going to transfer the money. His only play was to park at the casino, watch the armored car leave, and follow it. Mora's GPS guided him to the casino grand entrance.

The Silver Star Casino was a sprawling complex of buildings. He circled the entire complex a few times to get the layout. Being a large casino, it wasn't immediately obvious what door the armored car would pull up to; casinos didn't put up signs to advertise security procedures. Mora chose a location in the parking lot that gave him a view of several avenues of approach to the casino. It worked in his favor that the road system surrounding the casino was designed to funnel traffic to the casino. Mora felt good about the location he chose.

Now I sit and wait till I see the armored car arrive, he thought, then follow it to where they pick up the money. Not much of a plan, but it's all I got.

. . .

The team Angelo sent to Houston was gathered in one of their two adjoining hotel rooms, where they discussed the op, and repeatedly went over the details. Two of them were talking; the third just got back from dropping off Justini's Mercedes in Mexico, and he was sleeping. The fourth bled out on a north Houston highway service road, and that was the current topic of discussion.

Angelo was on speakerphone with them, as reluctant as ever to talk details on the phone. "I'm sending two down, they are almost there. Redo the plan with five and get it done. Check in with me before you leave the hotel room." *Click*

They just started talking about the plan again when there was a knock at the door. One guy stood up and said, "No shit they are almost there. I swear the boss is like a Swiss fucking clock." He looked through peephole and saw two familiar faces. He threw open the door, and welcome greetings were exchanged between guys that were glad to see help arriving, and the cavalry themselves.

. . .

Nico was part of the cavalry. He was trying to stay cool but knew how much was on the line. His thought when he joined his crew was to get right to business because *we only get one shot at this.*

"Nico! The boss didn't say who was coming. I'm glad to see you and Tony!"

Nico smiled. "Good to see you guys too. That was a fuckin' shame at the op. He was a really good operator." Heads bowed all around. "There will be time for mourning later, and we will take it. For now, bring me up to speed. The Boss wants me out front on this one, guys, so what do we know, Rob?"

Rob "Too Far" Ramone got his nickname for two reasons. First, his several combat tours had made him almost fearless, giving him the tendency to go too far. He was also a former Marine scout sniper, so when he was asked how far was too far to hit something with a bullet, he said, "Nothing is too far." The team member who was killed also had combat experience and was the lead in the op. Rob took the position over as the

170

next ranking member of the team. Angelo wanted Nico in charge; that was all Rob needed to hear.

"Okay, boss," Rob said, "here is what we have." He spun a laptop on the coffee table so Nico could see the Google three-dimensional map of what looked like a sparsely populated area. "For the op, we boosted a Tesla, made sure we got a full charge on it, and it is the op car."

Nico let loose a crooked smile. "Shit, I like it already. No one is going to hear us approach in that."

"Exactly. We got four suppressed AR-15s and suppressed Glocks for the crew with plenty of ammo for everything. We have a Glock and AR-15 for you, Nico. I'm using a suppressed Remington 700 sniper rifle with a night vision–enhanced scope on it the size of a loaf of bread. We don't know exactly what route the armored car will be taking to the target location, but the area is rural, and once you get off the highway, it's pretty obvious. We have a good spot picked out where we have concealment for the car. Sixty seconds after the car passes, we will drive to the target location. I have helmet-mounted night vision, so we'll be driving lights out."

Nico did a double-take. "Wait, what?"

Rob laughed. "You're gonna love it, Nico. In those goggles I can see like its noon. You're going to feel like you're riding Space Mountain at Disney. We'll park short of the property driveway. We get out there, but the four of you stay with the car till I radio an all-clear. I'm going to survey the situation, see what we are up against, and what activity is going on at the house. When I give the clear, you all approach from the driveway, quick and quiet. Fan out and drop anything that looks like it plays for the other team. Those ARs are quiet, but by no means silent. So, when the first hammer drops on an AR, chances are good everyone will know." Rob paused as Nico took it all in.

Nico finally weighed in after several moments of silence. "Sounds tight. I like it. Why the delay in us taking them down?"

Rob smiled. "My father always said, work smart not hard. With the night vision, I will be able to see when the gun belts are off, uniforms are off, and all the money has been transferred from the armored car to the box truck. You have any idea what thirty-mil in bills weighs?"

Nico smiled and nodded. "Let's make this happen for the one who didn't make it. Let's get it done so Mikey wasn't a waste." The team put on expressions of resolve to get it done in Mikey's name.

37

Eliazar stared at the phone sitting on his desk; for the last half hour, his gaze went from the view out his window, back to the phone, then back out the window. This was going to be one of the most important calls of his life. So important, he rehearsed out loud exactly what he was going to say, made some notes, and mentally gamed out many of the directions the conversation could go. Eliazar had already picked up the phone four times, only to set it back down again to go over his lines one more time. Each time he thought of something new; that only encouraged him to repeat the process again.

Operation Claymore's operational planning was complete, and the document was on his computer desktop ready to print. The proposed targets listed in the Operational Specifications were mostly cartels in Mexico, including the Serpiente Cartel. Eliazar structured the Claymore Operation as an operation designed to interdict the largest amount of drugs and human trafficking as possible, even more so than Crossbow. The facts had only to be stretched mildly by Eliazar to sell the focus of Claymore's efforts.

He claimed in the report that the focus area where the most damage to interdict could be accomplished would be from the Juarez/El Paso area and east to the Gulf of Mexico. The cartel activity was more concentrated in that part of the border of the United States, and the amount of fentanyl in that area was much higher. Eliazar, if he could establish contact with Serpiente, would be able to work out the same arrangement that the El

Paso agents had with Villareal. Seizures and interdictions would go up all over the border. As long as Eliazar worked with Serpiente to orchestrate small seizures of Serpiente product from time to time, the collaboration may be able to exceed John Bayan's success with Villareal.

This was what Eliazar was thinking when he finally dialed the phone that he just picked up for the fifth time. It was answered on the second ring.

"*Háblame*, who is this," from the other end of the connection.

Eliazar spoke in Spanish and with force, hoping to sound both respectful and confident. "Señor, I am with an intelligence agency, a U.S. intelligence agency, and I have a proposal I'd like to discuss with you." There was a long pause. Eliazar could hear background noise on the phone, so he knew they were still connected. He almost certainly caught off-guard a man who is not used to that feeling. As the pause grew longer, Eliazar realized he had not anticipated how much thought the man on the other end of the call would have to put into his response to a call such as his.

The man on the other end finally broke the silence. "Villareal. Did you work with them?"

Eliazar knew he was on unsure footing. "I need to know, am I speaking to Eduardo Gaston Mendoza?" The question was designed to let the other person on the call know that Eliazar was the real deal. Mendoza, like all cartel leaders, went to great lengths to keep his identity secret. The correct name and phone number were Eliazar's credentials.

After another long pause, "*Sí, señor.* And to whom am I speaking?"

"My name is Mario, and I am who I say I am. And if you are Mendoza, then we can help each other. For now, it is only important that I make you a proposal. I did not work with Villareal, and the men who did met the same fate as Villareal. My best guess is that they became greedy and tried to set up operations on our side of the border. That was a mistake, as you can't do that without stepping on someone else's territory. My proposal is that I provide to you all the same services that I know were provided to Villareal, with one big difference. The difference being, I propose we connect with a network on this side of the border. That ensures a smooth flow of whatever is moved into markets in the U.S. Your traffic goes up, the other cartels' traffic goes down. I will connect you with an organization in the States; I open the door, and you walk through. Law of supply and demand would dictate that the organization in the States would grow larger and need more from you as the supply from the other sources is intercepted." Eliazar was a bit surprised he was still on the phone with Mendoza. He knew this was the time to let Mendoza think.

There was another long pause. "I will consider your proposal, Mario. But for now, let's just say I believe we will be able to work together. Call me again in three days. If I want to proceed, we will need to meet, and you will need to bring me proof that you will be worth your word." *Click*

. . .

An agitated Michael Grim sat in his large office chair behind his huge office desk inside his enormous office with windows that overlooked the casino floor. It was almost cliché. The office was lavishly appointed and decorated, as if it was designed as a movie set. Grim had a hard time dealing with the mix of anticipation, apprehension, and what seemed to be the incredibly slow passage of time. He lost count of the number of times he got up from his chair, strolled over to the windows, and looked out over a casino floor he knew he wouldn't be in charge of twenty-four hours later. He had to change his plan a bit for the heist, as Justini was still missing. That left no one to alert him to the arrival of the armored car at the transfer site.

I'll go batshit crazy if I stay in this office another minute. Grim walked out of the rear employee entrance of the casino and to his car to spend the last few hours. He climbed into his car and parked in the casino parking lot. *Sit here till I see the armored car, then follow it to where they transfer the money. Not much of a plan, but it's all I got.*

38

Angelo noted the time on his phone. *Time for the guys to be on their way.* Not patient enough to wait for the phone call from Nico, Angelo dialed his number. Nico picked up on the first ring, something that happened often when Angelo called almost anyone. "It's almost go-time."

Nico sounded on edge. "Boss, I was just about to pick up the phone. The rooms are clean, everything is in the vehicle, and we are about to walk out the door."

"I'm really excited for you guys. You take this down, and all goes as planned, it will be something people talk about for a long time. Just make sure everyone understands they can never be the ones talking about tonight."

Nico said, "You got it, boss. They are good men. We will not let you down."

"Good luck." *Click*

. . .

Nico put his cell phone in his pocket and turned to his men. "Let's go, guys. Angelo says good luck."

The five men filed out a single hotel door, having swept both rooms to make sure they left nothing interesting behind. They were all veterans in one way or another; some were former military; some were soldiers in Angelo's operation. They had all been in this situation many times, but never of this magnitude. There wasn't a word said all the way to the car, or even when they all got in. A few of the bags were put in the trunk, and the rest were taken into the interior of the car with them. There were still a few last-minute preparations for each of them to make to be ready to conduct the op, but they knew there would be time once they got to the stakeout location. The car pulled out of the hotel lot and headed toward the highway.

It was ten minutes into the drive when Nico finally broke the silence. "Jesus Christ on a racehorse, who the fuck farted? Is there a doctor in the house?" They all had a badly needed laugh that broke the tension.

. . .

The Silver Star Casino wasn't the only scheduled pickup for the armored car to make that night, but it was by far the largest, and so it was scheduled to be last. Since they were doing a weekend nighttime round of pickups, they requested and received approval to make their first pickup of the evening a mall department store that shared a parking lot with a McDonald's, so they could get some dinner. They didn't have to work hard to convince the dispatcher. "What's the problem? It's our first pickup. The car will be empty."

There was one problem they had to overcome, one that Justini solved before he disappeared; a solution he never shared with Grim. The armored car company made a change to their vehicles a few months previous when they installed tracking devices on all the vehicles. The workaround Justini devised was for them to leave a chase car at the first pickup. One of the crew removes the tracker from the armored car, puts it in the chase car, and then the crew member in the car would hang back at the first pickup for a while. They had a timetable worked out so the chase car would follow them on the route but lagging way behind. The radio calls were timed to coincide with the tracker location. If they stuck to their timetable, they would be able to give the armored car almost an hour before it was overdue and anyone started looking for it.

. . .

The armored car pulled up to the department store, and a crew member immediately went into the store to make the pickup. The manager noted they were ten minutes early, but they had been busy that weekend, and he was glad they were picking up early. The armored car left immediately; the chase car sat in the McDonald's parking lot for another thirty minutes before the driver called the armored car on his cell. The armored car driver saw the caller ID and answered.

"Make the store radio dispatch call." The call immediately disconnected.

The armored car driver reached for the radio microphone, depressed the transmit button and said, "Central. Car two-four-nine is leaving stop one, enroute to stop two." *So far, so good.*

"Roger two-four-nine."

Two more pickups, chase car repositions, phone calls, and radio calls were made in the same fashion. By the time the armored car left its third pickup and was enroute to the Silver Star Casino, the armored car had a fifty-minute head start.

The armored car pulled up to the side entrance of the casino; it was closest to the collection cage and the count room door. The plan was working well: per Silver Star policy, casino employees, not the armored car crew, loaded the armored car. No one missed the third member of the armored car crew. The driver of the armored car checked his watch, then looked at the timetable, handwritten on a folded piece of paper he retrieved from his shirt pocket. The timetable was holding and the chase car was now a full fifty minutes behind the armored car. The last line on the timetable showed that if they added in the casino delay, the chase car would be an hour behind the armored car. It was a twenty-minute drive from the Silver Star to the armored car facility.

We'll have at least an hour-twenty before we are expected to arrive at the company gate. Add to that dispatcher confusion, calls to supervisors, police response time, and we might have two hours. By then, I'll be in the wind.

Two loud bangs on the side of the armored car, and the sound of the back door closing, let the driver know he was loaded, and ready to go. As he pulled out of the parking lot, the driver dialed his cell phone. "Leaving the casino now. See you at the transfer."

"We still have two radio calls to make, so keep the cell handy and listen up for anything unusual on the company radio." The call disconnected.

The armored car driver checked his watch again. He didn't need to consult the timetable again; he had the last number memorized.

We are right on time. The same time the tracker is delivered to the yard, we will be just starting to transfer the cash. Chase car should be pulling up to the transfer house just as we finish loading the box truck, and we all make our way out.

. . .

Javier Mora, la Sombra, watched the armored car pull away from the casino and drive toward the parking lot exit.

There it goes. I follow it to its destination, and I make my move. This is going to work.

. . .

Michael Grimaldi, Grim, watched the armored car pull away from the building and drive toward the parking lot exit.

There it goes. So now I wait the two hours for the planned meeting time at the transfer house. This is going to work.

. . .

An hour later, the driver of the chase car threw the tracker out of the driver's side window in front of the armored car yard and sped off toward the transfer site. His GPS directions told him he'd be at the transfer site in thirty-five minutes.

I'll get there in thirty, he thought.

. . .

The five-man team sat in the black Tesla, concealed from view off the road, waiting impatiently and listening to music. "La Grange" by ZZ Top began to play with the familiar guitar riff. Rob reached for the volume control and said, "I fuckin' love this song." Just then, the armored car drove quickly past the point where they were parked. "That's the vehicle."

Nico said, "Are you sure?"

Rob was wearing a ballistic helmet with night vision goggles attached, the one's discussed earlier in the plan. "Nico, I told you, with this night vision rig, I see everything like it was daytime. Besides the question, how many armored cars do you think we'll see tonight, I read the number on the side, and..." Rob's voice trailed off as he noticed another set of headlights coming from the same direction as the armored car. "We may have another attendee at the party." The second car sped past.

Nico asked, "What the fuck is going on?"

Rob smirked, "Let's go see." Rob pulled the car, its headlights off, out of its concealment, turned onto the road, and accelerated hard after the vehicles. The road turned almost immediately to the left and then back to the right.

Nico exclaimed, "Jesus, Mary, and Joseph!"

Rob laughed. "Keep it together, boss. I told you it's like driving in daylight when I'm wearing this thing." Rob could see clearly that the car had followed the armored car right up to the driveway to the transfer house, and then drove past, slowly. Rob said, "I think they have a tail."

Rob pulled the Tesla up to the spot at the bottom of the drive where they planned. He got out, went right to the trunk for his very impressive sniper rifle setup. He quickly tilted the night vision goggles on his helmet up out of the way, and lifted the rifle's night vision scope to his eye and began a slow sweep of the area. First in the direction of the tail car, then the house, then behind their position. "Everyone out of the car, locked and loaded. Stay quiet and low, radios on, earpieces in, I'm heading up the drive."

The drive sloped up and the higher elevation gave Rob a good view in all directions. He made out the tail car that had driven past; he saw one person now out of the car, holding a scoped rifle.

Rob communicated to his team via radio. "Sniper down the road, past your position about one hundred meters. Stay where you are but spread out. He may not be the only one. House in view now, transfer is happening, targets have shed their skins." Rob guessed they were mostly done, as two men were working fast to transfer the bags, and they had ditched their belts and shirts. He thought for a second and made a tactical assessment. "Number one, I think you leave one behind for security, three come to me, I will get my crosshairs on the sniper, you get ready to pounce, I think it's time. I'm seeing two tangos unloading, and one sitting on a porch chair. Could be more. What do you think?"

Nico responded, "You're our eyes. You sure he's not too far."

Rob smiled. "No one's too far."

39

As quickly and quietly as possible, three men made their way up the driveway, all with their AR-15 rifles aimed up and at the ready position. Nico could just make out Rob crouching, looking through his scope in the direction of the sniper.

Nico whispered, "Do you have him?"

Rob whispered back, "Absolutely, but like I said, my weapon is pretty loud so you need to go in silent first, and as soon as my target looks like he's going to engage, I'm going to end him. Once I pull this trigger, it's on."

Nico looked in the direction of the armored car; no one was in view. *Maybe they are changing clothes*, he thought. Nico used hand signals to maintain silence. He pointed at Tony and made a go-left signal. Then to Mark with a go-right signal, and then to himself, he signaled between the two vehicles up the middle. They all nodded and moved out. Tony was the first to see anyone; it was an armored car guard by the back of the car taking a leak. The noise covered Tony's steps, so by the time the guard saw him, Tony was a foot away with the rifle pointed at his chest. He signaled to the guard to be quiet by putting his left index finger to his lips, keeping his right index finger on the trigger, and then nodded in the direction of the house. As the guard passed the rear door of the armored car, the other guard exited, wearing casual clothing. Tony dropped them both with several shots a piece.

Hearing the suppressed AR fire, Rob squeezed the trigger of his sniper rifle, and was rewarded with the night-vision scoped view of the sniper going down hard. As Rob had advertised, the sound of the rifle was loud enough to get everyone's attention.

Mark, who had the longest walk around the box truck, reached the porch about the same time Rob fired. The guy in the rocking chair reached for a double-barreled twelve-gage shotgun. Mark stopped him cold with four shots to his chest. Mark moved to the door of the house, looked inside, and saw a group of young girls.

Rob swept the entire area with his night vision scope, but he saw nothing out of the ordinary. All four men checked the entire area and made sure all threats were eliminated. The entire encounter from first round to last was less than thirty seconds. Rob turned to flash Nico a smile when Rob's attention was diverted by yet another set of headlights heading in their direction. Rob shouted for everyone to take cover. To all of their amazement, the car turned, climbed the driveway and parked behind the armored car. It was the third armored car guard in the chase car. The driver of the car got out of the car shouting names. Nico hit the shocked man in the side of the head with a single, aimed round. The guard still had on his body armor. Just then a flash of light and a loud peal of thunder shook them all awake. They had work to do.

. . .

The night dispatcher logged all the stops and radio calls into the computer for the seven armored cars out running their routes. The location beacon on each armored car automatically logged positions, and the positions of each were also displayed in real time on his computer monitor. Everything seemed to be going well; maybe one was a bit behind schedule. Oddly, for the last ten minutes or so, the position of Car 249 was logged as just outside the gate of the armored car yard. The dispatcher first noticed when he got back from a bathroom break.

The dilemma was, he was working alone, and was strictly forbidden from leaving the building for any reason when he was the only employee in the building. The car locator showed that it was at the gate, but he clearly saw on the camera that there was no armored car there. Five numbers from the "Situation" list were called without answer. Finally, after this went on for twenty-five minutes, he dialed 9-1-1. The call didn't sound very urgent to the 9-1-1 operator, as was evidenced by the fact that a Houston P.D. police car didn't arrive on scene for another forty minutes.

. . .

Nico knew the clock was ticking, and they all had jobs to do. It did not go fully according to plan, so the loose ends had to be tied up, and Nico took charge. "Rob, you're in charge of all weapons, they all go in the armored car, your rifle included. Keep the scope if you like. Mark, sweep the house. DJ, take that last car that pulled up, go get the sniper's body, Rob will lead you in. Tony, start dragging bodies to the armored car, two of us will load them."

As each man was issued an instruction, he moved to make it happen. Nico stood on one spot in the driveway and surveyed the three hundred sixty degrees of his surroundings, making sure he didn't forget anything. The thunder was getting louder, and the lightning illuminated the scene off and on, as the thunderstorm approached.

Mark came out of the house. "Nothing but a bunch of girls in there."

Nico nodded. "Okay, Mark, your job was to drive the box truck, but I count five vehicles here, and five men. You're going solo, head out to Grapevine now. Drive the speed limit all the way, take the route we planned, and we may catch up to you." Mark ran to the back of the armored car, tossed his rifle inside, pistol as well, and climbed into the box truck cab.

Rob had removed his night vision scope from his rifle. He held it to his eye with his left hand, and the radio up to his face with his right. "The road turns to the left in about twenty meters. When you turn, you'll see the car another fifteen meters ahead on your left. Grab his rifle, it's on the hood. He's on the ground in front of the car. Put him in your trunk. Grab anything else you see as well and take a second to check carefully. If he doesn't have a cell phone on him, look till you find it. When you find it, crush it." DJ had no problem seeing what he was doing, as the more frequent lightning repeatedly erased the darkness.

Nico went over to the back of the armored car to make sure it was empty of all the cash. He let out a big breath when he saw that it was; he should have checked before the box truck left. Nico said loudly, "Guys, on me." They all assembled on Nico as he continued. "I'll take the armored car, DJ follow me in the Tesla, you two take those two cars to our auto guy in Houston, crush them both, and then make your way back to Dallas. Everyone stays in touch with me. I'll be in contact with the boss. Let's go!"

Everything happened in real time as Nico spoke it. Standing in front of the armored car now, Nico scanned in every direction one last time, making absolutely sure he was forgetting nothing. Nico grew up in the city, so when he was finally alone with the armored car, he marveled for a moment at how very quiet it was out in the country. A change in sound caught his attention. The rural quiet feathered into the sound of wind kicking up and heavy rain coming down. The thunderstorm drenched Nico as he took that last look around. Satisfied, he climbed fully soaked into the cab of the armored car.

Nico chuckled. *The rain should take care of most of the evidence.*

40

As Dan and Sindee walked through the doorway of their home, Dan closed the door, and wrapped his arms around his love. "The hotel was perfect, and the time there was perfect. Thank you, sweetheart." Sindee smiled and kissed him deeply. When they broke the kiss, Dan said, "We're going out tonight, I just don't know exactly where yet." Dan explained further at Sindee's confused look. "Angelo mentioned that I might want what sounded suspiciously like an alibi tonight."

Sindee sounded surprised. "Oh. Okay, I'll think of something. How much time do we have?"

Dan said, "I don't think we have to leave for a few hours. Dinner at Vincent's was my first thought, then I realized how bad an idea that was. I should never bring potential attention to Vincent's. The second-best alibi that came to mind was dinner with Mike and Toni Chelsea. But after what happened last time, maybe I should let a little time go by. I don't want to make more trouble for Mike."

Sindee's eyes lit up. "How about I group text the Made for You staff and tell them we are throwing an impromptu employee appreciation party at that brewpub we like in Southlake? It would be iron clad for an alibi, and it would be great for morale."

"I love that idea. Send out the text. What will we do with the next hour?"

"Go to your office and look at engagement rings online!" Sindee's smile was ear to ear.

"Sure, babe." Dan led Sindee to the office with Sindee stripping off her clothes as they walked. He plopped into his big chair. As he looked to his left, he was surprised to see a completely naked Sindee. She pushed his chair back, then climbed under the desk. "Are you looking for a budget increase for the ring."

All she could manage for an answer was "mm-hm." By the time she climbed on top of a seated Dan a few moments later, he was looking at eighty-thousand-dollar rings.

He looked into her eyes as she absolutely wrecked him in his office chair and thought, *I'm the lucky one here.*

. . .

At least thirty-five employees showed up at the brewpub, and surprisingly, a few showed up with their Made for You clients. Dan took each employee aside and made it clear to them how that was not at all a good idea. Sindee agreed that that would be the subject of an upcoming memo. Dan's alibi cost him less than twenty-five-hundred dollars, and everyone had a good time.

On the way home, Dan turned the discussion to a more serious topic: ground rules for moving forward. Sindee told Dan that she thought that would be a good subject for them to explore. Dan said, "I'm still going to do the occasional op for Angelo, at least for a while. I think it should be a rule that you don't ask me questions about exactly what I'm doing and where. The less in the way of details you know, the better for everyone. I will smooth things with Angelo, and once I let him know we are getting married, he will understand. I also think that getting married sooner, rather than later, is a good idea. But, what's most important to me is giving you the wedding you want.

"It doesn't have to be a big event; I just want the ring, the dress, and the occasion. I want to have the memory of it to remember for the rest of my life. Are you really going to buy me that ring we picked out earlier?"

Dan was shocked at her doubt. "Yes, of course sweetheart."

Sindee's gratitude was obvious in her voice. "It's beautiful, but it's just so much. I don't know how I'm ever going to thank you."

Dan smiled wide. "Baby, you know exactly how you are going to thank me. You're playing the scene in your head right now."

Sindee giggled.

. . .

The sound of a phone ringing into voice mail always annoyed Mendoza. He was the kind of man that when he called someone, they dropped everything and picked up the call immediately. Anyone making Mendoza call back more than a few times was punished. Mendoza dialed the cell phone of la Sombra at least thirty times. Each time, it rang several times, and then went to voicemail. *Sombra pick up. This makes no sense. The phone is on, it is ringing. Did he lose it, or was it stolen? Was he in an accident?* The longer this went on, the more Mendoza imagined scenarios where Sombra couldn't pick up the phone, and the more dire they got.

Suddenly, the line stopped ringing when he called. It went right to voice mail. Sombra's phone was turned off — or destroyed. *Shit, he either lost his phone, or he's dead.* Mendoza realized that Sombra may have been taken out. The shadow was good; but that was a lot of money. It took much planning to pull off a robbery like that and the people involved would have taken precautions. Mora was sent to surveil. Mendoza asked himself the question — and dreaded the answer enough to say it out loud: "What would I do to someone I caught spying on a thirty-million-dollar operation of mine?"

Mendoza thought he was protecting Mora by making him his

second-in-command. The position of right-hand man for the leader of the Serpiente Cartel was a position that paid well, and had many perks and privileges attached. Mora was a friend to Mendoza; they went all the way back to their army days. Mora had been a soldier under his command and Mendoza had recruited him for Serpiente. Now it was starting to look like he'd sent his friend on the mission that got him killed. *I will find the man that killed him and kill him very slowly.*

Mendoza's phone rang. For a brief second, he felt relief, assuming the call was from Mora. Looking at the call ID, he pulled in a deep breath, and let it out slowly. It was Grim.

There was what sounded nearly like panic in his voice. "I just left the transfer house. Everything is gone, even the box truck. Blood everywhere even though it's raining. They are going to connect me. I need to get out of town!"

Mendoza asked, "Do you have a bag packed?"

Grim said, "Yes. I was planning on driving the box truck to Mexico tonight."

"Okay, then, come to Mexico. We will meet you at the border, escort you here. You can lay low with me until we find your money."

Grim's voice returned to a more normal tone. "Okay, I'll be in touch when I get across."

Mendoza disconnected the call. "The gringo says the money is gone. He's coming here."

With him on the back veranda was one of Mendoza's trusted men, chosen by Mendoza to be at the hacienda with him while la Sombra was out of the country. "What are you going to do, jefe?"

"I am going to ask him some questions, and he is going to tell us everything he knows."

The armored car was like a rolling billboard advertisement. Nico couldn't remember a time in his life when he was more nervous than when he was driving to the hole. The route, the location, the timing, all turned out to be perfect. Even the hole was perfect. It was excavated by guys who didn't know why they dug it, but it was exactly to their specifications. DJ was chosen for the job of filling it in because in a previous life, he was a heavy equipment operator.

Nico parked the armored car in the hole while DJ boarded the heavy front loader left at the site. Nico swung the rear doors open on the armored car and the first bucket of earth DJ moved filled the back of the car. In an hour, DJ had the hole filled in, the earth smoothed and the site finished. When the construction crew returned to work Monday, it would be ready for the concrete pour that would cover the evidence for a very long time.

DJ and Nico took turns driving the boosted Tesla back to Grapevine, Texas. They didn't make it. The battery was running out when they saw the Buc-ee's in Ennis, Texas, about seventy miles short of their destination. Nico paid a truck driver five hundred dollars to take DJ and him to the Buc-ee's further north on I-35W at State Highway 114 in Roanoke, Texas. From there they paid a taxi cash to take them to Nico's neighborhood; they'd covered their tracks completely. DJ crashed on Nico's very comfortable couch and the two tried to get a few hours' sleep. Nico's text to Angelo when they buried the armored car read, "package on the way, garbage taken out, see you tomorrow."

Angelo texted back: "Balls."

191

41

If a serviceman was lucky, they were transported back to the states in civilian aircraft, with passenger seats and flight attendants. The procedure was to take off, pop one of the sleeping pills that were handed out like candy in the combat theater, and sleep for most of the trip in a comfortable seat. If you were Major Hatfield, on a clock to get back to the States for your White House award ceremony, you took whatever transport was available. In this case, a C-5 from the Ninth Airlift Squadron of the 436th Airlift Wing on its way to Dover Air Force Base was going to have to do. Unfortunately for Hatfield, this particular aircraft was configured with benches that lined the inside of the cargo bay walls, of which he was allotted twenty-four inches and a seatbelt.

When crewmembers closed the cargo ramp, Hatfield surveyed the cargo hold and was happy to note that there weren't many servicemembers on board. Everyone would be able to lay down for the flight. He also noted that the various types of cargo strapped down along the center of the aircraft included four metal coffins. Dan was going home, and so were they. More soldiers awarded the Congressional Medal of Honor went home in a coffin instead of wearing a seatbelt.

A few minutes later, the huge C-5 Galaxy transport lifted off the runway at Prince Sultan Air Base and generated a cloud of sand and dust as it did.

Twenty minutes into the flight, Hatfield unrolled his Air Force issued sleeping bag on the floor in front of him. It didn't look like it was going to be very comfortable for the long flight, especially with the rolled-up jacket for a pillow. *Thank God for these*, he thought, looking at the two, small, white pills in his hand. Hatfield washed them down with some bottled water and laid down in his makeshift bed. The last thing he saw before closing his eyes were the four coffins, strapped to the deck he was laying on.

Sorry, brothers.

. . .

Rough air from a line of thunderstorms off the Atlantic coast of America shook Hatfield awake with about forty-five minutes left in the fifteen-hour flight. When the pills wore off and Hatfield woke halfway through the flight, he made a trip to the bathroom, and then took one more pill. When the turbulence bounced him off the deck a few times, he woke, looked at his watch, and tried to estimate remaining flight time through the fog of sleep still slowing his brain down. It took a full minute of checking and rechecking before he was confident there was less than an hour left.

Fucking perfect.

He picked up his bathroom kit and headed toward the front of the aircraft to find a line of several men waiting for the bathroom. A rough patch of air knocked all of them to the deck; they all got up laughing.

I made it out of the sandbox; gonna die waiting for the head on this plane.

Forty minutes later, the C-5 touched down on Runway 32, slowed to taxi speed, and taxied to the assigned ramp to be unloaded. As the airplane pulled to a stop, guided by ground crew, more crew put chocks under the wheels, and the flight crew members lowered the cargo ramp on the back of the aircraft. Hatfield had already retrieved his duffel bag and briefcase from the luggage container, and was in the back of the aircraft, waiting for the ramp to touch the ground.

There was no time to notify Sharon; Dan had yet to tell her anything. He wasn't expecting anyone to meet him at the airplane. Dan's plan was to get to a telephone, let Sharon know she needed to meet him in Washington, D.C., as soon as she could get there, and give her an idea why. After several steps on the wet tarmac, Hatfield heard someone shout his rank and name.

"I'm Major Hatfield. And you are?"

The officer in air force fatigues saluted Hatfield and said, "Major Hatfield, I'm Captain Laredo of the Pentagon DOD Public Affairs Office. I'm here to make all the arrangements for you and your wife; help you navigate the next several days."

Still shaking off the grogginess of the sleeping pills, Hatfield finally noticed that Captain Laredo was still holding his salute as he spoke, waiting for Hatfield to return it in protocol. Hatfield returned the salute and said, "Sorry, Captain. I'm feeling the sleeping pill I took on the flight. Can you get me up to speed on what other people are planning for my life?"

Captain Laredo reached out his right hand. "I can take your duffel bag, Major. I have two rooms reserved for us at the Watergate Hotel in D.C. What I thought we could do, sir, with your approval of course, is drive to the hotel, decompress, take a shower, put on something comfortable, and I will lay out the itinerary for you in detail."

"Captain, everything in my bag smells like desert sweat. There's probably a half-pound of sand mixed in and maybe even one of those desert spiders you get so fond of in Saudi."

Laredo took the duffel bag from Hatfield. "I haven't been over to the Middle East yet, but I've seen pictures of those things. Not to worry, Major, your room has a variety of clothing in it for you, stocked bar, and we will order the most expensive things on the room service menu. Then we will talk business. But I have to say, just once, it's an honor to be working as your aide. I've read the CMH Citation and the unredacted report. Amazing, sir."

Hatfield sighed. "That all sounds great, Captain. You're batting a thousand so far. The only thing I'd like to add to that little plan is a call to my wife, who doesn't know I'm on this side of the Atlantic or why I'm here."

"Uh, yes sir, but I should tell you that I took the liberty of reaching out to Mrs. Hatfield. It was just a matter of the timeframe. When we received confirmation that you were on the transport aircraft, I called her, explained the situation in general, and gave her the flight information. She will be arriving in D.C. tomorrow evening. Her door-to-door transportation has been taken care of. She doesn't know the details of what happened in Iraq. I thought you would want to tell her."

Hatfield nodded. "I understand. You did the right thing. I appreciate you thinking of letting me give her the details. Okay, well, I want to call her anyway. Thank you for the head's up and for arranging her travel."

. . .

It was 10:45 P.M., and the two officers executed the plan perfectly. They ordered steaks from the room service menu, had a few drinks while they waited, and Laredo laid out the itinerary with Dan. With a ribeye, medium rare, in his belly, Dan felt ready to make the call to Sharon. Laredo excused himself for the night to give them privacy.

Sharon was relieved to hear his voice and cried as they spoke. They talked for twenty minutes. Sharon asked Dan if he was tired, and he replied yes, so Sharon cut the conversation short. She told him to go to bed, but he explained that he had a few things to do before he could hit the pillow. When Dan hung up the phone, he went through his nighttime routine, getting ready for bed. But due to the difference in time zone, even though it was 10:45 P.M., Dan was feeling the combination of being tired and yet wide awake, also known as jet lag.

He decided to pick out a decent outfit from his new wardrobe and head to the lobby bar.

42

Angelo had gotten little sleep. He wasn't going to bed before the box truck arrived at his house. Bringing it to his house was a risk, but it was one he felt he had to take. He didn't trust the money going anywhere else, and behind his house, the truck was completely out of sight. Once he got a look at all the bags in the truck, he decided to get a rough count, with Mark's mildly enthusiastic help. Angelo understood that Mark had just made a long, stressful drive and was probably thinking about a bed for the last half of the drive. But the count was important.

Angelo said, "Instead of counting sheep, you can help me count the take." Mark just smiled and nodded. The cash bags were organized by denominations, so there were bags of hundreds, fifties, twenties, tens, and fives. The pair laid out the bags in piles by denomination. Angelo wondered, *What the hell do I do with the ones? Maybe I'll take them to the strip club; now that's a great way to launder money.*

They counted one bag of each denomination, and then added the bags. It took just over an hour; Angelo could see the relief on Mark's face when Angelo announced the job was done. After some rough math, Angelo had a number. "If the bags are consistent, it was more than we expected. We're looking at about thirty-six point seven million."

. . .

By the time the armored car was finally reported missing, the alarm went out far and wide. It was a mystery, as every stop the car made was verified, as were the radio calls, and the tracker locations. It wasn't until the sun was coming up that the dispatcher noticed the times didn't match. He did some math, then told the police that by his best guess, when the Houston cop was holding up the tracker for him to see on the front camera, the armored car had a nearly two-hour head start. The dispatcher explained that to the detective overlooking his computer monitor, and she called in on the radio that it definitely was a robbery.

The detective asked, "Any idea how much was in that truck?"

The dispatcher's heart sank when he pulled up the expected pickup amounts. "Three pickups, less than one-hundred-thousand dollars. The last pickup was the casino, they phoned in an expected amount of around thirty-six million dollars." The dispatcher already knew from shop talk over the years that they had just been the victims of the largest armored car robbery in history.

· · ·

There are knocks on the door that tell an inhabitant who is knocking, and there are knocks that tell who is not knocking. When a cop knocks on the door, it's fairly obvious. Andy Powers looked out the peephole to see a woman in a business suit, flanked by two uniformed Houston Police officers. He didn't have to fake the look of grogginess; he had just been woken by that knock. Leaning on the now open door, Powers said, "Can I help you?"

"Andrew Powers, of the Silver Star Casino? Can we come in? I'd like to ask you a few questions."

Powers assumed by the suit that the woman was a detective. The detective badge she showed him removed all doubt. "Of course." Powers stepped aside and let the three into his living room. "I'd like to make coffee while we talk, if you don't mind, and I'm glad to make you all some as well."

"It's been a long night, Mr. Powers. I believe we will all take you up on your offer." The uniforms both nodded.

"I'll make a full pot then. So, what is this about?" Powers asked.

. . .

Detectives are trained not to give up too much information right away when interrogating a suspect. Knowing what Detective Christine Osgood knew, she wanted to tread lightly at first. Powers was definitely a suspect, even if he didn't look like one.

Osgood said, "There has been a robbery at the casino."

Powers replied, with what sounded like genuine shock. "Oh my God, was anyone hurt? What happened? What did Michael and Danny say? Have you spoken to them? Wait, why haven't they called me? Are they okay?"

"Well, that was one of the questions I have for you. We haven't been able to contact Michael Grim or Daniel Justini. Do you have any alternate contact methods for them that the casino doesn't have? Personal cell phones maybe, or other places they could be? Neither man was in their residence, nor were their vehicles, and both of their cell phones are going straight to voice mail."

Powers was getting emotional. "No, I... what's going on? I don't have any other way to contact them. What kind of robbery are we talking about? What's going on?"

One of Osgood's first goals was to get Powers a bit worked up, even emotional. People tend to think less clearly, blurt out truths when they are caught off guard. She thought, *Time to hit him with the full hammer.* "It seems the armored car picking up from the Silver Star was taken, with a substantial amount of the Casino's cash in it. We were unable to find the armored car, its contents, the crew, Mr. Grim or Mr. Justini. The last location on their cell phones was in the casino, which implies that they disabled location intentionally before leaving the casino. Last location on Justini was two nights ago, Grim's cell location was last night. At this point they are both persons of interest, as, frankly, so are you, Mr. Powers."

Powers' mouth dropped open in obvious shock and surprise, something not lost on Osgood. His reaction to her statement was the pivotal moment in the interview. The look on Powers' face changed slowly from shock to anger. "Listen. Investigate me all you like, I had nothing to do with that, but those two motherfuckers. I never liked either of them. Find them and put them under the fucking jail. Don't slow up your search for them in any way. Now, if you have anything else for me, I'm glad to talk. But if not, it would seem I have a casino to run, one that just got its ass kicked."

Osgood was fairly satisfied that she was listening to a man telling her the truth. But she never ruled anything out completely. "Would you be willing to take a polygraph?" she asked as nonchalantly as possible.

Powers replied quickly. "Of course."

Osgood nodded. "Okay, that's all for now, I guess. Thank you for your cooperation and for the hospitality, but as you said, I'm not slowing down." They all looked at the coffee pot, only half brewed, and then the trio made their way to the door.

. . .

Glenn Miller's cell phone text indicator went off, and he rolled over in bed to see who had made his phone wake him with an urgent text. It was an FBI Central Communication All-Personnel Message. The text read, "All agents be advised, armored car robbery last night, Silver Star Casino, Houston, Texas. Stolen cash in the tens of millions of dollars. Investigate any possible leads or connections to ongoing investigations, report any possible leads or connections immediately. FBI CenCom."

"Armored car in Houston? Nope. But thanks for waking me up on a day I could finally sleep in."

43

After he hung up the phone, Eliazar reviewed the phone call in his head, playing it back like a recording. After some analysis of the call, and then the entire situation, he was convinced that Mendoza was going to go for it. He decided to spend the day in his office, putting the finishing touches on Claymore with his new plan in mind. John Bayan came to mind as well, a man he had met many times, and was a friend, but never really worked with. He now fully appreciated the position Bayan had set himself up with regarding the Villareal Cartel.

Eliazar was concerned with making sure his ending was different than Bayan's. He turned his chair to face the computer; calling up the final version of the Claymore Operational Proposal, he read it again for at least the fifth time. Not only was he looking for holes in the proposal, he needed to know it backward and forward.

. . .

Nico, Dan, and Angelo sat down in the boss' office with coffees, courtesy of Maria, Angelo's housekeeper. She caught Nico staring at her ass again, and when they made eye contact, she smiled again. Dan noticed the whole exchange. So did Angelo. When they were settled into the office, Dan saw the obvious serious look on Angelo's face.

Angelo spoke in a voice that was intended to call the meeting to order. "Dan, I promised you the backstory on the housekeeper, and Nico, looks like you need to hear it too. I had a friend, worked for the organization in Vegas. One way or another, he fell from the good graces of the management of the organization. They decided he needed to go. So, they have a guy put some explosives on his car. They felt they needed to send a message for a reason I don't need to talk about. They might have asked me to do the job, but they didn't on account of us being friends. What happened was, he got in the car with the wife, son, and daughter, only the daughter ran back to the house for something she forgot. She comes back out just in time to see her family incinerated. She runs to the next-door neighbor's house.

It's a wise-guy neighborhood, and the neighbor is a guy I've known since we were a couple of kids boosting apples from a cart at the market. We came out to Vegas together, so he called me because he didn't know what to do. I drive to the house, and I recognize her right off. Walking up the driveway, I see her face in the window for a second, then disappear. I'm the girl's Godfather; I was there at her Christening. A few seconds later, she runs up to me and throws her arms around me. Only thing I tell my friend is "she's family," and we walk away to the car. She was fourteen, been with me ever since. I would murder a guy for giving her a bad haircut."

Nico and Dan glance at each other, then back to Angelo. Dan said, "We got it boss. That makes her important to us too." Nico nodded.

Angelo moved on. "So, I have some news for the Houston crew, which includes you Dan. Nico, pass it to the rest, no phones, you know how I work. Okay, the haul was good, it's around thirty-six and a half." Dan and Nico's eyes both popped wide open. "Yeah, boys, I feel the same. I pulled out a taste for everyone, but what I'm going to need from everyone now is patience. There is an arrangement I've made, one where we can wash it clean and send it offshore. It's perfect. But we have to do it a million at a time. This guy can take one million every other week; he'll make sure there is nothing in the way of tracked bills, or marks. Then he puts it into one side of his business and wires it right out of the other side of his business to offshore accounts. I'm going to need a couple of bagmen I can trust to take the cash to him, and right now, those bagmen are you two." Angelo's face went very serious. "This does not leave the room, *capiche*?"

Nico said with caution in his voice, "Absolutely boss, you know you can trust us. What is the place?"

Angelo smiled wide. "Oh, I believe you've heard of the place. It's the, uh, Silver Star Casino in Houston." There was a second of silence while the two men realized Angelo was serious. Then the laughter lasted a full minute.

Nico finally said, "Boss, I swear to you, there's more genius in that than anything I've ever even heard of."

Angelo said, "I didn't tell you the best part; bagmen get a bigger cut."

. . .

Michael Grimaldi had been given instructions for meeting Serpiente's men at the Mexican border in the form of an address in La Barranca, a small town just inside Mexico. As he pulled up to the address, he was immediately suspicious. A dozen men exited two black Expeditions, and all of them were armed. Grim was shown to the middle row of seats of one of the vehicles where he sat between two vicious-looking men for the drive to Mendoza's hacienda. The drive took nine excruciating hours; not a word was spoken to Grim during the entire drive. He stopped asking questions after the first half-hour.

Pulling through the hacienda front gates, the two vehicles came to a stop in the driveway and parked near the front door. Sitting ominously in the driveway were a high-backed wooden chair and a small table. The sun glinted off a collection of sharp metal instruments arranged on a tray on the table. Mendoza stood on the front porch next to an older, pock-faced man who wore a smile like a child in a toy store. Grim froze with fear at this ominous scene laid out before him and had to be nearly dragged from the vehicle. When they zip-tied his hands and legs to the chair, his trembling became violent.

"Please, please, Señor Mendoza, please don't kill me. I've had so much time to think about this." Grim forced an innocent smile from his face. "I think I figured it out. There is only one person who could have been responsible for taking that money."

Mendoza leaned down to Grim and whispered, "Do go on. Tell me what you know, and maybe you will live."

"Señor, it would have taken a crew and planning to intercept that money. Also to make everything go away. Nothing was left at the transfer house. Planning means they knew about it ahead of time. The territory belongs to a mafia boss in Fort Worth. He is the one who put the vice president of the casino in his position. The vice president is the only person who could possibly have found out about the score. And I guarantee the man in Fort Worth has the resources to pull off taking it apart."

"And the name of this powerful man?" Mendoza's voice oozed with sarcasm.

"Angelo Genofi. It's gotta be Angelo Genofi." Grim suddenly lit up with hope. "I know where he lives. I can take you to him."

Mendoza looked at the older pock-faced man and nodded. The child-like smile on the man's face grew wider and psychotic. Grim's mouth fell completely open as his last bit of hope washed away. "But, but, Señor Mendoza, I am telling you the truth."

Anger spread across Mendoza's face. "The truth. The truth? In a few hours, we will know for sure what the truth is. I will tell you *a* truth. You come here, empty-handed, without my money, and you expect to be greeted as a friend? That money is my money; it was always going to be my money. I can find this man myself. When I do, I will either take my money, or take his life. Perhaps both. That is *my* truth. In a few hours, we will know for certain about *your* truth."

A crowd had gathered to watch the old man work. Looking around, Grim realized that this was something they had done before; it was a spectacle like a public hanging. As the old man walked up to the chair with a medical scalpel in his left hand, Grim started to cry.

With his sinister grin, the old man whispered, "*Hola, mi juguete.*"

. . .

IT guy left the barn to get himself and Manny something to eat. They had been eating so much carryout, the outside trash barrel smelled like the dumpster behind a shopping mall food court. As was typical for Texas, it was November and the afternoon highs were still in the low eighties.

IT guy got in his Tesla, headed down the long driveway, and exited toward the nearby town. Manny was busy at one of the benches, taking apart the laptop taken from the El Paso house. The idea had been IT guy's; he thought maybe if they took them apart, sort of like an autopsy, they might learn if the components were customized or altered. Manny was skeptical until the laptop was opened, and they took it apart. Just like a welder shows their skill in their welding, or the way a surgeon stitches an incision reflects his level of skill, the inner customization will speak to the abilities of the techie who customized the tech. Manny was good, but unfortunately for the organization, he was not as good as the guy who added components to this laptop.

. . .

In the Computer Forensics lab inside CIA headquarters, an indicator light illuminated above the bank of surveillance computers. They were computers dedicated to whatever surveillance tasks were needed at any particular time. Several years prior, the CIA had a field operation that

almost turned into a nightmare when a laptop with critical information on it went missing. After that incident, the Forensics lab created
a small component that piggy backs on the modem and Wi-Fi system,
also equipped with a tamper detection feature. Simply put, if someone
opened up a CIA-inventory laptop, the component emailed an information packet back to Langley the very moment the laptop finds the
internet.

A technician wordlessly got up from his chair, walked down the row
of monitors, and stopped when he found the flashing screen. It contained
a message that a lost laptop had sent a burst of information back to the
lab. The tech printed out the information and had it sent to the person
who requested the surveillance.

44

Detective Osgood exited the luxury condominium building in downtown Houston, the residence of Andrew Powers, who just found out he was the new interim president of the Silver Star Casino. Her mind raced, trying to make sense of the array of unconnected facts she collected. *Collected so far.*

She took her cell phone from her front coat pocket, looked up a recent contact, and dialed. "Hey, partner, I'm hungry, why don't we get together and compare notes. I do some of my best thinking over a meal."

The voice on the other end of the call answered. "Yeah, you still downtown?"

Osgood replied, "Just left the Silver Star guy, Powers."

The voice said, "I'd like to go to the security guy's house next, its north of downtown. How about we meet at that diner in Crosby, off Highway 90 at Crosby-Lynchfield Road?"

Osgood saw that she was getting another call. "Sounds good. The Chief is blowing up my phone. It's gonna be a full-court press on this. I gotta tell you, so far, I feel like we have shit."

"Yeah, me too, but it's early. See you there."

. . .

Angelo rubbed his hands together, a signal that the conversation direction was changing. "Okay, we've talked about the good. Let's talk about the bad and the ugly. Nico, give me a rundown on how it all fell out."

Nico, let out a lungful of air just to say the words, "Oh, fuck, boss." He paused and then, "Well, let's just say we came within an inch last night of it all going sideways. It was all going to plan right up to the action at the transfer point. We were waiting in our cover position in the car. First the armored car, then a second car goes by. We pull out, park at the end of the drive, Danny gets out with a rifle that looks like something out of a fuckin' Rambo movie. It's got a scope that can see in the dark, ya know? He scouts the scene, tells us what to expect, and that he sees a sniper a hundred yards down the road.

Angelo stopped Nico's story. "A sniper? Covering them or opposing them?"

"Unknown, boss. But my guess was he was at least watching them. He was following the armored car. If he was with them, wouldn't he already know where they were going? But, yeah, Rob spotted him and kept him in his sights. So, we advance, take out two armored car guards and a guard at the front porch of the house. Too Far takes out the sniper. Just when we think it's all done, a third fuckin' car drives up the drive and parks in the middle of it all. *Stunad* gets out of the car, starts calling for his buddies. We drop him, pack up, collect the sniper, and drive all vehicles off the transfer property."

Angelo asked, "Who the fuck was the last guy?"

"He was the third armored car guard, and why he showed up late in a car I'm sure I don't know."

Angelo leaned back in his chair, racking his brain but coming up with nothing.

Nico said, "Boss, one more thing. All in all, I think everything else went pretty well, including the cleanup and the drives in all the vehicles. I been thinkin', trying to make sure we don't have any loose ends, and there are two that are possible. First, we had to leave the boosted Tesla at a huge gas station about sixty miles south of Dallas. We left nothing in the car, and we used gloves for the entire op. We might want to send someone there, see if it's still there. Second thing, and I'm stumped on this boss. The sniper, he and his weapon went into the armored car, with everything else. The thing is, boss, his car had Texas plates, but the guy had the look of cartel. The clothes, the tattoos, the five-hundred-dollar boots, the jewelry. He's in the armored car and his car is a cube on its way to be melted down, so that's tied off. But I can't make that fit, boss."

Angelo nodded. "Okay, I'm on it, Nico, but any way you cut it, you all did well. We have one more loose end, and that is Grim. My guess is he is on his way to another country. They will pin this on him if they catch him, and he's got nothing to give them. My guess is we never hear from him again. If we do, he's going to prison. Okay, I got one hundred large for each member of the crew. The rest everyone will need to wait for. And Nico, you need to remind them of something: be patient. They'll be set for life and will be a lifetime member of my personal crew. The only way we get caught is if we get ourselves caught. If one talks, we all get pinched. Tell them not to turn me into DeNiro at the end of *Good Fellas. Capiche*?"

Nico affirmed. "You got it, boss." He looked at Dan and noticed the puzzlement on his face. "Dan, Jesus, tell me you've seen the movie *Good Fellas*."

"Can't say that I have. Is it good?"

Angelo and Nico both laughed so hard, they nearly fell on the floor. "Yeah, it's a good movie," Angelo said. "You need to watch it tonight. It's a mostly true story about a part of the organization in the Northeast. They pull off a really big score, and then the crew starts going out, spending money, running their mouths. It was DeNiro's crew. He whacked them all, one by one."

Dan injected, "They failed to maintain a low profile."

Angelo held up a finger and smiled. "Exactly right, flyboy. Nico, our boy is coming along, eh? Anyway, my math goes roughly like this: four mil for each of the five guys on the Houston crew, six mil each for you and Dan. Mikey had no family, so I'll donate two mil in his name to that charity that builds houses for military that come back wounded, and my cut will be what's left."

The way Nico tilted his head to the side with a confused face made him look like a dog reacting to an odd noise. "Boss, wait. By my count, that's two-point-seven for you. That's smaller than my cut. What gives?"

"I did the least amount of work, and I'm set already, my friend. I want you two to think and be wise here. Explain this to the rest of the crew. Five or six mil does not make you rich. What it does is give you the satisfaction of knowing that you will never worry about paying the bills, or paying for a vacation, or making a car payment ever again. Any one of you can take that away from all of you. Just don't. Enjoy life now."

. . .

The late afternoon sun bathed the back veranda of the sprawling, rural estate of Eduardo Mendoza. When he constructed it, not long after bringing Serpiente from a low-level operation to the level of top tier cartel, he intentionally had it face to the east so that sunrise filled the front of the house. It was good feng shui to orient a house in that fashion; at least that is what the designer told him. But over the years, it had grown on him: morning coffee on the front porch sunrise and finishing his day with the back veranda sunset.

This evening, he gathered his trusted managers within the cartel; they were all seated at the large table waiting for him to speak. Spread across the front lawn were all of the drivers, bodyguards, and assistants. Guns were everywhere. Meetings like this weren't called often, and that put everyone on edge.

Mendoza addressed the gathering. "My friends, by now, you've all heard about the armored car robbery in Houston, and how it was millions of dollars. You probably all wished we were in on that. Well, we were." Mendoza let that thought marinate for a moment. Puzzled glances were all around the table. "I said 'we were,' because someone else stepped in and took it away from us. The gringo who was supposed to bring me the money paid a visit instead, and he was empty-handed. His path to death was long, but he did give us something. The American Mafia, a man who lives in Fort Worth, Texas, put a friend in as vice president of the casino. So right now, someone has stolen my money. They have also stolen something else very valuable. It grieves me to say, I believe we lost La Sombra as well."

Bewildered faces turned into shock and surprise. Many in Serpiente believed that Mora was invincible.

"Everyone needs to be shaking every tree, talking to every contact in the United States. If anyone has a contact in the Houston Police Department, the FBI, the Pentagon, whatever, I need to know. Tell no one that we know about the Mafia. Gentlemen, that money is gone. But the people who took it from us still breathe air. We may know who they are. Find me proof."

* * *

The phone on the desk was ringing on speakerphone. "Agent Franklin."

"Agent Franklin, this is Special Agent Miller with the FBI, El Paso, Texas, office."

Franklin said unenthusiastically, "How can I help you?"

Miller started fishing. "Yeah, I'm conducting an investigation in El Paso regarding a house your agency was using for some kind of operation."

"Uh, if it was in El Paso, I doubt it was a CIA op house."

Miller tried to sound nonchalant. "Well, we have fingerprints of one of your men in the house, and let's just say that the rest of the details fit the profile. Can you look into it for me? The address is 12605 Rancho Trail, El Paso."

"Sure, I'll check," Franklin said. After a ten-second pause. "Nope, we have nothing associated with that address."

"Okay, thank you, Agent Franklin. Have a good day." Glenn disconnected the call. *That address check was way too fast. What the hell is going on here? Why would the CIA be operating inside the U.S.?*

. . .

When Agent Franklin inputted the address on his computer, an alert box popped up with a message: *Agency Only, Report Contact to: Nick Tuber, extension 1249.* After Miller disconnected the call, Agent Franklin dialed extension 1249 on his desk phone.

45

Dan walked into the back door of his home to see a smiling Sindee stretched out on the long couch. He had seen that particular smile before, many times; it said, "I missed you." It was one of many smiles Dan had been cataloguing, and it was one of his favorites. Dan returned the smile and said, "Hey, baby, I missed you too."

Sindee, being coy, said, "Oh really, and how did you know I missed you?"

Dan returned her attitude. "Oh, I can tell. What I can't tell is what is under that full-length silk robe."

"Well then. Take me to the bedroom, pretend it's Christmas, and unwrap this box."

Dan chuckled. "I see what you did there." He held out his left hand, and Sindee took it as she rose from the couch. They walked together to the bedroom door, where Dan stretched out his right, indicating she should enter first.

Sindee turned to see Dan closing the door. She squeezed his hand. "Oh, leave it open. Mali is in the office. She'll be able to hear; I want to tease her."

"You really are such a tease." Dan said as he reopened the half-closed door. When he turned toward Sindee, she was facing Dan standing against the bed.

"C'mere, lover." Sindee purred. Dan closed the distance, slowly loosened the knot on the tie of her robe, and parted it. Gradually, Sindee's amazing body appeared, enveloped in a pink full-body stocking, complete with openings in all of the right places. He let the robe slip to the floor and gave her a slow look from head to toe and back. Sindee clearly wanted to give him a show; that was exactly what she did. She turned slowly, bent completely at the waist, and slowly crawled onto the bed.

. . .

Laying on the bed in each other's arms, the couple found themselves out of breath. Dan kissed her neck; when he did, Sindee turned her head to the side and caught sight of Mali standing in the doorway. What Mali was doing showed that she had been standing there for a while, enjoying what she saw. When they made eye contact, Mali slowly raised her hand from touching herself and blew Sindee a kiss with it. Sindee winked, and Mali turned toward the office, slinking away.

Dan rolled onto his back, drew in as much air as he could, then let it all out. Sindee had a feeling of satisfaction; she really enjoyed knowing that she had completely pleased her lover.

Sindee broke the silence. "Can we talk about a few things?"

"What's on your mind?"

Sindee breached the discussion carefully. "I feel like we are at a crossroads of sorts. I see that there are many different directions we are going, and all of them good. Things are growing and going in the right direction, but I don't want us to screw things up because we aren't paying attention to something."

Dan joked. "Okay, well, I don't think either of us is dressed for a business meeting, but if you want to waive the dress code today..."

Sindee cut in, "Oh, flyboy, I think you are dressed perfectly." She spoke while simultaneously sliding her hand to his crotch.

Dan put a hand on her hand. "Talk first. You know how that makes it hard for me to think."

"That's fair. I'll go first. Mali, Carleton, and I have spent the last few days doing a complete reassessment of the Maid for You structure, and the way customers are handled. I think we are better equipped now to expand without risk. There's no shortage of customers or workers. The webcam traffic just keeps ramping steadily up. The shows are bringing in about nine thousand dollars a week now. That's good, but it took months to get to this point, and that is doing three or four shows a day. I give a cut of each show's take with whoever I do a show with; two girls is always a better show and pays better. Mali is getting a day rate of pay for doing all the scheduling and books, so she is really happy with the money, as well as her job responsibilities. Okay, your turn."

Dan said, "Well, I don't have much to report, but what I do have is very good." Sindee rolled to her side and looked at Dan with anticipation. "One of the ventures with Angelo paid off in a big way. We will not have to need for money for the rest of our lives."

Sindee was a bit shocked. "Really?"

"Yeah. What do you think about that?"

Sindee rolled over and hugged Dan with all her might. She felt a weight lifted from her shoulders, the concern of wealth security. She knew if Dan said it, it was true. She kissed him, then looked in his eyes. A surprised smile popped on her face as she realized they had something else to discuss.

"Do you want to know what I have planned for Mali?" Dan started to guess, but Sindee stopped him. "Wait! I want it to be a surprise. Just make sure you let me know when you are on your way home after the next trip."

"Ohhhkay. Will do, sweetheart."

46

Special Agent Miller sat at his desk, staring out of the third-story window. He had a great view of the thunderstorm that was ruining the afternoon of all those early evening arrivals at the Top Golf franchise a half-mile away. On his mind was a thought that seemed to be racing in circles in his head. *What the fuck is my involvement here?* He picked up the phone to get an update from his counterpart at the Houston Police Department. Scrolling through his Recent Calls, he found the number he was looking for.

"Detective Wampler."

Miller said, "Hey, Detective. Special Agent Miller. Do we have anything new?"

In an exasperated voice, Lamar said, "Oh, God, Agent Miller, I wish. That house is like a black hole of facts. Every angle, I mean every single angle has been a dead end. The blood in the garage turned out to be human, and the DNA logged, but there was no database match."

Miller felt the frustration build. "I'm at the point of asking if we even have a crime here?"

"You mean besides a shit-ton of vandalism? Hell, I don't know. Medical examiner came out to the scene; he said there wasn't enough blood on the floor for a person to have bled out. But in case you are thinking, maybe he got injured and died in a hospital, I checked. Shocker, another dead fucking end."

"Well, that was good thinking. There was no vehicle at the scene, so if he was only wounded, he could have driven away."

"But, another dead end," Wampler said. "Do you have anything?"

There was a short pause as Miller decided whether or not to talk about the fingerprint. "I hate to even bring it up, because it's the kind of lead that can be your worst nightmare. Deep rabbit hole kind of lead." A few seconds of silence reigned until Miller broke it. "There was a print at the scene that had an old hit on the computer. DUI arrest from—"

"Yeah, San Francisco," Wampler interrupted. "I didn't bother to call his number, if his prints are in El Paso, he isn't in San Francisco."

"And the number of the person who made bail?"

"I called it four times; no answer. Did you get something?"

Miller had the feeling that he was about to step through a doorway. "Yeah, I talked to her. The lady rented him a room. Liked him. Said he was real smart. So smart, she said, he was recruited by the CIA."

Wampler sighed. "Oh boy. Why do I just know I'm going to wish you'd never told me that. Is that it?"

"Is that it? Don't forget, you asked. I called the CIA Liaison office, and the rapid 'no' I got when I gave them the El Paso address told me everything. They were conducting some kind of operation in that house, but what and why, I have no idea. Should we continue to pull on this thread?" Another few seconds of silence; it was a question they were both considering.

Finally, Wampler said, "Go home, I'll call you tomorrow."

. . .

There were two departures from the Del Rio International Airport every day: small jets that were regional airline feeder aircraft, and both flights were to the Dallas-Fort Worth International Airport. From there, Eliazar could get anywhere in the world. He got to the airport early, as it was very important that he get to Washington, D.C., that day. The next day was important: he was pitching Claymore to the directors. The single entrance door of the small terminal building had the words "Jack L Robertson Terminal Building" above it. Eliazar had walked through that door many times and had the same thought each time: *Who the fuck is Jack Robertson?*

He walked through that door and up to the single, small airline ticket counter. When he got close, he glanced at the single flight monitor screen on the wall to his left. In red letters, "DELAYED" was displayed next to his flight. He stopped walking, just stared at the board, and thought, *Oh fuck*. He took a few more steps to the counter, where he was greeted by a smiling, young woman in an airline agent uniform.

"Can I help you?" she squeaked.

"Yeah, uh, how late is the flight?"

The agent's face turned serious. "It is going to be about two hours delayed, but it doesn't look like it will be delayed further.

That was all the information Eliazar needed or wanted. "Okay, thanks. I have my boarding pass already." Eliazar turned toward the small, TSA screening checkpoint and took a few steps before an idea stopped his feet. He thought, *I'm going to call Mendoza a day early.* Eliazar exited the terminal through the same door, and walked out to the parking lot, where he could be sure no one and nothing were listening to him.

Agent Mario Eliazar didn't use the cell phone in his pocket. In fact, he carried four. Eliazar fished the correct phone from his soft-sided, black leather briefcase, selected Mendoza's contact, and a few seconds after he put it to his ear, it rang.

Mendoza picked up on the second ring. *"Háblame."*

"Señor Mendoza. I know I'm a day early, but I'm on my way to Washington right now to speak to my bosses. I don't want to rush your decision; I am merely calling to see if you have already made up your mind. You strike me as a man who could come to the right decision quickly."

"Yes, my friend, I have already decided to explore your idea with you."

Eliazar was excited but kept his voice professional. "That's great, Señor Mendoza. I believe we should meet face-to-face, and I am guessing you would like to meet in Mexico."

"Sí, my friend, we will meet at my modest hacienda. Call me when you are back from Washington, and you would like to meet. I can send a plane to Del Rio to pick you up."

Eliazar thought, *Woah. He's checking up on me already. I never told him where I live.* "Okay, I..."

Click

47

Dan was having a hard time getting out of bed to get ready for the trip he was assigned. The difficulty involved the beautiful woman who was on top of him and what she was doing to him. Sindee liked to wake Dan that way on any day that he was leaving the house. She woke before he did, and the thought of the way he looked in uniform was all it took to make her wet. Her first thought after touching him was *I love that men get ready before they even wake.* Now she was on top of him, moving just slowly enough to make it last as long as she could. She was enjoying every second, making sure Dan was, as well.

"Do you think about this when you are in the cockpit?"

Dan smiled. "Baby, I have to concentrate in the cockpit. When I think of you, concentration is not possible."

That excited Sindee even more than she already was; she picked up the pace.

. . .

Sindee was now lying next to Dan with her head on his chest. "You're going to be back tonight?"

"Yeah, I just go to Chicago and back. We call that a Chicago turn. I won't be back until late, maybe home about nine o'clock. What do you have planned for today?"

Sindee said thoughtfully, "Mali and I have a web show late morning, then this afternoon I have a new Made for You client appointment, then a late afternoon web show.

Dan was surprised. "Wait, did you say a morning web show? Do you get much traffic on morning shows?"

Sindee giggled. "Oh, you'd be amazed. We wait until late morning when the executive types are settled in their offices. They get a little work done, can act like they have something important to do, and tell their secretaries they aren't to be disturbed. I usually start in business attire, then something smoking hot underneath. Business types all have that 'fuck my hot secretary' fantasy." Sindee let that thought marinate in Dan's brain for a while, and she could tell that he was picturing it. With all that he had seen and felt, and all that Sindee had done, she knew he'd be able to play the scene in his head easily.

Dan was a man who liked routines in his life. Piloting passenger aircraft relied heavily on the use of routine. With Sindee now in his life, Dan had to alter some of his routine planning. On the days he left on a trip, he told Sindee he needed to adjust his calculations about when he needed to get ready. Time with her had to be factored in, or otherwise he would be leaving the house late. Often, actual negotiation with Sindee was needed to ensure that Blue Sky Airlines got the on-time departure they wanted from Captain Hatfield.

Sindee saw the look on Dan's face change to his business face. "Listen, my sex goddess, I need to shave, shower, and get out of here. If you make me coffee while I shave, I'll let you assist me in the shower."

She let loose her sexual smile. "Assist you? Sounds good. I'll have coffee and you, coming right up."

. . .

"Osgood."

"Detective Osgood, this is HPD Dispatch. Chief of Detectives wants you to check out something on the north side. I'll send you the address. This is a bit sensitive; it seems a property was called in to 911. Uniformed officers are on the scene. What they report is a group of about twenty-five underaged girls, all Mexican, or other Central American countries. The property has a house that appears to be secured in such a way that they've been held there captive. Looks like human trafficking. Chief thought because you're a woman and fluent in Spanish, you might be the best person for interviewing the girls before Border Patrol takes them to a processing facility. He also wanted you to know that if you need anything at all for the girls, expenses are authorized.

Must be bad, she thought. "Okay, send me the address, I'm leaving right away." Osgood disconnected the phone call. She couldn't help thinking about her mother, who came across the border many years prior in a similar fashion.

. . .

Andy Powers liked that pay phones still existed; his problem was that they were becoming increasingly rare. Even more rare was a payphone in a location that didn't have a dozen cameras covering it. Powers had spent hours on the computer, and then in his car, lining up a dozen pay phones that he thought were in isolated enough locations that surveillance didn't cover them. He rotated through his list so that no one pay phone was used any more frequently than once in a few weeks. There were only a few people he communicated with using them, all of whom had his list.

Powers numbered the phones one through twelve on that list. All Powers had to do was text a single number from his burner phone to the person he wanted a call from, then wait for the phone to ring. Andy, like Angelo, had no trust in cell phones. *What the fuck am I going to do once the pay phones go away altogether?* he wondered as he sat in his car. He was parked to the side of the highway gas station, waiting for the pay phone to ring. Surprised at how quickly it rang, he jumped out of the driver's side door and answered it.

Angelo spoke. "So, are we on for everything that we talked about? No changes?"

"Yes, no changes," replied Powers.

"Okay, exactly as agreed." *Click*

48

The bartender explained to Major Hatfield that the Watergate Hotel used to be a great hotel but had gone downhill a bit in the last decade after changing hands a few times. The present owner, he said, was some Swiss hotel group, and the rumor was that they'd be for sale again within a year.

"How long have you worked here?" asked Dan.

"When I got back from Nam in 1970, I applied for a job here. Worked my way up to bartender. That seat you are sitting in was G. Gordon Liddy's favorite seat. I served him myself several times."

Dan blew a low whistle. "Wow. Well, thank you for your service in Nam. What branch?

"Army. Hundred and first Airborne, Screaming Eagles. Usually screaming because we just jumped out of a fuckin' airplane wearing a hundred-and-twenty pounds of gear. What brings you to this fine establishment, Dan?"

Dan drew in and blew out a big breath. "Well, I can say it now because it's in the news. I'm here for a Congressional Medal of Honor ceremony at the White House in a few days." When he said that, two things happened. The bartender's mouth dropped wide open, and the two other men at the bar turned their heads to look at Dan.

Stammering, the bartender said, "Are you... are... are you the recipient?"

"Yes, sir. Major Dan Hatfield, United States Air Force."

A voice from down the bar spoke up. "There's three of us here for that. Us too." The man motioned at himself and the man next to him."

The bartender spoke, excited, "Well, fuck me. None of you are paying for anything tonight. Holy shit, guys, I need to hear the stories."

Dan laughed. "Our tabs are on the government. None of us were paying anyway." They all laughed at that.

Over the next two hours, the men related their stories, and drank. At one point, Dan asked when the bar closed that night, and the bartender told him that on that particular evening, it didn't close until they wanted it to. Dan was the last to tell his story, and as he finished, he felt a hand on his shoulder. He turned to see a beautiful blonde woman had sidled right up to his left side.

"Mind if I sit next to next to you, Major?"

Dan was surprised, and also uncomfortable. He hadn't had many women in his life, and the only serious one was Sharon. That made him uneasy around women, and in this situation, it was visible to her. She sat down and said, "Don't worry, Dan, I won't bite. Not in the bar anyway. I heard your story, and I have to tell you..." She leaned over and finished the sentence as a whisper in his ear, "...I want you to fuck me all night any way you want."

Dan pulled back and said, "I am married."

"So what? Is she here?" she said.

Before Dan could speak, the Marine Corps sergeant next to him spoke up. "I'm not." He motioned to the lobby with his head, and she winked. The two disappeared a few seconds later.

The bartender said, "Your wife must be a helluva woman."

◆ ◆ ◆

The bed was amazingly comfortable compared to what Hatfield had been sleeping on in Saudi; the bed and the scotch from the lobby bar combined to lure him into sleeping very late the next morning. When he woke at almost noon, he thought, *Thank you, Captain Laredo. Don't know what I would have said into a ringing phone at eight A.M.* Reaching for that phone, Dan called room service and had a coffee and pastry service sent up.

Sharon was on his mind, since he was going to see her when she arrived at the Watergate late in the afternoon. His choice of assignment was also on his mind, as the two subjects were linked. Even though they told him he would have his choice of any assignment, he knew they wouldn't approve anything dangerous. He also didn't want an overseas assignment of any kind, so his choices were limited. Dan settled on pilot training in Del Rio, Texas. That arid part of the United States would probably not be Sharon's first choice. But what Dan was thinking is that it would be a flying assignment they would approve, he would keep building hours, and would be able to slide right into the airlines as soon as he finished his air force commitment.

. . .

Sharon grew up in Carmel, Indiana, an affluent Indianapolis suburb. Dan grew up in Indianapolis in a not-so-affluent neighborhood, until he was parentless. He did well in high school and on the SAT; combined with his economic situation, Dan qualified for a lot of financial aid, which he used in the flight program at Purdue University.

Sharon was expected by her parents to get a degree, and they had no problem paying for it. She settled on the Restaurant, Hotel and Institutional Management degree program. Dan joined the Air Force ROTC, and Sharon was smitten with him and his uniform when they met. Being in the same class year, they graduated in the same ceremony. Dan and Sharon were married shortly after college graduation, a feat made possible by the deep pockets of Sharon's father.

Sharon and Dan spent the next few years at a few different bases as

Dan progressed through the air force pilot training regimen. Eventually, Dan ended up at Shaw Air Force Base, near Sumter, South Carolina, as a new F-16 fighter pilot. By the time Major Hatfield acclimated with his unit, the Twentieth Fighter Wing, the unit was scheduled to rotate to Prince Sultan Air Base in Saudi Arabia, to participate in Operation Desert Storm.

Throughout the process that brought them to Shaw, Sharon repeatedly expressed her unhappiness with where she was. By her standard of living, military officer's quarters were beneath her. Dan tried to make her happy, but the truth was, the life of moving from one base to the next, and not staying in any one place for longer than eight months was not easy for anyone. For Sharon, it was hell. All Dan could do was keep reminding her that it was only for a few more years, and then it was the life of an airline pilot's wife. That standard of living would be much higher, he repeated many times.

When Dan deployed to Saudi Arabia, Sharon was alone in their quarters at Shaw. With it just being herself, no kids, few bills, and Dan in the field, Sharon lived comfortably while he was away. But life apart was a new hell for Sharon, one that she coped with by meeting with the other wives on base who were also missing their husbands. All of this she would share with Dan in their correspondence; there was little he could do from a huge canvas tent with a plywood floor in a desert six thousand miles away.

Then the call came from Captain Laredo, explaining that Dan was coming home and would be in Washington, D.C. the following morning. He gave her travel details that he recommended she write down, and later she was glad she did. Only a few hours later the phone call was like a blur in her memory. Dan was coming home due to heroic combat action to receive a medal. That's all she was told, but that was enough for her. Her husband was returning home — and as a hero.

The phone call that evening from Dan was hope for her that the long nightmare of her life was over. Her hope carried her all the way to the Watergate Hotel in Washington, D.C., and into the arms of Dan. The few hours after that were a roller coaster of emotions for her. The realization that she was going to meet the President and the First Lady. The fact that Dan wanted to ask for Del Rio, Texas, as an assignment, of all places. Then there was the make-up sex of two lovers reunited.

But once she had a moment to think, Sharon's thoughts were of that God-forsaken base she had already spent time at: Laughlin Air Force Base. She was not at all happy that Dan was wasting his golden ticket to move them to the arid Southern Texas area. Of course, as the hero that he is, Dan would be a God walking among the living in Laughlin. *What will I be?* she thought.

. . .

Captain Laredo was such a perfect orchestrator of events, Hatfield wondered how many times he had done this before. The only thing the captain insisted upon for Dan was that Dan and his wife be in the lobby of the Watergate at exactly nine A.M., ready to be on camera for the national media. To Dan, that meant 8:45 A.M. Apparently, to the Marine Corps sergeant he met at the bar, it meant 8:59 A.M. He was perfectly dressed in his dress uniform, and the blonde was barely dressed. The kiss indicated exactly what they had been doing since the night in the lobby bar.

The three service members and Dan's wife boarded a van with government plates. The next stop was the front guard gate of the White House. The short duration of the stop told Dan that they were expected. After they exited the van, Dan overheard a reporter giving an on-scene report saying it was the first time multiple recipients would be awarded in the same ceremony in many years. The seriousness of that was not lost on Hatfield.

Once inside the White House, Captain Laredo led the trio to a large room with a podium in the center, an area off to the side for participants, and a large gallery containing family and press of about one hundred people. Sharon was sitting in a front-row seat, next to several other people who were obvious civilians. In the same coincidental order, the three told their stories to the bartender, they were presented with their citations. Hatfield was last again, and it was as if they were saving the best for last.

As the President read his citation narrative, Dan tried to concentrate, but as the narrative was read, he couldn't help but be caught up in the story. Dan's brain filled in all the details as it was read, and he only regained the present moment in his mind as the president of the United States read aloud, "... conspicuously by gallantry and intrepidity at the risk of your life above and beyond the call of duty."

Major Dan Hatfield turned toward the president, the commander-in-chief of the Armed Forces, who placed the Congressional Medal of Honor over Hatfield's head and around his neck. Sincere applause erupted from the people in the gallery. As Hatfield proudly surveyed the group, he noticed that even the members of the press corps were applauding enthusiastically. Sharon was giving him a look he hadn't seen since their meeting at Purdue University, when she first saw him in uniform.

49

Many pilots believe that the Chicago area controllers and the Chicago O'Hare International Airport controllers are among the best in the world. The sheer density of air traffic in the Chicago area requires them to be very good at what they do.

Dan operated many flights in and out of O'Hare, and he shared that opinion. He also believed that the reason the controllers were so good was because the airspace required that they be of a high skill level. He had said many times before, "If you sucked at controlling, you wouldn't last long in Chicago."

The combination of high air traffic density and precision controlling often led to another phenomenon: wake turbulence encounters. The turbulent air behind a flying aircraft is somewhat like the disturbed water behind a boat that is moving. Aircraft leave a wake behind them as well. They can be dangerous for small aircraft, but for a one-hundred forty-thousand-pound Boeing 737-800, wake turbulence encounters were usually nothing more than a short, sudden burst of turbulence. Unless the aircraft ahead was something much heavier. The Asia Pacifica Cargo 747-400ER was flying into Chicago with a full load of cargo. When it took off from Shenzhen, China, it weighed almost one-million pounds. It was much lighter when Captain Hatfield caught his first glimpse of it; after the long flight and burning off fuel, it still weighed almost seven hundred thousand pounds.

Hatfield had no trouble seeing that the aircraft ahead was a "Heavy" aircraft, a classification for aircraft with a takeoff weight over three hundred thousand pounds. His next glance was to the wind arrow on his navigation display. It showed the direction and speed of the wind at their altitude, as calculated by the Flight Management System. Hatfield did not like what he saw. It was lined up with his aircraft and the Heavy ahead.

Captain Hatfield said, "Do me a favor, call the flight attendants, make sure they are all seated."

First Officer Chelsea replied, "Sure, boss." But he didn't get the chance. At that moment, their aircraft "found" the wake of the 747; Hatfield's 737 was rocked hard and violently.

While Chelsea made contact with the flight attendants, Hatfield keyed his microphone and asked, *"Chicago Approach, Blue Sky 3429, what kind of aircraft are we following?"*

"Blue Sky 3429 is following a 747 heavy. Caution wake turbulence."

"Thanks, approach, we found it already." Hatfield's voice had just a touch of annoyance, but it was easily noticed by the approach controller, who spoke on the radio for a living. Just then, they found the wake again, and this encounter was longer and more violent than the first. "Are they sitting down?"

Chelsea replied, "Yeah, boss, they said they sat down fifteen minutes ago."

. . .

Ten minutes later, Captain Hatfield was steering his aircraft off of Runway 27 Right on the Chicago O'Hare Airport. Chelsea had his pen in hand, ready to write down the complex taxi instructions that would lead them to their assigned gate. The high-density air traffic resulted in high-density ground traffic at O'Hare, and the controllers did not like to have to repeat themselves on the always-busy radio frequency.

There was one other problem created by the amount of ground traffic: taxiway wear. The combination of frequent aircraft, heavy aircraft, harsh winters, and severe spring/summer weather created rough taxiways with numerous quick-fix repairs. Hatfield's aircraft bounced over fifteen minutes of taxiing before they turned into the congested ramp.

. . .

Sindee was seated behind Dan's desk, dressed in a sharp, navy blue, pencil-stripe business suit. Several weeks prior, IT guy set up three cameras in the office, giving the web show three distinct, strategic camera angles. Sindee described the general script of the show to IT guy, who selected the proper equipment, and then professionally installed it. Sindee's idea was that Dan's office provided a different "set" for her to be able to have web shows in, shows that had an office theme. A hard look at the revenue numbers proved that the popularity of that theme was big with her most affluent fans: businessmen. At Dan's request, IT guy installed a small access panel, behind which was a disconnect for the cameras. Dan knew he may someday have to make someone, such as Angelo, feel comfortable that the cameras were not functioning.

At the moment, the cameras were working perfectly. Sindee played the role of upset, exacting boss, not happy about her secretary's work product. Mali was the apologetic secretary, but apparently, she had been warned one time too many. Mali came around behind the desk, bent over it next to Sindee. Mali slowly pulled up her very short skirt, revealing that she was not wearing underwear. Sindee then informed her that she will also be punished for violating the dress code. Dan would have been surprised to see what Sindee placed in his desk drawers for use during the show.

. . .

Angelo's heart sank a little when he saw the text from Powers. The text was a single number, and Angelo retrieved his list of Powers' pay phone numbers from his desk drawer. There were few people that required Angelo to do anything, but Powers was supposed to confirm the first cash drop at the Silver Star. That was something even more important to Angelo than Sindee's web show, which had just begun on Angelo's oversized computer monitor. *At least the call will be short, but damned if I don't have to turn off the computer's sound.*

When Powers picked up the handset, Angelo got right to business. "So, are we on for everything that we talked about? No changes?"

"Yes, no changes," replied Powers.

"Great, exactly as agreed." *Click*

Turning toward his computer monitor, Angelo took in the sight of Mali bent over the desk, when another of Angelo's phones rang. Looking at the caller ID he winced. *Damnit, I gotta take this.* It was IT guy. As he connected the call while glancing at his computer monitor, Angelo thought, *Hey, I wonder if they could do a show in my office. I'd pay real money for that.*

"IT guy, talk to me."

IT guy started. "I emailed you a few pictures I'd like you to take a look at while we talk."

Angelo was now exasperated. "Right now? Aw fuck, okay." Angelo took one last look at Mali getting a proper spanking, then opened his email program. On top of the list was an email from IT guy with attachments. Angelo opened the attachments, scrolled through the images, and immediately had questions.

"Okay, boss, what you are looking at are images from the camera I put in the tree at the El Paso house. This guy visited the house, ran off some kids, and then stayed for a few hours. Look at that jacket with 'Police' written on the back, and then take a look at the car, and the rest of his look. My ass he's police. He is something else. And in that last picture, he's walking out with what looks to me like a computer server under his left arm."

Angelo said, "Whatever's in the bag looks heavy. Did you run his face through the database?"

"Sure did, boss. Got nothing on him, and the images are good. If he was in the database, it would have matched. But boss, there's more. Funny thing is, there's really only one guy in El Paso to take that server to, he's really good, and he's a friend of the organization. I've known this guy for years, so I reached out. An hour after this guy visits the El Paso house, he walks into my computer guy's shop, server in his arms. My computer guy mirrored the server drive and gave a copy to his client."

Angelo jumped in. "Can we get a copy of that data?"

"Boss, it's me you're talking to, remember? I already have a copy, but here's the thing. The server was just a backup server for the computers we already have. So, we didn't get anything new. But, now we know there is someone out there who knows everything we know."

Angelo was deep in thought. "How the hell do we find out who this guy is?"

"Maybe you should just ask me, boss. I have his address. My computer guy in El Paso had it. The guy lives in Del Rio. Other than that, my computer guy wouldn't talk about his client."

Angelo was ecstatic. "IT, nice fucking job! Listen, don't add him to the database just yet. We don't know what this guy is. Great work, seriously great." *Click*

Angelo quickly dialed a different number. "People guy. I have someone I need you to do a workup on. I'm going to text you a name, an address, plus a pic of his face. It's all I got." *Click*

. . .

It was only a moment before the aircraft door was going to be closed when Dan's other phone rang. Of course, it was Angelo.

Angelo asked, "What are your next few days like?"

"I'm about to push back to head back to DFW, I'm home late tonight, and then I have three days off."

"Okay, good. Meet me tomorrow, regular place, regular time." *Click*

Dan heard the call disconnect and put his phone away. It was time to be Captain Hatfield. It takes many people to get a flight out of the gate, and if they work together, they might actually achieve the coveted On Time Departure. The flight captain is like the conductor of the orchestra. He makes sure to pull all the different sections together so the music being played matches the score placed in front of him.

Captain Hatfield managed the push back from the gate, taxi out to the runway, and takeoff. By the time they reached cruise altitude, Dan was alone with his thoughts. Dan was the non-flying pilot back to DFW, just working the radios, and his F.O. had training coming up, so at cruise he studied his manuals. The only sound in the cockpit at cruise, besides the radios, was the white noise of the air that rushed over the windshield. Dan's mind wandered, thinking over the last year, unconsciously wanting the past to direct him to the best future for him and Sindee. He thought over the jobs he had done for Angelo and thought back to his days in Iraq, causing him to ponder the question: how much longer will I work for Angelo? *Why would I stop?* He chuckled at that thought.

. . .

The hacienda was huge, and the living area inside the house was cavernous. Mendoza preferred to occupy the living room when it rained, and it was pouring. The lightning and thunder didn't let up. It made the mood of the gathering even more ominous than it already was. Mendoza sat, sipping tequila, and thinking, a smoldering neglected cigar next to him in the ashtray. Enough silence had passed that the other three men in the room were beginning to get visibly nervous. Mendoza picked up on the body language; it was what he wanted. He had not told them the reason for the meeting.

Finally, Mendoza spoke. "Draw thirty thousand in U.S. dollars from the secretary for expenses. Pack for a week. Take a vehicle with Texas plates and a smuggling rig to bring guns with. I want you all to have a pistol for each with plenty of ammo. Make sure the secretary knows when you will be going, so we can arrange that you will not be disturbed crossing the border. You are going to Houston; you will be checking into some things for me. The secretary will have a workup for you. I don't know how long you will be in the U.S., but it could be weeks. Say your goodbyes. *Comprende?*"

"Claro, claro, claro que sí" rose from voices around the table. When Mendoza stood, it was the sign for them to be on their way, so they shot to their feet rapidly.

Mendoza's last words to his team: "Stay low, stay out of sight, bring no attention to yourselves. The guns are a precaution, so leave them hidden in the car unless you need them. What I need is your eyes and your reports. Leave tomorrow morning early." The men all nodded and left for the secretary's office.

50

The headquarters of the Central Intelligence Agency was located in Langley, Virginia, on the banks of the Potomac River. Different levels of security clearance and job responsibility allowed employees access to only the areas of the building for which they were cleared. Nick Tuber and Mario Eliazar had clearances to nearly the inner-most areas of the building. Very few people even knew the most inner areas existed, and if they did, they weren't allowed to talk about them.

Tuber's office overlooked the Potomac, and he enjoyed the fact that when Reagan National Airport was landing to the south, a steady stream of airliners flew past his window. Tuber had considered taking flying lessons after he retired just for enjoyment, but the life of a professional pilot was not his calling. He was one of those people who had the itch to work as a spy his whole life. Spy was what he imagined when he was twelve years old; his current job looked nothing like his childhood imagination.

Tuber understood now and took great pride in the knowledge that his current position carried much more impact and responsibility than the glamorous life of a field agent he daydreamed about in middle school. Tuber got on an elevator and selected a floor that his ID allowed.

After some security protocols, and a different elevator, he arrived at a floor containing secure meeting areas. These were the areas where people could speak without fear of eavesdropping but were used for discussions that were merely "Classified." There were still more secure areas for "Top Secret" and higher classifications. Eliazar was already there, as was the

Central American Region assistant supervisor. Tuber sat down at the end of the long rectangular table where the other two had already set out papers and laptops.

As he sat down, Tuber asked, "Did you get coffee?"

"Probably more than I need."

Tuber got right to business. "Okay, let's get started."

Eliazar reached for a stack of folders in front of him, then separated three copies of the same packet. He set one each on the table in front of himself and the other two men. The top cover of each folder was labeled "Claymore — Classified."

Eliazar began. "This is my proposal for a follow-on operation to Crossbow. In its essence, it is an intelligence operation developing human intel assets in Mexico for the purpose of drug interdiction. Crossbow established connections with a specific cartel in Mexico, the Villareal Cartel, and used this connection to obtain information regarding the structure of the entire of Mexican drug cartel operations. Claymore will springboard on the work that was done in Crossbow." The men in the room paged through the written proposal as Eliazar continued. "At the time our men disappeared, the head of the Villareal Cartel was murdered, and his number two man disappeared, along with a bodyguard. The Villareal Cartel was rumored, among the other cartels, to be working with the CIA. Within a month of this event, the assets and territories of the Villareal Cartel were seized, stolen, invaded, or otherwise absorbed by the other cartels. That also includes personnel, and that is where our opportunity lies."

Both men's faces showed puzzlement at the last remark. Eliazar explained. "When the personnel who were formerly associated with the Villareal Cartel spread out into the other cartels, it created a situation where numerous contacts of ours were injected into the other Mexican cartels. In general, the cartels in territories adjacent to the Villareal territory did the best in the looting of Villareal, and I can say we now have contacts numbering in the dozens in four other cartels.

Okay, I can see where this is going, thought Tuber, exchanging glances with his assistant director. "Alright, you have my attention. I will give you the go-no-go decision in a few days, but I'm leaning toward go. The money is already there in your existing budget and the budgeted funds already in place for Crossbow. At the very least, we will close the file on Crossbow as long as you have everything you need already. Is that right?"

Eliazar replied, "I do, in fact. I have everything I need to move forward."

Tuber wrapped up. "Okay, head home. You'll hear in the next day or two."

Eliazar neatened up his papers and put them in his briefcase as Tuber and his assistant filed out the door. On the elevator, Tuber said to his assistant, "That jackass might actually be on to something. If he can make this work, show real results, he may be able to change the direction of his own career right before it was about to crash into the ground. I'm going to green-light him, but I'll give him a couple of days to worry about it. It might motivate him better if he thinks his ass is hanging out even farther than it is."

◦ ◦ ◦

Creating a cloud of dust in its wake, a pickup truck drove down an unpaved road in rural Mexico with a driver, a rear seat passenger, and a front seat passenger who was speaking on his cell phone. The truck was a basic model, crew cab Ford F-150, black in color, and a few years old. It was the perfect vehicle to drive anywhere in Texas and not draw attention.

"Jefe, I got the team ready to go right now. Would you like us to leave this evening? We could be in Houston by tomorrow afternoon.

Mendoza replied, "Thank you, hermano. Yes, that would please me. What time do you anticipate being at the border?"

"About two A.M., Jefe. GPS, it says 2:07 A.M."

Mendoza said, "I will update the secretary myself. Thank you, hermano. You have the workup; call me when you are arriving at the first address." *Click*

51

Deep in thought, Special Agent Miller stared out the window of his office. *How many times have I been in this spot? Am I on to something, should I keep digging, or am I just jerking off? Is this a big fucking waste of time?* His desk phone ringing startled him back to reality.

"Agent Miller, this is Assistant Director Gavin of the Counterintelligence Division. How are you today?"

"Fine, thanks. How are you, and how can I help you? *Fuck me, I was wondering if I was going to get a phone call like this.*"

AD Gavin explained, "I'm well, thank you. The reason I'm calling is because you are investigating a location in El Paso that overlaps with an investigation of ours. What I need you to do is send me everything you have uncovered in your investigation, and then move on to other, more pressing projects. I can assure you there is nothing you need to be investigating with regard to that house. Other agency assets have that covered."

There was a pause, and Miller realized it was his turn to speak. "Of course, Assistant Director, I will get you all I have this afternoon."

"I sure do appreciate that, Agent Miller. I appreciate your efforts, they will not be forgotten, and I can vouch for our efforts as an agency being fully covered without your participation."

Miller tried not to let the disappointment he was feeling come out in his voice. "Understood, Assistant Director, have a great day."

"You as well."

Miller disconnected the call and put the phone on the desk in front of him. *Holy shit, that call was full of FBI-speak. "Overlaps"? "Fully covered without your participation"? "Move on," coming from an Assistant Director? So, the AD calls me instead of the Director, because that would be too big a leap in chain of command, and also gives the Director deniability of the phone call. I was just told to back off for general reasons that tell me nothing about what is really going on. If I take this to my boss, and it turns out he was jumped in the chain, it is going to make certain people look bad and maybe burn down my career. If you piss off people who get promoted...* A ringing phone shook him out of his thoughts again.

"Miller here."

"Agent Miller, it's Detective Wampler. Do you have a minute? I may have found a few bits of evidence related to the fingerprint from the scene."

You have got to be shitting me. "Okay, talk to me," Miller said.

"Well, I went at this from a few angles. First, we know where he went to college; most people go to college pretty close to home. So, I went onto a few of those high school yearbook websites and found a name match from a small high school maybe forty miles away. Got a yearbook pic, but it's a few years old, right? So, I have a name and location; I make a few calls, find out the parents are dead, no one knows of any siblings. Sounds perfect for the computer nerd upbringing. So, then I think, maybe he has a storage area in either the location of him leaving for the CIA or in El Paso. I put together a list of fifty or so storage areas in El Paso and San Francisco in the area of his university."

Oh fuck, here it comes, Miller thought.

"I made a ton of phone calls but didn't find a storage area in San Francisco in his name. I moved on to calling the El Paso locations. I started with the locations closest to the house and scored on the third call. One unit, in his name, unpaid for 6 months. I visited the location, and the owner of the family-owned business said the man always paid in cash but hadn't visited them in six months. The timing works with when the incident at the El Paso house happened. The owner said the unit was about to be auctioned. I asked her what she would want for it right now, and she said five hundred. I paid up, and they are going to let me use their grinder to cut the lock. Ever watch *Storage Wars*? You want to come with me now to take a look inside?"

Miller took it all in. He filled his lungs with air, blew it out slowly, shaking his head as he did it. He knew what he should do: follow the directive given by the Assistant Director. He also knew what he wanted to do; tear apart that storage area and solve the mystery.

"Miller?"

Hearing his name shook him from his thoughts. "Yeah, I'm here. I'm just thinking about a phone call I got a while ago telling me to forget about this case, that there were other people covering it. Thing is, it came from a guy just a little too far above my pay grade. Now you bring me this shit!" Those words were delivered in a way that made them funny, and both men had a chuckle. "Listen, give me an address, and let's meet there day after tomorrow. I want to give the appearance I'm working on other field work before I try to get myself fired." *Glenn, what the fuck are you doing?*

53

At a few minutes before one P.M., Sindee strolled through the front door of Vincent's, followed closely by Dan. Sindee, of course and as usual, turned every head in the place. Dan loved the way they all reacted; every man's head turned just a little quicker and lingered a little longer than the women's heads. Sindee decided on a black-and-gold theme that day. Black four-inch heels with black stockings, and a tight black spandex dress, just short enough to show the tops of the stockings. Gold necklace and earrings, and a small black cap that sported a small black feather on top. She could have walked into Gucci's in Rome and still would have turned every head in the store.

When Vincent saw them, he made the very European gesture of the simultaneous genuine smile and tilting his head to the side. Even though he certainly saw the reservation, he was genuinely happy to see them and greeted them warmly. "Aah, the beautiful couple graces my establishment yet again. How nice to see you."

Smiling wide, Dan said, "I can't stay away from your place for very long, Vincent, and it has been too long this time."

Vincent took Sindee's hand and kissed it gently. "I have honestly seen an increase in bar revenue on the days when you visit, Ms. Simpson. My patrons stay longer simply for the opportunity to take in your beauty."

Sindee's mouth opened when she heard the comment. After a pause, she breathed, "Really?"

Dan could see her flush at the comment. *Vincent may think she's blushing, but I know her better. That is arousal.* Dan thought. "I know my way to the back. Vincent, if you would accompany Sindee to the bar, I would appreciate it."

Nodding, Vincent said, "Captain, it would be my pleasure." Sindee took his offered arm and they both walked to the bar with the air of royalty. Dan stood there taking in the sight of patrons at the bar parting for the two. A man got up to give her a seat at the center. She was handed a drink as she sat down; the bartender made it as soon as he was able to pull his gaze away from her visage when she walked in the door.

I am never going to stop coming here, thought Dan. The last image he took in before turning toward the massive mahogany doors was Sindee literally being the center of attention of every person in the bar area. She was acting as if she didn't notice, but Dan knew for certain, the attention was turning her on completely. Dan still had a smile on his face as he reached for the brass door handle and swung open the heavy door. Angelo smiled when he saw Dan, but Dan could see the disappointment on Angelo's face when Dan closed the door behind him.

Angelo asked, "Where is your definitely better half?"

"She is sitting at the bar. She loves the attention."

"I was looking forward to seeing her. It's the highlight of my day."

"And you certainly can, I'll fetch her when we are done. Don't you see her enough online?" Dan flashed a big, knowing smile.

Angelo smiled like a Cheshire cat. "You bet your ass I see her a lot online, but it's never enough. I doubt I've missed a show. That reminds me, I want to ask you a question right now, so I don't forget. Last show I was watching, it was Sindee and Mali doing an office gig–secretary thing, and it was hot as the fuckin' sun. Got me thinking. If a client, say who was well-to-do, was to want, say, an in-person show, you think something like that could be arranged?"

Dan chuckled. "Asking for a friend, right, boss?" They both laughed.

"I'm sure it's possible. I'll run it past Sindee, but I know what she is going to say. Let's be honest, even you know what she's going to say." They both had a laugh at that, too. "Just so I know, let me ask you a few relevant questions. Are you audience-only, or do you want some interaction? Is Mali who you prefer, or one of the other girls? What if she wants to record? I'm guessing no to that."

Angelo held a hand up. "Okay, I'll answer the questions and you let me know later. We gotta stop talking about this soon, so I can concentrate. I want Sindee and whoever she thinks will do the best show. Sindee is watch-only; her partner should be up for anything. And you know, I'd like her to record it but just for me. I want the file on my computer and no other copies. You can use it as a shakeout run if this is a service you want to add."

Dan said, "Aah, I see what you did in the end there. You are actually doing me a favor? Okay, boss, done. So, let's talk about what brought us here."

"Right after we order." Dan didn't see Angelo press the button, but knew he had because a waiter appeared from the kitchen door. Angelo, then Dan, made their lunch orders in the usual fashion, while the waiter stood listening with hands behind his back.

I love everything about this place, Dan thought.

The waiter disappeared, and Angelo put on his business face. "My IT guy put a camera in a tree at the El Paso house to keep an eye on the place. It picked up a guy going into the place several days ago, taking some kind of computer equipment out of the place. He takes the computer to a guy in El Paso, a friend of the organization, asks him to crack it open. Turns out, it is a backup of all the computers those guys were using in that house, the same computers we have here. So, he knows everything we know, except we don't know who he is." Angelo handed Dan an iPad with two images open. "Here's two pics from the camera. Here's the guy's face, and this is the car he was driving. Can't see the license plate, though, and he doesn't appear in any of our databases."

Dan wondered what he meant by that, and it showed in his face.

Angelo appeared to take offence, but in a joking way. "Captain. The organization isn't just a bunch of goons sitting around social clubs talking about pasta. We are so much more than that. We have our own intelligence system. Some of it we own, some of it is people who access what we need from various outside sources. We ran this guy on everything we have, got nothing; so, he is either working with the cartel, or he's CIA. He has a house in Del Rio. I'd like a better picture of this guy, pics of anything you can get about his house or vehicles, whatever. I got something for you." Angelo slid an envelope across the table. Dan took it, opened it, and took out an ID and credit card.

"Gold card, huh? Membership has its privileges, right?" Dan holds up the ID, studying it. "Texas driver's license in the name of Greg Boyington? Pretty convincing, but boss, do you know who Greg Boyington is?"

"You mean, was. He's as dead as the shrimp in my scampi. That ID is convincing because it came from the DMV. Easier to pay an employee than to go to all the trouble to try to fake it. That name was my people guy's idea. You need to know that name cold, so his idea was to give the ID the name of a pilot you would know, but not too famous. Use that ID and credit card for things like car rentals. You're going to need them for this; I'm assuming you're gonna get this done from an El Paso overnight?"

"Actually, San Angelo is a closer drive."

Angelo slid a small box across the table to Dan. "Okay, San Angelo then. One last thing, here's a new toy for you. My IT guy checked it out, got it all set to go. It's about the best, small digital camera you can spend money on. Use it on the trip and get me what you can." Just as Angelo slid the unmarked box across the table, the kitchen door opened, and the waiter emerged with a large tray. As he set out all of the offerings to Dan and Angelo, Angelo addressed the waiter. "Can you get word to the bar that Ms. Simpson's presence is requested here? And bring some calamari, bread, and olive oil for her, along with a glass of something white, something nice.

Only a few moments later, Vincent opened the large door for Sindee, who walked through wearing a sexy smile.

"I guess you boys got to missing me?"

Angelo smiled wide. "Darlin'? You have no idea."

54

A late fall afternoon in Texas can mean brutal temperatures. The truck Mendoza's men chose had functioning air conditioning, something that all three of them grew up without in rural Mexico. Unlike most of the Americans they were driving past, they saw the air conditioning more as a blessing, where the Americans saw it as a necessity.

Raffiel, the driver, had not been in the cartel employ long enough to have a nickname given to him any more ominous than Raffie. He had an unspoken loathing of America. He loved his native Mexico and blamed many of her problems on America. When he was approached by a friend who worked for Serpiente, he was told that this was a chance to take back from America what Mexico deserved. He was hooked immediately.

The change in the economy of the landscape as he drove from rural central Mexico to rural southern Texas only served as a reminder of why he felt the hostility he did. Looking at the GPS display, he saw they were less than five minutes out from the first address. Raffie turned to Tomas in the passenger seat. "Make the call."

Tomas pulled his phone from his pocket and dialed the number for Eduardo Mendoza. *"Digame."*

"Jefe de jefes, we are ten minutes from the first address."

Mendoza said, "Put me on speaker. I wanted you to call me early so I can give you some details. This location was a place where girls from the south were transferred to travel into the United States. It is connected to one of the men who took the money, so it may be connected to the money. I want you three to take a look at the place carefully. Tell me what you see."

Tomas spoke up. "It's the country out here, jefe. Ranch houses and cattle, but spread out. We are coming up on the house road now. There is yellow tape crossing the driveway, and more yellow tape down the road. Looks like something happened here."

Mendoza ordered, "Go up to the house."

Raffie drove through the yellow police tape and up the driveway to the house. Tomas said, "We drove through the tape, jefe, and we are parking in front of the house now. Parking area is big enough for trucks. The windows on the house are boarded up, sealed. This is the place, jefe. Raffie is going inside; Sam is going to the place down the road. There are little yellow flags planted in the ground all over the place, the kind the police use to mark bullet casings. Some casings are still on the ground, there was a firefight here. I see tire tracks, some of them heavy truck, dual tires, could be an armored car. Others are cars. It has rained here since the vehicles were here, but I can still make out some of the tracks."

Raffie came back to the truck after a quick search of the house. "Jefe, inside the house is clean. It does look like a transfer house. It's got sealed windows and doors. Looks like someone was killed on the porch."

Tomas said, "Even though it rained, there's blood in the driveway in a few places as well."

Sam came running up the driveway, out of breath. "Down the road, there's yellow tape around a place where a car was parked. There's a mess on the ground near there too. Looks like someone got a head shot with a high-powered rifle. The tire tracks look like only one car parked there. Wait!"

They all froze as three girls emerged from behind the house. The girls begged the three men to help them. Raffie said, "Tomas! Get them some water and whatever food we have in the truck, anything we have.

One of the girls spoke. "We heard you. We have been hiding since it happened. We had some food from the house, but it ran out yesterday. Can you help us?"

Raffie asked, "What happened?"

"We could see nothing, we only heard guns and shouting. One gringo came inside the house for a minute and left. We didn't see anyone else but we could hear them. They were all gringos."

Mendoza listened to everything that was said, and then he stepped in. "The girls are of no value to us. Give them one thousand dollars each from your cash and a ride into Houston. Then proceed to the next address, good work, men." *Click*

. . .

Mendoza disconnected the call. He turned to Gloria and said, "Sombra took his long-range rifle with him. That was the last location before his cell phone went dead. So now we know it's true, what we suspected. Sombra went to that location, following the armored car. It seems the armored car was hit there, the crew was killed, and the money was taken. The same people that took the money killed Sombra. Mí Sombra."

Gloria asked, "What are you going to do, *mí amor*?"

Mendoza considered that notion. "I'm going to send someone to meet the team in Houston. Bring them some firepower. Then we will avenge Sombra."

. . .

Back in his office, Dan looked at the company trip trade website, trying to find a San Angelo overnight. He called out, "Hey, sweetheart, can I see you for a minute?" Half a minute later, Sindee swayed into the office with a scotch rocks in hand. "Oh my God, you are the best, thank you." Sindee sank to her knees in front of Dan, seated in his high-back office chair. He stopped her. "Baby, there's something I want to talk to you about. Angelo has been watching your shows. All of them, actually. The last one you did, an office scene with Mali, apparently gave him an idea."

Sindee purred. "Oh, I'll bet it gave him a lot more than an idea."

Dan replied, "I'm sure you're right. But his idea was this; he wants to know if you wanted to branch out to doing on-location shows. Specifically, he'd like you and Mali to do a show in his office." Dan could see from the look on her face and the shift in her body that the idea was really heating her up. "Angelo thought that if you were going to do online shows from other locations, you could use his show as kind of a dress rehearsal."

Sindee asked, "He wants it recorded?"

"Well, yes, but he gets the only recording file. He wants it for himself. Oh, and he wants to pay. I guess we should decide what the fee is and see if this is something we can break into, or if it's even legal. And something else, my lover. Angelo wants to be audience only with you, but he'd like whatever partner for the show you choose to be up for anything. I think we need to think about breaking out into something like this, but we need to be careful."

Sindee pursed her lips as she considered the idea. "Tell him, yes, of course. If it's for him, then of course we can do it. Let's work out the details tonight in bed. He said, 'up for anything'? That describes Mali, so I will bring her as my partner."

55

Just a few years prior, a luxury bus company ventured into the niche of providing first-class style accommodations on a few routes within Texas. They grew in their route structure to include a few cities outside of the state of Texas, as well. The Fort Worth to Houston route seemed to Nico to be the perfect alternative to driving every other week to Houston with a bag containing one million dollars in cash. Bus tickets could be paid for in cash, there was no TSA to clear, and the cab at the other end could also be paid for in cash. Cup of coffee in the cup holder; big, comfortable seat leaned way back; footrest up; and iPad in hand, Nico enjoyed the opportunity to just relax. It was something that routinely did not happen in his life, and now it would. At least for the next fifteen months.

* * *

The CIA computer tech was as frustrated as Supervisor Tuber was. His written report to Tuber left Tuber with more questions than answers. All Tuber was understanding was that a laptop had, on its own, reported back to the computer department, and that Tuber was listed as the supervisor to contact when it did. Tuber read the email four times and was still no closer to getting his questions answered.

Tuber decided to get the tech on the phone. "All I'm understanding so far is that someone lost control of a company laptop, and the laptop reported back to you. But why are you calling me with that? It wasn't my laptop."

The tech tried to explain again. "As you know, all of our company equipment has an anti-tamper device installed that is designed to send a burst of information back to us here at headquarters in the event that someone tries to open it up or break into it. This laptop is an asset for an op with restricted access, so I don't know who had it or what they were working on. But when the report came in, your name and telephone extension were listed as the contact person. The laptop is capable of determining its exact position, and that is supposed to be included in the information burst report. In the case of this laptop, the position info was odd. Using the internet address the burst was sent from allows me to draw a three or four-mile-wide circle on the map of where the laptop is. It did send its last known GPS location, but that was months ago in El Paso, Texas. What I can try to do—"

"Wait, wait, wait," Tuber interrupted. "You're saying you can get an idea where it is now, but the last accurate location the laptop knew it was at was months ago in El Paso? Where does the internet address put it now?" *This could be Bayan's laptop, or at least someone on the El Paso op.*

"Like I said, it's not an exact location, but it is somewhere northwest of Fort Worth. I can draw a circle on a map with a high level of confidence that the laptop is inside the ring."

Tuber thought for a second. *Finally, we might have some fuckin' answers to what happened in El Paso.* "Send me another report, only this time make sure all the info is in it, and it's written in plain English. I don't fuckin' speak computer. Drop everything else you are doing; this is important."

Tuber hung up the desk phone and picked up his cell phone. "Eliazar, we've had a development. It seems that a computer from the El Paso op just reported in to the computer department here. They can't pin down its exact location, but they know its near Fort Worth."

"Sir, consider this my request for assistance from Special Assets. I'm on the regional flight from DFW to Del Rio. I will go straight to my office when I get home. If we can find out who has that laptop and how they acquired it, that will answer a lot of questions."

"Get right on this, Eliazar. I'll email you everything via the secure net. It'll be waiting for you when you get home." *Click*

. . .

A few hours later, Eliazar was in his car on his way home. He dialed Mendoza's number. "I'm back in Texas, and I'm free tomorrow. When would..."

Mendoza interrupted him. He heard everything he needed to hear. "Tomorrow is fine. I'll send a plane to Del Rio. Be at the corporate ramp at ten A.M. Bring anything you like except a *pistola*. And you won't be going through customs." *Click*

. . .

"La Sombra was my eyes and ears. There's no one in the organization I trusted more than Javier. And now he's gone." Mendoza was having a private conversation on the back veranda with his wife, Gloria. In addition to being his wife, Gloria was also a valuable employee of the Serpiente Cartel. She was smart, organized, and very good at handling details.

Gloria said, "Eduardo, yes, he is gone. He worked well for you for years, but you need to replace him. You have many men, but my mind keeps coming back to the same man."

"Roberto Reyes?" Mendoza guessed, and Gloria nodded. "Yes, I think he is the best choice. Please, get him here to meet with us as soon as you can. I want to talk to him about his new position, then send him to Houston with hardware for the crew."

. . .

Captain Hatfield said goodbye to every passenger that left his jet at the San Angelo International Airport. He told the first officer during the flight that he had someone he had to visit, so he wouldn't be on the hotel van with the crew. After he left the crew, Dan headed to the rental car counter.

Dan followed Nico's lead and asked for a minivan when he was greeted by the rental agent. The agent took Dan's credit card and driver's license, and printed up a rental contract for a white, harmless-looking minivan.

"Would you like the additional insurance coverage on the van, Mr. Boyington?"

Dan chuckled a little. "Oh, no thank you. And I'll return it with the gas tank full."

Three hours later, Dan pulled the minivan into Eliazar's neighborhood. *Nico is right about the minivan thing. I've seen a half-dozen of them in the neighborhood, and I just got here.* Dan parked the van across the street from the target home, confirmed by the map app he was using on his phone. Both garage doors were open; the sedan from the El Paso picture in one, and a Corvette in the other. Dan climbed into the middle seat area of the minivan, turned on the digital camera, and took pictures. *House with address visible, license plates of vehicles, oh wow.* The front door of the target house opened, and a man exited the house, one who strongly resembled the man in the El Paso surveillance picture. He walked from the front door, out to the mailbox, and pulled out a large amount of mail. Dan used the digital zoom and took a dozen pics of him. *Perfect.*

Dan waited until the man went back in his house, then he pulled the van away from the curb, retrieving his phone as he drove. When he was about a mile away from the target home, Dan pulled over into the parking area at a gas station. He dialed his other phone. "Boss, I'm enjoying my vacation. I took lots of vacation pics, I even captured a dozen of an interesting animal in front of its habitat. I'll be sending them in a few minutes. Check your email."

"Perfect." *Click.*

. . .

True to his word, Dan emailed the pictures from the digital camera to Angelo. The top of the email showed that Dan also emailed the pictures to IT guy. Angelo opened the attachments and blew a low whistle. *Dan always comes through. These pictures are perfect.*

Angelo selected a phone and dialed People guy. "PG, I'm sending you some pictures right now. Two license plates I need you to run, and a face pic. Get me a name right away, and a full work-up when you can. It's important." *Click*

He sent the email to PG with the pictures, and in less than five minutes, Angelo received a reply. The body of the email said: "Boss, the sedan on the right comes back to some kind of government vehicle. The Vette comes back to Mario Eliazar. Address on the registration matches that address in the pics."

Angelo forwarded the email to IT guy. He added the note, "Run the name Mario Eliazar through the database on the computers, see what pops up. Get me a report on what you find and make me a one-page summary of what is in the report."

He knew he'd soon have the life details of one Mario Eliazar. Angelo pushed his chair back from the desk, leaned back in it, and started trying to make sense of it all. *So, El Paso is a CIA op, off the books and unknown to CIA leadership. They had a good thing going. Then they step on our toes, we make them disappear. CIA figures out their guys are missing, along with all their intel. Eliazar is there to clean up, so he's at a higher level than the El Paso guys. Eliazar knows everything now, so is he going to restart the op?* Angelo nodded. *I'm going to contact him.*

56

The men arrived at Vincent's one at a time. They were instructed to enter, not say a word to anyone, and go straight to the big doors of the meeting room in the back. Five men entered the meeting room, each of them greeted by Angelo, in his regular seat behind the table. When the fifth man entered the room, Vincent closed the heavy doors. On the table there were several opened bottles of Italian red wine. As they all sat, one at a time, they realized there was an extra glass in front of an empty chair.

Angelo looked around the room; he felt like a proud father, but also felt the pain of having lost a son. He cleared his throat once and the room fell silent. "Gentlemen, let's get started. There are a few people involved who are not in this room, who get a cut from the pot. There were also expenses that were taken care of. Mikey Robinson was ex-Army Ranger. He did four tours in Afghanistan and Iraq. Mikey left no family; just a wife that left him after he went back for his third tour. I'm gonna donate two million in the name "M. Robinson" to the charity that makes homes for wounded veterans. Anyone object?"

Everyone looked around the room; there were no objections. Angelo raised his glass. "To Mikey, our fallen brother. I would give up my cut to have you here with us today. To Mikey." He raised his glass higher, and they all returned the toast, saying as one, "To Mikey."

"I want to say something now that I want you all to let sink in deep. Each of you is going to get a four-million-dollar cut." There were huge smiles all around. "Now that I have your attention, I want you to remember this: four mil does not make you rich. What it does give you is the satisfaction of knowing that you will never worry about paying the bills or paying for a vacation or making a car payment ever again. I have a taste for each of you today. On the table at the end of the room are five packages, one hundred Gs in each. We need to launder the rest of it, so just be patient. Enjoy your life, but don't go blowing a bunch of money that could bring unwanted attention back on us. Any one of you saying or doing the wrong thing can take that away from all of us. So, just don't. First person that talks, dishonors us all, and Mikey will have died for nothing. This subject never leaves this room, and you will all have a special place in the organization. *Capiche?* Now, is there anyone in the room that has never seen the movie *Goodfellas?*"

All the men looked at each other and laughed, nodding with the understanding that they wanted the end of their story to be different than the movie.

. . .

Two days after the meeting at CIA, Tuber called Eliazar to give him the greenlight. "You have six months to show me results. There's been a development I need to read you in on. Is your phone encryption on?"

"Yes."

"We have a general location of the El Paso laptop now, say about a four-mile-wide circle northwest of Fort Worth. I approved your request and have dispatched a two-man team from Special Assets. They will be on the ground and hunting in a few hours. This is all in your hands now. I've already emailed you all the follow-up information. The Special Assets team will be reporting to you."

. . .

The two men carrying black duffel bags across the airport tarmac had a lot in common. They both served in the U.S. military: one in the army and one in the marines. They both had served multiple combat tours in Iraq and Afghanistan. They were also both deeply patriotic. They loved their country and wanted to continue to serve in some way that allowed them to make a difference. A way that didn't require that they swallow sand or carry one-hundred-pound packs in one-hundred-ten degree heat. When their military tours ended, both men were contacted by a CIA recruiter who ended up offering both of them everything they wanted.

One said, "We are a long way from Bagdad."

Two replied, "You always fuckin' say that, beginning of every op."

"It's always fuckin' true, and you know it." One said with a smile.

"Sure as hell is."

"I fuckin' love how they take care of us," One said. "I've got no idea what's in the bags we're carrying, where we are going, or what we are doing. But, sure as the sun will rise tomorrow morning, and fully illuminate your ugly, jarhead face, there are two folders sitting on seats in the back of that jet telling us everything we need to know. Just like these bags will have everything we will need, and I don't even have to look."

Two stopped walking. "Hey, lay off the shit-talk about the marines. I'll tell you why I joined the marines. I wanted to be in the army, but when they did my background check, they disqualified me. They found out my parents were married when they had me."

One dropped his bags on the ramp and cracked up laughing. "Pretty good, motard, pretty good."

57

It was late in the day, and Angelo was still in his office. *It's been a while; I might go to the club tonight.* One of the phones on his desk rang, and the caller ID showed it was a call from IT guy.

"Boss, we may have a problem. That laptop was modified in such a way that if it's tampered with, it sends an info packet back to the CIA, and it appears to have done just that. I looked at the data that was sent, and it included the IP address. It tried to send the Barn's location, but the room is shielded, so it doesn't know its present location. It sent its last known location, which was El Paso. All of my IPs are masked, so if they do a simple check of the IP, it comes back as Madagascar. But if they are good, and I'm sure they are, they will be able to figure out the actual location down to about a three- or four-mile radius of the house."

Angelo said, "Sure as hell, they'll send someone. I'll get you some overwatch." *Click.*

He picked up a different phone and dialed Rob Ramone. "I need to see you at my house within the hour."

· · ·

Too Far drove out to the rural Texas home of IT guy, under orders from Angelo, to provide security for the property. As he pulled up to the rural property, Too Far noticed that the elevation rose toward the far property fence. Then he noticed something that was a very welcome sight. As is common for Texas, he saw the elevated deer stand on the highest elevation of the property. *Fuckin' perfect, I thought I was gonna be on the ground.* There was still an hour or so of daylight, and Rob wanted to get in the deer stand in darkness. That would be easily done with night vision. *I'm going to Walmart for supplies. Might be up there a few days.*

. . .

When Dan left the aircraft in DFW after the flight from San Angelo, Sindee asked him for an exact time that he'd be home. He assumed the question was posed just so Sindee would have herself ready for him. Thirty minutes later, he walked in the back door of his home, rollaway bag dragging behind him. He could see from the back door of the house that the master bedroom door was open. Dan smiled, thinking Sindee would be on the bed waiting for him. He was half right.

Dan was greeted with the sight of Mali kneeling on the bed, blindfolded, headphones covering her ears, in a smoking-hot black nightie and thigh-high stockings. Sindee stood by the bed; she put her right index finger to her lips to tell Dan to keep quiet.

Sindee whispered in his ear. "I told her we were going to play with some sensory deprivation. Drop your uniform, everything, right now." Sindee watched with anticipation as Dan quickly shed his clothes. The sight of Mali, knowing what was about to happen, Sindee's red corset and boots, all combined to make Dan as ready as he had ever been. The sight of that had an effect on Sindee that Dan could see. The look of primal hunger on her face told Dan she was as excited as he was, maybe even more so. Sindee whispered again, "Kneel on the bed behind her."

Mali's head tilted when she felt the weight of someone moving on the mattress. Her head leaned back when she felt two hands from behind on her shoulders. Her mouth dropped completely open when she felt a third point of contact with her body, and she arched her back to greet the touch.

Sindee walked on her knees across the bed to a position in front of Mali, and Sindee's hands on Mali confirmed for the beautiful Asian woman that a third person was in the room. Mali ripped the headphones and blindfold off of her head, and turned to confirm it was Dan. She turned back to Sindee, made eye contact, and mouthed the words, "Thank you."

Dan thought, *I guess Mali doesn't want to be deprived of anything right now.* Dan didn't do much thinking during the hour that followed.

· · ·

Mesa Verde Moving and Storage was a typical facility with hundreds of rental storage units of various sizes. It was one of the first in the El Paso area; it started as a moving company but expanded to provide storage capabilities when its original owner saw the niche and exploited it. In 1962, land in the El Paso area was cheap, and storage buildings were relatively inexpensive to build. Thomas Sevenfeathers was proud of his Native American heritage, but realized at that time that Sevenfeathers Moving and Storage was not a wise choice of business name. He and his sons, who now run the company, had considered changing the name since times changed. Every time it was discussed, they always came to the same conclusion: name recognition was more important.

The name threw Special Agent Miller off, as he expected a Hispanic owner when he walked through the door, not the two clearly Native American men. Before he spoke, he noticed the portrait on the wall bearing the caption "Thomas Sevenfeathers, Founder." Glenn shook it off and introduced himself. "Gentlemen, nice to meet you, I'm Special Agent Miller with the El Paso office of the FBI."

The elder man said, "We know who you are. Wampler already called us."

They stared at Miller in a way that to Miller felt like they were looking right into his soul. *I guess Wampler already has contact with them, I'll let him lead.* "Okay, great, we will just wait for him to arrive. Nice place you have here." No one spoke.

· · ·

Nico took a seat in the office of Andy Powers, now the acting head of the Silver Star Casino. Nico patted the large briefcase he carried and said, "Here's the first delivery. So, how do you do this, if you don't mind me asking."

There were a few seconds of silence before Powers spoke. "Well, I guess there's no harm in telling you. One of the things the outfit likes about casinos is there is never really a full accounting of the money that changes hands. So, there's that. In this case, I get plenty of money transferred directly from overseas accounts for incoming gamblers. That is commonplace now. So, money comes in, there are cage withdrawals, people gamble, chips are brought back to cages, money goes overseas. If someone deposits cash, then desires it be wired to an overseas account, we accommodate that too. Happens more frequently than you'd expect. I also get repeat customers. The first deposit, the one we are doing today, is the trickiest. I show some cash deposits, I show some cage withdrawals, I then show some cage cash-outs, and I have some of it sent overseas. I keep those accounts open. They have more activity next week, with more money being deposited and more being sent back and forth overseas. I figure I can handle a million every other week until it is all done. But rest assured, when I'm done, that money will be going through several accounts and several cage transactions to end up sitting in a Kuwaiti bank as clean as Ivory Snow."

Nico chuckled. "Yeah, uh, did you know the Ivory Snow baby was Marilyn Chambers, the porn star?"

Powers said, "No shit? Learn something new every day."

58

It had been nearly two years since Major Dan Hatfield was awarded the Congressional Medal of Honor by the President of the United States. After leaving Washington, D.C., the air force gave Major Hatfield a full month of leave to enjoy with his wife before they had to make their way to Hatfield's new assignment.

Laughlin Air Force Base, in Del Rio, Texas, was situated close to the border with Mexico, and a few hours' drive west of San Antonio. It was southern Texas, rural, small town, no shopping malls, and much of the words spoken there were in a language that Sharon Hatfield didn't speak. She was in hell. She tried hard to put up with it all, but her major coping mechanism was the vision she painted of the future in her head.

Eventually, Dan separated from the air force. Sharon tried not to seem overly excited about it and did her best acting job to portray the sympathetic wife of a husband who was making a major life change in direction. But inside, she was ecstatic. *Finally, we are moving on and moving up.*

At Sharon's insistence, Dan called a friend of his from flight school at Purdue University, Ed Ronkowski, with questions about Blue Sky Airlines. Ed had just interviewed with Blue Sky after flying for a regional airline for six years, where he built up his flight time and experience. Dan knew that Ed was interviewing with the major airlines and thought Ed would be able to help him since he separated from the air force and would be interviewing as well. Sharon survived Laughlin and Del Rio by reminding herself that there was life after the Air Force, and it was waiting for them. She met Ed while they were all at Purdue and liked him. But she liked Dan more and ended up serious with Dan.

The drive from Del Rio to Fort Worth was long, and they didn't arrive at the hotel until late evening. Even so, Sharon was all business. She searched for real estate agents near the hotel, which was chosen by its proximity to the area she wanted to live. The Lewisville, Texas, area was just north of the Dallas-Fort Worth International airport, there was much in the way of new subdivisions being built, new shopping surrounding the area, and it was located near several large malls. Even the kind of malls with high-end shopping. One look at the sprawling Grapevine Mills Mall, and Sharon was sold. But that was all on the internet. That evening in the hotel, Sharon compiled a list of phone numbers and agencies to call the following morning.

On her fourth phone call, at 8:14 A.M. the next morning, Sharon found an agent that had the next few days free. Sharon gave the agent her list of desires for a house and the price range. An hour later, the agent met them at the hotel with a fist full of listings. After a quick stop at the nearest drive-thru coffee shop, they were on their way in two cars. Three days, and about twenty-six houses later, Sharon finally found a house that she loved. Everything else didn't look good enough from the street or was too "closed" or too "small" or too "far from shopping." After Del Rio, Dan said he'd be happy with any of the houses, and it was clear to Sharon that he was frustrated. He breathed a huge sigh of relief, as did the agent, when Sharon said she liked the house, and wanted to put in an offer. The only comment Dan made about the house was that he loved the huge double shower.

A little over a month later, Sharon stood on the front lawn of the house like the captain of a ship, passing out orders to all who walked within earshot of her. There were movers, a landscaper, house cleaners, and a guy who was measuring all the windows downstairs for drapes. It was just Sharon and Dan, but she insisted on purchasing a four-bedroom home. Dan seemed to really like the large, detached garage that opened onto the alley behind the house, and the large office in the front of the house, but aside from that, he didn't seem to have any other opinions. In only three days, Sharon had coached the house into a condition that was nearly complete. Dan's suggestions for the office and the garage were "ridiculous and unnecessary," and she prevailed on everything else that she wanted.

Dan interviewed at Blue Sky in shortly after the move-in. He learned at the interview that it was his air force service record, and most importantly, his Congressional Medal of Honor that made him a shoo-in. It was as if he was already hired from the moment he introduced himself. This was how he described it to Sharon, which pleased her. She would soon be an airline pilot's wife. It felt like her life was finally coming together. Ed got a job offer the day of Dan's interview; Dan got his official offer a few weeks later.

The problems started when Sharon got her first taste of what a newly hired airline pilot actually makes after taxes and deductions. When the first paycheck was deposited, Sharon called Dan and said, "There's something wrong with your paycheck." Dan explained to her that no, there was nothing wrong. It's what a new hire makes. Sharon was shocked. She was under the impression that airline pilots were paid serious bank. She didn't understand that pay rates started low and increased every year. But she didn't stop her shopping trips to the mall, and the arguments over money began soon after.

After Dan finished the initial training, the pay increased a little, but Dan also quickly learned how to pick up extra flight time, something that Sharon encouraged. For his first year at Blue Sky, Dan picked up so much extra flight time that he hit the maximum number of hours the

Federal Aviation Administration allowed any pilot to fly in a year. And yet, the checking account was always pennies at the end of the month. Sharon wasn't happy with the money, but she also wasn't happy with the frequency she was seeing Dan. More money meant less Dan. Less money meant more Dan. Dan was becoming increasingly disappointed with not being able to make her happy, and it was becoming increasingly obvious what she missed the most.

The day they had their first big blowout, Dan told her he didn't think anything would make her happy. She stormed out of the house in a tantrum. Knowing no one else in this part of Texas, she called Ed Ronkowski to ask him some questions about how long before the pay would be comfortable. He invited her over to talk. Sharon was impressed with Ed's home. Ed came from a wealthy family, and his house was everything Sharon dreamed of having while living in Del Rio and counting the days until their escape.

. . .

The three-day trip Dan started the next day had a very early show time. Because he was new, he got the trips that the senior pilots didn't want, like this trip with the seven A.M. sign-in time. Ed Ronkowski was a new hire like Dan, which made them both junior on the first officer seniority list. Dan was tired; he had not slept well the previous night because Sharon had stormed out during an argument. She didn't come home until the early hours of the morning when Dan was getting ready for work. Needless to say, Dan was glad to see his friend at the gate next to his; Ed was signing in for his trip.

Dan greeted Ed as he walked up to his gate. "First Officer Ronkowski, what's up?"

"First Officer Hatfield. You can actually fly an airplane, right? One without bombs?"

Dan laughed. "Of course I can, but I'm not flying today. All I do is one leg to Memphis, and I'm going to ask the captain to fly. I didn't get a lot of sleep last night."

Ed thought for a second, and said, "Dan, that sounds like a plan I'm going to steal. I didn't get a lot of sleep last night either."

"It's good to see a friend today. Been a rough couple of months at home."

"Really?" Ed said. "I'm early, so I've got some time. I've been doing the airline thing for a little while; maybe I can help."

"I'm not sure if you can help with this. You're a bachelor. I'm trying to make Sharon happy, and that is hard on new hire pay. You remember how Sharon was at Purdue? It's way worse now."

Ed said, "Oh yeah, I remember. You know I wanted to date Sharon, but you had that ROTC uniform that sucked her in like a magnet. Don't worry, the money will come soon enough, and when you upgrade to captain, it will step up in a big way. Sharon will come around."

Dan checked his watch. "I gotta go move some fuckin' metal. Hey, if things don't work out, you can have Sharon. Take it easy." Dan turned toward the boarding door, towing his bags behind him, and headed toward the jetbridge.

Ed laughed under his breath. As Dan walked out of sight, he muttered, "Sure enough, Dan. I'll take her right off your hands."

59

The team from Special Assets was in rural Texas, and they were hunting IT guy. Just as One suspected, the duffel bags were loaded with everything they needed. Opening the bags on the airplane, the first thing they saw was blue jeans and suit jackets, which was the uniform for business casual in Texas. The magnetic company logo signs for the rented pickup truck made them land developers. There were also binoculars and detailed maps of the target area. The instructions folder was thorough and complete, right down to the Operational Security page that had them turn off all cell phones.

Driving toward the target area, One asked, "Why a pickup truck?"

"A Ford F150 is all about blending in. Hell, half the bird shit in Texas lands on F150s. You can't open one eye anywhere in the state and not see at least five of them."

The road ahead climbed a steep hill, and when the truck reached the top, Two pulled the truck over to the side of the road. They both climbed into the bed of the pickup and looked out over the sprawling landscape of ranches, hayfields, and cattle. Both men slowly swept the visible earth, looking for something that stood out, that wasn't quite right. They both knew that when they found the oddity, it would be subtle. They were not hunting amateurs. They knew it would be as small an anomaly as extra power lines, extra phone lines, unusual antennae, or outbuildings, although those were everywhere.

Just then, a county sheriff car pulled up. The two men waved at him as he pulled up, in the friendly fashion of two men who had nothing to fear from law enforcement. "Hey. Y'all okay?"

"Yep," One said. We're land developers, just surveying the area. Getting some eyes on the ground."

The sheriff asked, "Where you boys from?"

"Nacoona," Two lied.

The sheriff's face lit up. "I got lots of family there. Do you know any of the Pickens family?"

The Special Assets exchanged looks. "Okay, you got us," Two said. "We're really from Dallas, but when I tell people that in the country, I might as well be saying New York City."

The sheriff laughed. "That's okay, I ain't from Nacoona neither. You two? In a rented truck with a magnetic sign, in outfits that shout 'new money'? I'll bet neither of you has ever seen Nacoona. What are your plans here?"

"Spending maybe three or four days looking around," One said. "Maybe longer if we find something that interests us."

. . .

This is fuckin' huge, thought Angelo. He understood that this phone call could change the direction of himself, the organization, and everyone in it. From the emails and other information on the computers, getting Eliazar's cell phone number was easy. Angelo looked at it on the one-page workup People Guy emailed over, along with the rest of the briefing on Mario Eliazar, CIA. The decision to ring that phone was much more difficult than finding the number. Angelo knew that the most difficult detail for the two to reconcile was going to be the fate of the El Paso crew. He knew that he was the man responsible for ending the lives of three men that Eliazar probably knew and worked with. *I'm gonna have to handle that first thing.*

271

Here goes nothing. Angelo dialed the number. It was answered on the fourth ring. The call was connected, but Angelo heard only silence. "Is this Mario Eliazar?" Angelo said.

"Who is this?" Eliazar's voice sounded suspicious.

"Someone who can help you." Angelo's goal was to get Eliazar interested.

Eliazar said, "Oh? Help me? With what?"

"Cleaning up El Paso and moving forward." There was silence on the phone. Angelo decided that since Eliazar hadn't hung up, this is where he had to go all-in. "You don't know who I am; in fact, I know that you have no idea. So, I'm going to confirm a few things for you and then educate you on a few things. Then I'll make my proposal. Your crew in El Paso killed a good friend of mine, an old friend, who didn't deserve to die. They added to that mistake by killing him in a gruesome way. My friend was a man who served his country, lived a good life, had a family and grandkids. That, all by itself, was reason enough for me to take them out. But then, they tried to kill another friend, something we were able to stop. The only reason our paths crossed at all was that Villareal was moving in on the U.S. side of the border. So, your supervisors have you cleaning up El Paso and trying to make sense of it. You now have a clear understanding of what the El Paso crew was really up to, and the kind of money they were bringing in, all while having their electric bill paid for by your agency. I've done a lot of talking so far, are you taking notes?"

There was a moment of silence on the phone call. Angelo was going to wait as long as it took for Eliazar to speak. Finally, Eliazar said, "Yeah, I'm listening. You said something about helping me."

Angelo continued. "About that. If I was you, I'd be trying to set up the same deal that your guys in El Paso set up. I know they were making themselves a lot of money, and so can you. I propose you find your cartel to get in biz with; I'm sure you already have. You provide the same services to them that your El Paso op did, and you could even restart the intel op as a cover. I can handle any amount of weed and blow you can move over the border; you get a cut on both sides, and you and I can work out your fee from me. One more thing. I'm sure you are going to need to produce to your bosses those responsible for El Paso."

Silence edged out the conversation.

"I'll take that as a yes," Angelo finally continued. "Albert Einstein once said, 'In the middle of difficulty lies opportunity.' But he didn't say it to me. That quote was said to me by a very wise Sicilian man who took a boy with no father and no mother under his wing. You need to ask your cartel contact who their biggest pain in the ass is, and then set them up as the one that took down El Paso. I'm sure that was a lot for you to take in on a single phone call, so I'll let you go think about it. I'll be destroying this phone when I hang up, so don't bother tracking it. It's clean; I'm not an idiot. You're going to need time to process this, so, I'll call you from a different phone tomorrow. Make sure you answer it."

. . .

Eliazar was in his car, driving to the airport for the flight to meet Mendoza. The phone call from his mystery helper had his head spinning. *Jesus fucking Christ.* Before the guy could hang up, Eliazar blurted out, "Yeah, uh, call me tomorrow. Wait a second. Are you serious? Any weight?"

The voice on the other end replied, "I'm dead fuckin' serious. Always. Any weight in weed and blow. I don't deal in fentanyl, never will." *Click.*

Eliazar looked at his phone. *What the fuck just happened? Is this a solution to everything, or is this a new problem? If he's serious, he just presented me with solutions to a few huge problems. Yeah, I knew John Bayan for years, but we weren't exactly friends. If this guy isn't full of shit, he makes Claymore seamless and a cash cow for me. It's a little shocking how much all*

273

this he has figured out. Even about tying off Crossbow. I'll bring that up with Mendoza. It helps us both.

The car behind him honked; he was so deep in thought that he was driving twenty-five miles per hour in a forty-five.

60

Eliazar was almost to the hacienda compound of Eduardo Mendoza, head of the Serpiente Cartel. Of all of the meetings Eliazar took during his years with the CIA, he felt the most exposed on this one. He shook his head at the irony; a phone call from someone he didn't know just made sense of the entire pitch he was about to give to Mendoza. Eliazar knew he could provide Mendoza with the intel he needed to get products north of the Rio Grande while helping him take down rivals and expand his territory. Now he had a buyer in the United States for unlimited weight. Eliazar chilled at the thought; Mendoza would want to meet whoever this man is. But then he realized, this man would want to meet Mendoza, as well. Eliazar would promise to broker a meeting.

The car he was in turned down a private road, was ushered through a gate, and stopped in front of Mendoza's lavish hacienda. Mendoza was on the front deck, ready to welcome Eliazar into his home. Eliazar felt as if he was standing on the threshold of the rest of his life. He exited the car to a smiling Mendoza with an outstretched hand.

◆ ◆ ◆

The Special Assets team drove a grid pattern hunting the Texas ranchland. For them, it was a simple math problem. Average forty miles per hour, and two hundred miles of roads could be covered in five hours. It only took the team three hours before they spotted the ranch. Outbuildings were a very common feature on the Texas landscape, but this one stood out.

"Pull over at the top of the hill," One said. "I want a closer look at the place we just passed."

When the truck reached the highest elevation of the road they were on, Two pulled the truck onto the shoulder. One lifted high-power binoculars to his eyes and studied the property below.

One narrated what he saw. "It's your average Texas ranch, maybe twenty acres. Standard Texas one-story ranch home, rectangular-shaped property. It's the outbuildings that stand out. Four shipping containers, I can see the welds on the front. Yup, definitely welded together. Doors are welded shut, too. Who the fuck does that if it's for equipment, or livestock, or whatever? There is a regular entry door installed on the container closest to us. I can see two air conditioners from here, so whatever it is, people work inside. The whole thing has some kind of covering, probably to help keep it cool. It has its own electric service pole and meter... um... two hundred amp service."

"Shit," Two chimed in, "that's serious power for an outbuilding."

"Yeah, I'd say— Oh, but would you look at that."

"What is it?"

One asked, "We're looking for some kind of computer lab, right? I see two fiber optic ultra-high-speed lines going to some fucking shipping containers. When I follow the lines back to the pole, it looks like they were run just for this property."

Two perks up. "Yeah?"

"I think we have them."

"I think you're right," Two agreed. "What are you looking at in the way of people on the site? I see two cars. You see anything more than that?"

"Just the two cars. I think we should come back around dusk and gear up. We'll take a closer look. Check the property first, then turn on the phones and phone this in. I don't want to be wrong."

. . .

Rob "Too Far" Ramone knelt in the deer stand, studying the two guys who were surveilling IT guy's ranch. The stand gave him a great view of the F150 that stopped at the top of the hill. Ramone saw the sign on the side of the truck and tracked their movements. *Land development, my ass. Definitely ex-military, definitely two-man team, definitely hunting.* Without taking his eyes off the men, Ramone retrieved his phone, and dialed Manny in the Barn. "Manny, listen. I'm eyes on the guys who are looking for you. Looks like they think this property is of interest. Be ready to evacuate."

Ramone received a tour of the Barn a year ago, so he knew about the trapdoor in it that connected to an escape tunnel, which exited fifty feet from the Barn in an area camouflaged by a few trees. It was designed for times such as this when the use of the only other door in the Barn was compromised.

"Manny, there are weapons in the tunnel," Ramone said. "If I tell you to evacuate, arm up. I'm overwatch, I'm not going to do anything until they make their move. Just be ready, I'm calling the boss." *Click*

Ramone dialed. "Boss, I'm looking at a two-man team taking a hard look at the Barn. It looks like they found what they were looking for."

Angelo huffed. "They are CIA conducting an op on U.S. soil. It can't be official and must be something the CIA would never admit to. Those fuckin' guys set foot on the property, take them out. I'll send cleanup." *Click*

. . .

Miller and Wampler spent most of the day going through the storage area.

Miller, dripping with sweat, said, "So far, if you had to imagine a storage area rented by a regular guy who was hired to do a job very far away, so he stored his uninteresting life in a storage area while taking just what he needed to D.C., it would look exactly like this."

Wampler nodded. "A hundred percent, and honestly, I'm not even sure what we're looking for."

"Amen, brother." Miller opened up a box of books. The box had the appearance of belongings the owner felt were important; neatly packed, some of the books were wrapped in bubble wrap. Miller selected a large book that turned out to be a scrapbook or memory book. The pages were packed with pictures, news articles, acceptance letter to San Francisco State University, and other documents. Just as Miller was thinking, *This is a big, fucking waste of time*, he turned to the last page of the book and found himself staring at a job offer letter from the CIA. "Found something."

Wampler made his way to Miller and examined what Miller was looking at. Wampler said, "Okay, so we know for sure he works, or worked, for the CIA, yet they claim he didn't. You get a call telling you to drop it from a guy who shouldn't have called you. What the fuck are we in the middle of here?" He wiped the sweat from his brow. "Fuck this shit. Let's go get something to eat."

. . .

Wampler and Miller took Miller's car to get food and returned to the storage area to dig further. When they turned the last corner in the maze of storage units, both men shouted, "What the fuck?" The storage unit door was open, and the space had been completely emptied. Not a scrap of paper left. Miller said, "Let's go to the office."

They drove back to the storage location rental office, walked in the front door, and were greeted by the two Sevenfeathers brothers.

Wampler asked, "Did anyone come in, let you know they were going to the unit we are investigating?"

"Yes, four guys. FBI. Showed us FBI IDs. Said they were with you and had a truck."

Miller and Wampler exchanged glances, sighed, then ambled out of the office.

Miller said, "Fake FBI credentials. And how the fuck did they know we were here? These guys aren't going to be the types that leave a trail. I think they did us a favor. I think we found the only thing of value in that unit, and now we don't have to tear the rest apart or get rid of that shit."

Wampler nodded. "I'm gonna expense that five hundred dollars. I thought maybe I'd get more than that out of the unit."

61

With the midday sun high in the sky, a light breeze made the back veranda a very comfortable place for Eliazar to explain to Mendoza exactly how he would make treason profitable for both of them. He laid out the plan for the two of them, but it was the math that had Mendoza's attention.

"So, Señor Mendoza, what I will provide will roughly double the total amount of product you will move across the border, while at the same time cut your losses to less than ten percent."

Also seated at the large table were Mendoza's wife, Gloria, and his new number-two man, Roberto Reyes. They sat and listened to Eliazar pitch the boss a proposal that Mendoza already decided to go with. It was the next comment that got the full attention of all three.

"Further, I have a buyer for your product who will take any amount of weight that you can move of marijuana or cocaine."

Mendoza was impressed. "Any weight? Any? I think I would like to meet this person. Can you arrange a meeting here at my hacienda?"

"Of course," Eliazar replied. "I'll reach out to him as soon as I get back."

. . .

The sun dropped below the horizon, and it started to get dark at the Barn. Too Far looked out of the deer stand at the two-man team through his night vision scope. They parked their pickup outside the entry door of the Barn, and both men got out wearing tactical gear and carrying suppressed AR-15s.

Too Far touched the SEND button on his phone. "DeFillippo, you and IT need to get out, and I mean now."

One of the men entered the door of the Barn, while the other waited outside. Too Far put the crosshairs of his sight on the man's right thigh. "Body armor isn't going to save you today." Ramone squeezed the trigger, sending a high-powered rifle round through the man's leg, ripping open his femoral artery. The man squeezed the trigger on his AR-15, which was on full automatic. Twenty rounds were fired into the dirt before the screaming man crumpled to the ground. Too Far now put his sight on the door. He held it there for a few seconds until the second man appeared in the doorway, his rifle at his shoulder, ready to fire. Ramone squeezed his trigger again and put the bullet through the man's neck. He let go of his AR-15, and with both hands on his neck, dropped to the ground next to his partner.

Ramone dialed Manny. "It's safe. Take the weapons, go to the house, and wait for my call." He disconnected the call and dialed Angelo. "Secure here, two down, need cleanup." Ramone hung up and climbed down from the deer stand. As he walked up to the two men, he could see right away that they were professionals. Matching boots, matching tactical gear, and ARs that were clearly customized all told Too Far that whoever they worked for had outfitted them well. He walked over to the truck and noticed it was a rental.

Twenty minutes went by before headlights appeared on the driveway. A van pulled up to the Barn with a carpet cleaner sign on the outside. The driver walked up to Ramone. "We are cleanup. You have two?"

Ramone pointed. "Right over there. They need to disappear."

"You got it. They are going to the cemetery."

Ramone was puzzled. "Cemetery? You dig them a grave at a cemetery?"

The man explained. "Sort of. Our guy works at a cemetery, operates the machine that digs graves. When we have a special, he digs a grave deeper, we toss the specials in. He fills it back in to the regular depth, and the next day, someone drops a casket on it. These guys are going to disappear."

Ramone raised his eyebrows. "Wow, that's thinking outside the box."

They all laughed. Ramone went to the bodies, checked their pockets, and took the truck key, phones, and their wallets. "Thanks, guys. I'm gonna return this truck to the rental car place."

. . .

"I have two weeks of vacation. Let's spend it in Paris." Dan and Sindee were lying in bed in each other's arms. "We could stay someplace near the Eiffel Tower, see the sights, take a boat up the Seine, drink too much wine, and eat too much food. Chocolate croissants and coffee in the morning."

Sindee could barely contain her excitement. "Oh, shopping in Paris. Louis Vuitton, Yves Saint Laurent, Gucci, Chanel."

Mali walked out of the bathroom. "Paris? Am I invited? Just kidding, Paris is for lovers." She walked over to Dan and kissed him on the head. "Sindee, enjoy Paris with your man. He is a really good fuck."

. . .

Mendoza's jet was fueled, the pilots were on board, and the highly attractive flight attendant stood in the doorway, motioning for Eliazar to leave the building and board the jet. Just as he reached for the door handle, his phone rang. *No caller ID. I hope that's the guy.* "Eliazar."

"It's your new friend. How did your meeting go?"

Eliazar replied, "It went well, and I think we have an arrangement. But he wants to meet personally with you as soon as possible."

"I'm available any time. Arrange it, then call me back at the number I text you." *Click*

Eliazar dialed Mendoza. "How soon can you meet with my guy?"

Mendoza replied, "Tomorrow, here." *Click*

He called the American back. "I don't even know who you are. How do I know you can back up your words? I bring the wrong guy to a meeting at a cartel leader's house or bring the wrong guy to the table to deal with a cartel, I end up dead."

"Well, you have already committed enough overt acts, and I already know enough to bury you, so I know you are all in here. My name is Angelo Genofi, that should be enough for you to look up my resume. I will get myself to his place tomorrow, just get me GPS coordinates." *Click*

Eliazar dialed Mendoza. "The meeting at your hacienda tomorrow is on. His name is Angelo Genofi. He is who he says he is."

. . .

There are several ways to make a name for yourself or gain notoriety in a cartel. Roberto Reyes started very young as a lookout, and then a delivery boy for Serpiente. One day when he was sixteen years old, he was called to a meeting at the hacienda of Eduardo Mendoza. Roberto grew up in the barrio in Juarez. He learned early that the drug business was a way out of the barrio. That meeting at the hacienda, however, showed him just how far someone could go, and he wanted what he saw. Asking around, he learned about the men in leadership positions in Serpiente, and he paid attention to the stories of how they got there. The common thread in all their stories was a capacity for violence.

Reyes made it known to his jefe shortly after the meeting that he was going to run the cartel one day and was willing to do anything to get there. Now, here he was, seated at a table with Mendoza and his wife. Reyes built the reputation that got him there through dozens of dead bodies.

Mendoza said into the phone, "Okay, tomorrow we will meet. Angelo

Genofi, you say? Tomorrow." *Click* "Roberto, what do you think about this situation."

Reyes thought for a moment. This was his first big test. "I would say, jefe, that this situation presents several opportunities. The opportunity to become the biggest, most successful cartel. If it is true, that Angelo Genofi has stolen from you, that is an opportunity, as well. Eliazar isn't going anywhere. But if Genofi was to leave the picture, someone else would just take over, and we could work with them. It would be Eliazar's responsibility to connect us with the new buyer."

Mendoza nodded to Gloria, then said to Reyes, "I have a few men already in Texas, but they lack firepower. I want you to pack two AKs and as much ammunition as possible into a smuggle vehicle and meet up with them. Gloria will make the border and communication arrangements."

62

Nico listened to Angelo tell him about the trip to Mexico the next day, then respectfully voiced his counsel to Angelo. He disagreed that the trip to Mendoza's hacienda was a good idea or even necessary. "My job is to protect you, boss."

When Nico closed his eyes later that night, his last thoughts were about the trip. When Nico woke early, his first thoughts were, *The boss's job is to think business; mine is security. He thinks there's no need for security on this. He thinks the relationship is the security, because it will bring them both a lot of money, and they both had something the other needs. He's got a point, but I don't like it. We're flying commercial, so no weapons; not that we'd be allowed anywhere near Mendoza with them anyway.*

Nico did some homework on the area of Mexico, the city of San Luis Potosi, and the route to the hacienda. They were being picked up, so they wouldn't even have their own vehicle. *Jesus. I don't think my ass has ever been hanging out this far before.*

As agreed, Nico was at Angelo's gate at eight A.M. Angelo was dressed in a tailored business suit, nothing flashy, and no tie. It gave the vibe of professional, not uptight, and missing the insecure personality of some-one wearing a lot of jewelry. Nico was dressed the same way; the outfits were Nico's idea, communicated to Angelo. *We don't want to stand out. Oh, fuck, who am I kidding. Two gringo guineas in rural Mexico being driven around by a cartel crewmember.*

"Maria, can we talk for a minute before I go?" Angelo said in a voice loud enough to hear a few rooms away. Maria walked into the office with a cup of coffee for Angelo. "Thank you, Angel. Is everything set for the party tomorrow?"

"Yes, sir. Your tux is ready, the caterer is set with a finalized menu, the bar service is set, the rental company has the tent, table, and chair requirements, and the decorator is set."

Angelo smiled. "Maria, you are a world-class event planner. You make me look so good with the way you throw parties that people call mine. Can you be a doll and email me the menu and guest list? I'll look them over on the trip to Mexico."

. . .

"This is Tuber."

"This is your contact from Special Assets. You requested a team for an op in Texas. That team has now missed a third check-in, and that requires a response from my office. I need to ask you, did your request contain all the pertinent information, or did you give us a brief that undervalued the threat level being encountered by my assets?"

Jesus Christ, who the fuck are these people in Texas? Special Assets personnel are top tier.

"Supervisor Tuber?"

"Uh, yeah, I'm here. I was just thinking, and no, I don't believe we gave you anything but a completely accurate brief."

"As you know, Special Assets operators are among the best and are very valuable. If anything happens to them, it will be investigated fully, internally, and if any negligence surfaces, there will be consequences."

Tuber said, "Of course, keep me informed."

"Why?"

The question caught Tuber off guard; he is a man that rarely explains himself. "Oh, well, um… I still have an ongoing situation in Texas and am trying to resolve it. The disposition of the assets may change things."

"We will take your request under consideration. Good day."

. . .

Mendoza and Angelo's meeting was all business. Gloria sat at the table and listened. After the introductions and pleasantries, Mendoza opened the meeting with a question. "I am told that your capabilities allow you to handle any weight in marijuana or cocaine we can deliver to the United States. Any weight is an impressive claim. There's no way you could know for certain what I can deliver, and with Eliazar's help, it will be even more. I don't need exact details, but I do need to have some idea how you can handle volume, and if it is scalable."

"There are large warehouses going up all over the Dallas-Fort Worth area," Angelo explained. "The organization already has thousands of square feet of warehouse leased for multiple purposes, with thousands more available at a moment's notice. Your product will be coming into the U.S. in containers and trucks. My warehouses can offload any amount of product you bring in. Between those loading bays, and the large truck stop the organization owns in north Fort Worth, we can distribute wide and fast. Trucks for major shipping companies, names you know, stop there. We meet the trucks going to the locations we want them to go to, with large bags full of what we want them to carry. There are drop locations for dozens of other cities in the U.S. My shipments go all over America and every location is asking me for more. If a trucker drives the speed limit, follows the rest rules, he almost never talks to a cop. Every driver knows, if he gets caught, he should take the rap. I will cover his legal, his expenses, and give him a bonus. I haven't had to do that yet. The only thing we have to discuss is pricing. Wholesale minus twenty percent."

Mendoza said, "I believe we can do some prosperous business. We will put Mario in the middle, and in the future, there will be little contact between you and me. Wholesale minus twenty is fine. I will be putting your claim of any weight to the test."

"Agreed." Angelo rose, as did Mendoza, and the two shook hands. Angelo nodded to Gloria, then left the veranda through the door to the cavernous living room. He joined Nico there, and the two walked out the front door to the large SUV that picked them up from the airport. Not a word was spoken on the ride, as it was one of Mendoza's men driving them to the airport.

. . .

Nico sat next to Angelo in the back of the SUV as it bounced over the rural Mexico road. *The boss seems happy, so it must have been a good meeting. But I'm not going to relax until we are on a plane back to Dallas.*

. . .

Angelo was alone with his thoughts of the day while sitting in the back of a small, regional jet. *Things are really going well. The armored car is clean, I got an ironclad way to wash the money. This thing with Mexico could be huge. I'm gonna need to talk to warehouse and trucking tomorrow. Well, day after tomorrow. The party tomorrow at the house takes precedence. I'll give the guest list and menu a quick once-over in case there's anything or anyone I want to add, but I'm sure it's perfect. Maria is the best.*

63

I want to make the most out of Dan's day off at home. It was early morning and Dan was still sleeping. Sindee was busy on her laptop in bed looking for hotels in Paris, and settled on an apartment that was a vacation rental. It had a balcony on the sixth floor of the building with a view of the Eiffel Tower. Sindee knew that one of Dan's favorite things was the "balcony blowjob." *He's going to get one every night.*

Sindee assumed when they first talked about the trip that they would be flying as non-revenue passengers, using the travel benefits of Blue Sky. Dan told her to book and pay for round-trip, first-class seats to and from Paris. Money was no longer an issue. With the tickets also checked off her list, she returned to the several engagement rings she saved in her internet browser.

Okay, that is the one. It was under the renegotiated eighty-thousand-dollar budget that Dan gave her, it was stunningly beautiful, and it was more than Sindee ever imagined she would be wearing. Like she heard Dan say many times, it was easy for him to treat her like a queen because she treated him like a king. This was a ring fit for a queen. Just as she sent Dan's phone the web link to the ring on her laptop, he began to stir awake.

Time to start my king's day off properly. She dipped under the covers, a sly smile on her face. *This day is going to be great from start to finish. The party at Angelo's house tonight is going to be epic.*

. . .

Vehicles arrived at Angelo's house all morning. Maria met each one, directed them where to go, and what to do. Angelo's backyard was transformed into an event location with tents, draped tables, and floral decorations. The event of the evening was a yearly fundraiser, hosted by Angelo, and the attendance was A-list. The Mayor of Northlake was on the list, along with local businessmen, professional athletes, and other notables. At just after eleven A.M., Angelo stepped out of the back door of his home, wearing a robe and holding a cup of coffee. When he made eye contact with Maria, he smiled, and nodded his approval to her. Her smile back was confident and proud. Events like this were Maria's chance to make Angelo look good. He was a man she owed so much to. Maria could see the look on Angelo's face, and realized it was one of a proud father. At the start of her life, he was her Godfather. When she came to live with him, he became so much more. She hoped the look on her face reflected the love she had for him as a proud daughter.

. . .

"Oh my God, it's like when I saw you in your uniform the first time." Sindee looked Dan up and down and ate up the sight of Dan in a tuxedo. She was still naked in the master bath, putting the finishing touches on her makeup and hair. "I'm glad I'm not dressed yet." She took him by the hand and led him to the bed.

Dan asked, "Are you afraid you won't be able to get through the party if you don't get some right now?" He said through a crooked smile as he took off his pants and laid them neatly at the end of the bed.

"I'm afraid you look a little too much like James Bond right now, I'm afraid of how hot you have me right now, and I'm afraid for the sheets in Angelo's spare bedroom if I don't have you this second."

. . .

The Grapevine Mills Mall in Grapevine, Texas, is surrounded by a vast parking lot. It's almost never close to full, aside from the days before Christmas. The two vehicles parked together in a wide-open corner of the parking lot looked harmless enough to the few shoppers, and even the mall security guard, that drove by. Four men sat in the F150, with the engine idling just to run the air conditioning. They were there twenty minutes as Roberto Reyes laid out Mendoza's plan to the three others.

"Raffie and I are going to take the truck back to Mexico," Reyes said. "Sam and Tomas, you take the car to do the job. It is a smuggling car; you will find AKs and ammo under the back seat. Tomas, I texted you the address of the target, but look at the link I texted with the overhead view of the house. It has a driveway that goes around the house to a garage in the back, out of sight from the street. Drive the car through the front gate, around to the back, and go in the house through the back door. Kill anyone you find in the house. Put the guns back under the seat. You will also find new license plates and tools under the seat. Change the plates somewhere you are not seen, drive straight to the highway, and text me your ETA to a border crossing so we can make arrangements."

Raffie said to his friends, "You guys got this. This is for Jefe Mendoza."

Both men just nodded. Reyes said, "He's right, this is a job ordered by the jefe himself. You will move up when you get this done. Tomas, I just texted you a picture of the target, but as I said, kill everyone."

. . .

Well, he did brag about his parties. Now I can see why, thought Dan as he looked around the backyard of Angelo's house. The women in attendance were all beautifully detailed in their appearances and dress. Oddly to Dan, it was the appearance of the men in attendance he found interesting. There were many normal-looking men, all in formal attire. But there were also many professional athletes, some of whom he recognized, some he did not. When a person is the size of a refrigerator and is surrounded by people trying to talk to him, it's a pretty good bet he plays professional football. The fact that said refrigerator is wearing a perfectly tailored tuxedo is what Dan found impressive.

His eyes found Sindee, who was like a magnet the way the crowd gathered around her. By the look of it, there were already two business types and two professional athletes who had attempted to gain her attention. Dan left her side to get them both drinks, but when he returned, he stood at a distance for a moment simply observing her ability to keep the rapt attention of multiple men simultaneously.

Dan knew that the kind of attention Sindee was getting raised her internal temperature to a boil. When they finally made eye contact, her eyes opened wide, and her mouth hung agape in such a way that communicated to Dan that she was turned all the way on. He held up the two drinks in his hands, and then closed the distance between him, the woman who loved him, and the soon-to-be-disappointed men talking to her.

Dan walked past Angelo, who was talking to the Mayor of Northlake, Texas. Angelo stopped Dan long enough to introduce him to the mayor, who made a joke about how he and Angelo looked like twin brothers. Dan said, "Wow, you two really do look like bookends." As Dan disengaged from the conversation, he saw Angelo make eye contact with Nico, then point to the house. Dan reached Sindee's side just as Angelo and Nico disappeared through the back door of the house.

The crushing metal sound of a car accident is a very distinct noise. Everyone at the party heard it, and when they did, they turned their heads toward the front of the house.

64

Tomas drove past two teenaged boys wearing matching T-shirts. They stood in the street in front of the target house. His only thought was that they might be witnesses who would have to be taken care of after the job in the house was done. One of the boys held out a hand as they drove past. Not knowing there was an event taking place, Tomas and Sam didn't understand that they were valets.

Tomas took the turn into the target house driveway, then hit the gas harder to ram the security gate. When the front bumper of the car passed the sensors outside the gate, the barrier system operated as perfectly as it was advertised. A vehicle approaching the gate with excessive speed activated the barrier's rapid deployment system, extending the heavy cylinders three-and-a-half feet vertically. The car breached the gate, then struck the barriers, and was stopped completely. The impact crushed the front of the car, dislodging the engine from all of its mounts, and caused deployment of the airbags. The two men expected none of that and were, for a few seconds, traumatized.

Tomas shook his head, punched his passenger in the shoulder, and shouted, "*Vamanos!*"

On the front seat were two AK-47s; they were wearing Glocks as they exited the now-useless vehicle. They met at the front of the car, where they could now see why the car had suddenly stopped. Sam motioned with his right hand that they should follow the driveway to the back of the house.

Shoulder-to-shoulder, Sam and Tomas turned two corners in the driveway to see something that stunned them as much as the airbags. Instead of the empty backyard they'd both seen on the Google Earth image, there was a large, formal event of some kind, with at least one hundred people. The sound of the crash brought the crowd to silence, and that is how Tomas and Sam found them when they got to the backyard. Both men quickly scanned the crowd for the target, and both quickly concluded that they'd found him. As they both opened up on the man in the middle of the crowd, they hit the Mayor of Northlake, and the two policemen in plain clothes next to him, with several rounds each.

. . .

Angelo and Nico had taken only a few steps into the kitchen. Angelo wanted to run a few ideas past Nico about increasing their trafficking potential when they heard the sound. Some kind of a car accident happened, and it sounded very close to the house. They both ran to the office in front of the house to see a car had impacted the security barrier posts at the front gate. While they looked on, two men stumbled out of the car, both carrying AK-47s.

Nico shouted, "Boss, the safe room!" Both men turned and headed for the door, which was in the middle of the house. Nico opened it, entered the room after Angelo, took an AR-15 off the wall, and two extra magazines from a shelf. "Stay here," said Nico, as he turned and made his way to the back door at a run.

Angelo hesitated for a few seconds, then grabbed an AR and two magazines. Before he got to the back door, he heard automatic weapons gunfire. He stepped out the back door and saw Nico exchanging fire with one of the armed men. His eyes found the second gunman, closer to him, and they made eye contact. The gunman's eyes opened wide as he turned his rifle, fired at Angelo, and sprayed the house until the bolt locked back on an empty magazine. Angelo felt three impacts, got the wind knocked out of him completely, and fell back into the doorway of the house.

. . .

When the noise of the crash happened, Dan instinctively took a step to put himself between the house and Sindee. The sight of two men walking up the drive with AKs a moment later put Dan in action. He said to Sindee, "Stay down."

Only a second later, the gunmen opened fire on the crowd. Dan took off at a run, quickly making his way around the crowd, along the back of the yard, and out of the view of the gunmen. He watched Nico come out the back door and fire on the gunman farthest from him. Then, before he could get close enough to stop him, the second gunman opened fire on Angelo, who stood in the back doorway.

His magazine now empty, the second gunman reached for another magazine just as Dan got to him. Dan tackled the gunman with a fierceness that one of the footballers in attendance would later describe as epic. Face down on the ground, the gunman reached for his holstered Glock. He never got it out of the holster. Shaking his empty magazine from his rifle as he ran, Nico reloaded his AR-15, and put five rounds into the back of the gunman. Dan picked up the discarded AK, took a magazine from the back pocket of the dead gunman, and loaded the rifle. He shouted to the stunned crowd, "Everyone get in the house!"

Dan stopped for a second to locate Sindee, who he saw running toward the house. There were at least a dozen people on the ground and only a few were moving.

Nico, teeming with adrenaline, shouted, "Let's go."

The two of them walked down the drive, ready to confront any other threats. They didn't find any, but they did hear the welcome sound of multiple sirens getting closer. They turned back toward the crowd and saw only about half had gotten inside the house. There were multiple people trying to render aid to the wounded.

"Dan, the boss is in the safe room. Go find Sindee."

Dan looked at Nico with a stricken face. "Nico, Angelo isn't in the safe room. I saw him get hit in the back doorway."

They both ran to the house. Nico pushed his way through the crowd to the back door, and when he entered, he saw Angelo on the floor, tux jacket open, and shirt bloody. The body armor Angelo was wearing was meant to stop pistol rounds, and while it did slow them down, it didn't stop the three rifle bullets that penetrated his chest.

A doctor knelt next to Angelo, providing medical attention. He looked up at Nico. "He's got a fighting chance if we can get him to a hospital stat."

Dan and Nico shoved their way through the crowd in the house to the front door. Emergency vehicles were piled up in the front of the house and in the street, as the gunmen's car had the driveway blocked. Nico opened the door and yelled for them to come in through the house. The emergency responders found Angelo first, before more made it to the carnage in the backyard. More than two dozen EMTs and firemen did triage in the backyard, identifying who to transport, and who was already deceased. Police ordered that no one leave the scene; Angelo's house was still filled with people.

It occurred to Dan that the one person he hadn't seen during the attack, or after, was Maria. He stood next to Sindee in the kitchen as they watched the wounded being wheeled or carried through the house.

Dan shot Sindee a concerned look. "Stay right here. I don't see Maria. I'm not sure if she knows that Angelo's been hit."

Dan pushed back through the crowd. Being the person she was, Dan assumed he'd find her in the backyard, assisting in some way. She was in the backyard. He found her from the doorway. There, in the middle of the yard, was a body under a sheet. The sheet didn't cover the red flowing dress Maria was wearing or the fashionable white heels that Sindee complimented when she saw them.

Dan turned to go back to Sindee when Nico found him. "Dan, I'm going to Baylor Grapevine, that's where they are taking the boss. Find Maria. She can help you with anything that needs to be done."

"Nico. I found Maria. She is in the backyard." Dan pointed to where she lay.

Nico's face twisted in pain, and tears filled both men's eyes. "I'll tell the boss."

65

It was two A.M. when Dan's phone rang with Nico's caller ID. Dan and Sindee were still awake; Dan was pretty sure he wasn't going to sleep for a few more hours and a few more scotch rocks.

"Nico, talk to me, how is Angelo?"

Nico sighed. "He just got out of surgery. The guy who worked on him in surgery was the doctor that was on the floor with him at the house. Just happened to be a thoracic surgeon on the guest list. Someone was looking after the boss. He said Angelo will be fine, the vest helped, and the rounds didn't damage anything important. Did shatter his collarbone, though, so he's going to be in the hospital and sedated for a while."

"Thanks for the update, Nico. Sindee and I are grateful. Damned glad to hear he's going to be okay."

"Hey, Dan, I'm leaving the hospital now. Can I come by your place?"

"Sure, I'll see you in a few." Dan disconnected the call. "That was Nico. Angelo is in rough shape but he's going to be okay. Nico wants to come over right now." Sindee nodded, rose from the couch, retrieved another scotch glass from the bar, and a bottle of twelve-year-old, single malt scotch. She placed both on the coffee table.

Twenty minutes later, the doorbell rang. Dan got up and welcomed Nico into the house. Nico sat down in front of the empty glass. Sindee asked, "Do you need ice, Nico?"

"You are such a doll. The scotch I need, the ice I would like. Thank you."

As Sindee headed to the kitchen, Dan said, "I'm not sure what you want to talk about. Is it okay to talk in front of Sindee?"

Nico said, "Sure. She should be here for all of it." Sindee walked back in, handed the glass with ice to Nico, picked up the bottle, and poured. "Thanks again, sweetheart. Before I get into it, how are you two doing? I mean, you aren't injured? Just shook up?"

They both nodded. Dan said, "Yeah, that would all be true. Do we have anything to worry about? Do we have any idea what the fuck that was today?"

"Well, first off, we have a made guy who was attacked today in a very visible way. I'm sure you can guess how the organization feels about that. They are shaking all the trees and this is what we know for certain so far. The car has Texas plates, but just recently crossed into the U.S. The back seat was modified to smuggle across the border, in this case weapons and ammo, and a change of license plates. Our guys at Border Patrol gave up the name of the guy who handled the car when it crossed, and we paid him a visit at home. He's on the cartel payroll, the particular cartel being the one we just visited in Mexico. We own him now. The cops fingerprinted the dead motherfuckers. Both are Mexican nationals with histories. So, we have a real good picture of who did this. What we are missing is the why."

Dan asked, "Does Angelo have protection in the hospital?"

"The organization is providing everything. This might be a good break for us, but the police are way off the mark. Northlake P.D. is taking the lead on this, and they are moving forward with the theory that the mayor was the target, and everyone else was collateral damage. He was the first guy they shot, and they took out his bodyguards as well. Their theory fits the details pretty well, right down to the house address, Google Map link of the house, and picture of Angelo they found on the gunmen's phones. The picture is so low quality, they think it is the mayor."

Dan was trying to take it all in. "Jesus, Nico, the mayor made the joke to me that he and Angelo looked like brothers, and they really did look like the same guy. So, Northlake P.D. is running down the theory that a Mexican cartel put a hit on the mayor?"

Nico's shoulders went up. "Something like that. They haven't connected all the dots yet that we have, but they probably will. I'm sure the FBI will get involved, if they aren't already. And by the way, Angelo is still sedated. I wasn't able to tell him about Maria yet, but I know what he is going to say on that. He's going to want blood. A lot of it."

"I'm sure he'll get it. So, where do we stand now?"

Nico paused for a second before he continued. "Well, we have some personnel issues to discuss."

Dan was puzzled. "I'm not following you, Nico. What personnel issues?"

Nico explained. "The organization is exactly that. An organization. They asked me if I could run things while Angelo recovers. We have to have someone making decisions, handling issues. They asked me if I would take the job. I told them you would be a much better fit for the position. They—"

"You told them what?" Dan was flabbergasted. "Me? Why the hell would you tell them that? I don't know the first fucking thing about running Angelo's outfit."

"Dan, I want you to think about this. You told me once that an airline pilot really gets paid for his experience and his ability to make decisions. The boss and I have talked about you many times. He trusts you, and he recognized right from the start how smart you are, how well you think on your feet. At best, yes, I'm Angelo's number two, but he has always been the detail man. That's not me, that's you. The organization also likes you because they know when Angelo is healthy enough, you will step away, and, of course, you'll be rewarded handsomely."

Dan looked over at Sindee, who just threw up her hands. He then looked back at Nico, who appeared to be waiting for an answer. "You're serious?"

Nico said, "My friend is laying in a bed at Baylor, hooked up to dozens of wires and tubes, with three new holes in his body. So... yeah, I'm fuckin' serious. And there's more. It's along the lines of the reward I was talking about. One of the bodies in Angelo's backyard was Tony Upton."

The name did not register at all with Dan, but he heard Sindee make a sound like a hurt puppy. When they made eye contact, she was already crying. He held his arms out and Sindee melted into them, sobbing. Dan asked, "Who was he?"

Nico explained. "He was the owner of the club where you two met. Well, he was supposed to tell everyone he was the owner. The organization really owns the club. Upton was someone Angelo met on the golf course. He had no past, no baggage, so the boss hired him to run the club as the owner. He was a great guy, the girls loved him, so the best flocked there. He got paid a percentage of what the club took in, so he was always fair with the girls."

"So, the organization wants me to run the club, too? That makes two jobs I'm unqualified for. Jesus, Nico."

Nico shook his head. "Not run it, Dan. If you step into Angelo's shoes for a little while, and all goes well, the organization will sell you the club for one dollar, and they won't ask for a cut. It's making good money right now, and if you run it like Upton did, it will continue to make money. You've got the perfect assistant sitting next to you, and the organization will provide anything you need for outside help."

Sindee turned in Dan's arms to look up into his eyes. She was no longer crying. She looked into his eyes and nodded. He looked over at Nico, who also nodded. Then he looked up at the center of the ceiling above him.

Nico said slowly, "Dan, you can do this. It isn't that hard when you are smart, like you are. The boss saw that in you; I see that in you. With my help, you could step right in."

Dan closed his eyes and shook his head. Dan's rational brain, his air force brain, told him that Nico's assessment, and conclusion, were correct. He was the logical and capable person to take over. His pilot brain told him that when in stressful situations, just stay cool, do the job, and make good decisions. His emotions were telling him to jump into the role, make everything right, and get payback for Maria and Angelo. There was no escaping it.

Dan sighed hard and said, "Okay, Nico, give me a briefing, and don't leave anything out.

Nico smiled. "You got it, boss."

Boss? Dan thought. *Boss. Boss it is.*

Made in the USA
Columbia, SC
15 November 2024

46381366R00183